# HER DEADLY FRIEND

# HER DEADLY FRIEND

### GLOUCESTERSHIRE CRIME SERIES
### BOOK 1

## RACHEL SARGEANT

This edition produced in Great Britain in 2024

by Hobeck Books Limited, Unit 14, Sugnall Business Centre, Sugnall, Stafford, Staffordshire, ST21 6NF

www.hobeck.net

A CIP catalogue for this book is available from the British Library.

ISBN 978-1-915-817-34-1 (pbk)

ISBN 978-1-915-817-33-4 (ebook)

Cover design by Jayne Mapp Design

Printed and bound in Great Britain

# PRAISE FOR THE GLOUCESTERSHIRE CRIME SERIES

'All in all a good read with an interesting storyline with a clever unexpected ending.' ThrillerMan

'Always good to read an author who develops their own style of writing and I think Rachel is one of them.' Pete Fleming

'I enjoyed it immensely.' Sarah Leck

'A tantalising crime thriller.' Angela Paull

'Her Deadly Friend is a fast paced twisty read from one of my favourite authors.' JoJo's Over the Rainbow book blog

'I flew through Her Deadly Friend ... I'm looking forward to seeing where she takes this series next.' Hooked From Page One

'The writing is flawless and the plot is so twisty and original that I didn't see any of it coming.' The Book Magnet

'A good read, a shocking conclusion and I'm looking forward to book 2 in the series.' Lynda's Book Reviews

'I do love a riveting police procedural thriller! And this definitely hits the spot!' Miranda's Book Scape

'pacy, twisty' Janet, Two Heads Are Better than One Blog

'I hope that there will be a follow up to this novel, I enjoyed this one a lot' Steph's Book Blog

'An outstanding book.' Monika Reads

'This is another cracking read from team Hobeck who has an enviable stable of excellent authors' Lesley Wilkinson, book reviewer

'It's very twisty-turny, and full of surprises right till the end.' I Heart Books blog

'A very cleverly plotted thriller.' A Mother's Musings

'A very clever plot with plenty of twists and a fabulous conclusion.' Deb's Book Reviews

## ARE YOU A THRILLER SEEKER?

Hobeck Books is an independent publisher of crime, thrillers and suspense fiction and we have one aim – to bring you the books you want to read.

For more details about our books, our authors and our plans, plus the chance to download free novellas, sign up for our newsletter at **www.hobeck.net**.

You can also find us on Twitter/X **@hobeckbooks** or on Facebook **www.facebook.com/hobeckbooks10**.

*To the landmarks of Gloucestershire*
*for inspiring my fictionalised version of this wonderful county*

# PROLOGUE

## Twenty-Nine Years Ago

"I didn't do it." I fold my arms, look Mrs Hardcastle in the eye and breathe in the stench of furniture polish that pervades every visit to her office.

The head teacher stares back, her face giving nothing away. But it's obvious whose side she's on. As usual, Amy Ashby and her mother get to occupy the comfy chairs while Terri and I have to stand.

"Well, someone did," Mrs Ashby says, high-pitched and pious. "Or are you suggesting my daughter did this to her own viola?"

All eyes go to the musical instrument on Mrs Hardcastle's desk. The bridge is snapped and there's grass and soil caught in the strings. The varnished surface is speckled dark red and there's no denying what it looks like. Beside it lies the bow. Two broken sticks of wood joined by a length of splayed, white horsehair. And between the fibres, more crusty flakes of blood.

"What have you got to say for yourselves, girls?" Mrs Hardcastle asks.

Terri looks at me and we both shrug. Before we can offer any defence, the lesson bell tolls and we all jump, even Amy. The corridor outside fills with the shrieking chatter of girls released for break time. Wish I was with them, but there's no chance of that. Reckon I'll be saying goodbye to break for the rest of the week.

Mrs Ashby places a manicured hand on Amy's sweatshirt sleeve. "Tell Mrs Hardcastle what you told me."

I look at the carpet and roll my eyes. You don't see Terri or me getting our mums to fight our battles.

"They took my viola," Amy says in that whiney victim voice that drives me mad. "They're always bullying me."

"No, we're not," Terri snaps. "Sorry, miss," she adds under a withering look from Mrs Hardcastle.

"They hit her with the bow." Mrs Ashby raises Amy's wrist to show the bandage. "Made her *bleed*."

"We never touched—"

The head teacher waves me silent. She pushes her chair from the desk and peers at me through her bifocals. "Please don't insult my intelligence by denying you took the viola. Any number of witnesses saw you, and these stains look suspiciously like blood."

I feel the colour flood my face. "That's not what happened."

Mrs Hardcastle picks up her notepad. "You were seen opening the case and whirling the instrument over your head. Then you and Terri taunted Amy, throwing it between you. Do you have a different version of events to present?"

"Well..." I glance at Terri sadly. "It was a bit of fun, that's all."

Mrs Ashby makes a scoffing noise and takes Amy's hand.

Amy bites her lip and blinks fast. I try not to scowl, but her stupid waterworks got old months ago.

There's a sigh from Mrs Hardcastle as she adjusts her spectacles. "You might not have meant any harm..."

"Clearly they did," Mrs Ashby interrupts.

"However, considerable damage has been done," Mrs Hardcastle continues. "I'm putting you both in detention every night for a week."

"But, miss, I've got netball practice," Terri protests.

I see a triumphant smile pass between Amy and her mother, and feel my fury rising. "That's not fair," I blurt. "Amy's a liar."

There's a gasp from Mrs Ashby, her neat little features becoming quite theatrical.

"Two weeks detention, then, Stephanie?" Mrs Hardcastle says.

"Believe me, I'm telling the truth," I wail, but know I'm wasting my breath. Bang to rights.

# CHAPTER ONE

Christa parks and gets out of the car. After the warm bank holiday weekend, early May is back to chilly mornings. She reaches into the back seat for her raincoat but changes her mind. She'll brave it; she wants to look her best.

There's just one other car in the car park. Hardly surprising. The only people usually out at this time are dog walkers. But they won't come here. She reads the sign: *Welcome to the Georgian Gardens. No dogs. No picnics.* The other car – a small hatchback – must be Morag's, arrived already. Christa's heart speeds up; she's really going to do this.

Her ballet pumps pick up dust from the chalky ground. Trainers would have been better but could never have worked with this outfit. She smooths the sleeve of her linen jacket – bought online – powder blue to complement her skin tone. Her belly gives a flip of excitement, knowing Morag will like it and say something nice.

From the car park, she heads along the path, mentally following the directions Morag gave her. A speck of gravel pricks her heel and she has to empty her shoe. Some women –

Glastonbury types – wear wellies with skirts. She'll do that next time. So much to learn.

The kiosk at the garden entrance is shut, as is the gift shop behind it. A notice on the door advises: *Visitors prior to 10 a.m. are requested to pay via the honesty box.* A scale of charges follows. Her old lawyer's instinct kicking in, Christa resolves to pay on the way out. She'll decide for herself what monetary value to place on her visit. If Morag's there with the advice she needs, she might even make a bigger donation.

Her last trip to a garden was Chatsworth at least ten years ago on a rare day off from the legal firm. The kids played hide and seek. And so did she, but a different kind of hiding. Even back then Sam deserved better, and realised it eventually – left and took the kids.

Christa stumbles over a loose stone and parts company with a shoe. Dust sticks to her moist finger pads when she puts it back on. Oliver is fourteen years old now and Sophie nearly twelve. Since they left, there have been seven years of Skyped parenthood. When Christa was little, people at church had pity in their eyes for the mixed-race kid without a daddy. She's ashamed she's done no better for her own children.

Further on is a conservatory surrounded by heavy pots of miniature roses. She presses her hand against the cool glass and peers in. There's no one inside, but she looks for a moment longer, prickling with the irrational sense that there's someone, somewhere, watching.

Her breath catches in her throat as she rounds the corner of the building and sees the extent of the Georgian Gardens in a basin of land below her. A vibrant wild flower meadow occupies the far side. To the right is a vast bed of tulips in shades from apricot to magenta.

A quack rings out and she realises it's the first sound she's heard apart from her own excited heart. Two white ducks bob in a pond in the flat area at the centre of the basin. She halts when she senses movement in a gap in the shrubbery. It doesn't look like the place Morag described for their meeting. Another early morning visitor? She shakes off a chill. There's nobody there. Must be a trick of the light.

Further on, steps lead down into the garden and she passes a folly in the form of a white turret with a red roof. A nursery rhyme drifts through her mind: *The King was in his counting house.* She must have learnt it in school, because her mother sang only in Cebuano at home. Mum taught her Filipino language to Oliver and Sophie, too, when they were little. Even Sam loved to listen.

On the ground below the folly, Christa pauses to admire the shiny foliage of rhododendron bushes. In a few weeks these plants will pop with scent and colour. She smiles. Morag said something similar. *Your time to flourish is almost here.* Who would have thought Christa's rescuer would be a stranger in a café? It just shows: never judge a book. Perhaps this morning Morag will reveal more about herself. Christa's been curious for a while, but it's not the kind of thing you ask. But there must be something. Morag gets it too well; it has to be from personal experience.

The sign for the bluebell wood is where Morag said it would be, and Christa leaves the garden basin to climb the wide, flat steps that have been fashioned from soil and logs. After half a dozen or so, she starts to count them. When an overhanging briar catches her head, she grasps her hair and untangles it before damage is done.

Thirty-two steps until she reaches the floor of bluebells. The wooded, earthy smell owes more to forest than to flower, but the blooms are magnificent – more of a luminescent mauve than blue.

There's birdsong. An animated, frantic twittering above

and around her in the trees. Her skin tingles. Her arrival must have spooked the birds, that's all. There's no reason for the sense of unease that's crept upon her.

As Morag described, the path leads to a timber construction, their agreed meeting point. A notice says it's a bug hotel. Logs, wooden tubes and straw fill a grid of compartments. She runs her hands down the bobbly surface, thinking how Sophie loved creepy crawlies as a toddler. Does she still like them? Tears prick Christa's eyes. How can she not know that about her daughter?

There's no sign of Morag – maybe the car in the car park isn't hers – but Christa is a few minutes early. She rests her back against the timber box, feeling its edge through the thin fabrics of her jacket and dress. The bluebells look even more vivid from this vantage point. A snatch of sunlight touches them through the trees.

There's a rustling sound behind, but before she can turn around, something slams into her back. The impact sends her staggering forwards and a dull pain throbs between her shoulder blades. Shock fizzes through her arteries. Trembling, she finds herself on all fours, breathing fast and sweating. Phlegm bubbles in her throat and tastes of metal. She spits blood onto the grassy path. Dizziness darkens her vision until she sees no more colour and everything turns black.

# CHAPTER TWO

An Openreach van pauses on the St Giles roundabout to let me inch forward and join the traffic. The driver's not bad looking. He grins and waves, and I wave back. Life in the old Steph yet. But then I catch a glimpse of myself in the rear-view mirror. Even with sunglasses hiding most of my face, I look grim. The van driver must think he's helping the aged.

A text from Jake pops up on the hands free. *Hope you're feeling better*. I'm feeling like horse manure but I'll send him an upbeat reply later. Can't have him worrying about his mother when he's got his mock A levels starting. I thought by returning to work I'd convince him I was back to normal, but he must have heard me tossing and turning again last night. And he knows I spent the hottest May bank holiday on record with a blanket round my shoulders watching back-to-back *Escape to the Country* in a darkened room. I've barely eaten since Saturday, and keeping down the cups of tea he brought me was an epic struggle.

Ignoring the agony at my right temple, I drive forward to

join the Painswick road at the lights. Jake reckons I should go to the doctor. Typical teen, loves the drama.

It's nose to tail heading out of town. The hill up to Painswick is steep and long. My Golf can do it easily, but someone at the front of the traffic queue can't. It kills my neck and shoulder to move the gearstick down to second. I should have taken one more day's leave, but the thought of being alone while Jake's at school brought me out in fresh pain. I'm not good on my own.

The phone goes and the in-car screen tells me it's my boss, DCI Kevin Richards.

I answer. "I'm on it. ETA five minutes." I end the call before he has a chance to reply. He's used to my ways.

Answering the phone has sent my neck into spasm. With one hand, I reach to the passenger seat and wrestle paracetamol out of my handbag. I've had four already this morning and should switch to ibuprofen next time. I've seen what a paracetamol overdose can do. The failed suicide's boomerang. It knocks you out, lets you wake, and then, just as you start to think life's worth living after all, it catches you on the rebound and finishes you off. I know it takes more than six tablets, but there's no point in stressing my already overstressed liver.

It's another fifteen minutes of slow traffic before I finally signal right and turn into the Georgian Gardens. I haven't been here since Jake was little and came for his friend Bradley's birthday party. I helped Terri – Bradley's mum and my best friend – set a treasure hunt through the woods. One of the gardeners tried to stop us picnicking by the duck pond, but, well, let's just say the old Steph charm worked its magic. We texted for a while afterwards but nothing came of it. He's in Cheshire now, managing the estate of a Premier Leaguer.

A PCSO on sentry duty waves me through the cordon. I don't know her but most of the community support officers know me – or my car. My dad got one of his mates in the trade to do the purple paint job. There are two pandas in the car park and three civilian cars. I get out and drag my headache uphill, feeling cold deep into my bones through my leather jacket.

As I shuffle my way past a kiosk, a middle-aged woman wearing a quilted jacket and an officious smile rushes towards me. "We're closed, I'm afraid. Police orders. There's been an incident."

I show her my warrant card. "I'm a detective inspector with West Gloucestershire Police."

As she peers at it, a grin comes over her face. *Here we go again.* "So you're Inspector L—"

"Just call me Steph." I cut her off. I got bored of that quip about twenty minutes after my promotion two years ago. "What's your name?"

"Elizabeth Bowers. I'm one of the volunteers here. I open the garden shop on weekdays." She points to the building behind the kiosk. Through the window I see stacks of more-money-than-sense tea towels and gift sets of soap. And Royal Wedding mugs, of course. Nine days until the big day, and ten until the unsold merchandise hits landfill.

"Has anyone interviewed you yet?" I ask.

"A lady police constable took my details and told me to stay here in case she needed to ask me more. But I wasn't present when the incident occurred."

"Which way is the incident?" I ask, adopting her turn of phrase.

She straightens up. A tall woman, at least five feet nine. "If you'd like to follow me."

"Just point me in the right direction," I say.

She suppresses a look of disappointment. "They're in the bluebell glade. Go past the café. When you get to the folly, take

11

the steps down. It's signed from there." She scrutinises my face. "Summer cold, is it?"

"Thanks for your help." I force a smile and move on.

The most gorgeous black Scottish terrier with its lead wrapped round a concrete planter jumps up and wags its tail when I approach the conservatory that houses the café. I massage its pointy ears and let it print dusty paws on my black jeans. Through the glass, I can see PC Izzy Hutton sitting opposite a woman in wellies and a green anorak. The woman's complexion is florid, either from a life spent outdoors or from the sobbing she's doing. I say goodbye to my new doggie pal and carry on. No need to interrupt Izzy; she's one of the best at getting a statement while simultaneously doling out sympathy.

When I reach the red and white folly and look across the garden, another headache starts. To get to the bluebell glade will involve a steep, downward walk followed by an even steeper climb back up. There's nothing for it but to press on, and I put my head through more throbbing before I reach the steps up to the glade. A uniform appears at the top of the steps and watches me make the climb. It's a PCSO in her early twenties. I don't recognise her but she knows me and addresses me in my preferred way.

"Morning, Steph. We've got a nasty one."

"How?"

"Stabbing."

I climb another three steps before I have to stop again. The PCSO is still watching me, her arms folded. She's a sturdy girl but stab vests don't do much for anyone's figure. Even Amal Clooney would look like a trucker in constabulary standard issue.

"Who found her?"

"Dog walker, Tracey Chiles. Izzy is interviewing her now. Once she got over the shock, she was more bothered about being caught with a dog in the garden. Kept waving her poo bags at us. 'I always pick up, officers, I promise.'"

I smile at her attempt at an old lady accent, but reckon she's pitched it about two decades too old for the woman I saw being interviewed in the conservatory café. Does she class everyone over thirty-five as geriatric?

"Are Forensics with you?" I ask and hope not. Siobhan Evans is doctor to the dead. She'll take one look at me in this state and book me in for an autopsy.

"At least another quarter of an hour," the PCSO says. "Big smash on the M5."

My sigh brings on another stab of pain.

"Feeling all right?" she says, giving a sympathetic tilt to her head.

"A touch of hay fever. Nothing much. Victim?"

"Female, smartly dressed. Doesn't look like the type to be out for a morning stroll, especially not in slip-on shoes. There's no ID in her bag except a Debenhams card in the name of Christa Talbot."

"You went in her bag?" Brave of her to mess up forensics; obviously hasn't experienced a Siobhan Evans bollocking.

"Not me. The woman who found her didn't have a phone so she got the one out of the victim's bag. She took out the purse and Debenhams card while she was at it."

I make my next bid for the summit but halt after a few steps when my ears start pounding. "Where are the phone and purse now?"

"Back in the handbag, according to Tracey Chiles, the dog walker. Would you believe she left her own phone at home because it's only for emergencies? Oh the irony. But you know what old folk are like."

My sixty-something parents are never off their smart phones. Dad couldn't run his building business without one. I charge up more steps and pause on the last one, thinking up another question to let me stall for longer and catch my breath.

"Don't suppose there are any car keys in that handbag?" I ask.

"We don't know, but one of the cars in the car park is unaccounted for. The other two – a silver Polo and a brown Volvo – belong to dog walker Tracey Chiles and Elizabeth Bowers, the volunteer woman in the shop," she explains, adding, "I'm on it," before I suggest a call to the DVLA about the third car.

She reaches out her hand. I'm not sure whether it's to shake mine or haul me up. "I'm Jess Bolton, by the way. Pleased to meet you at last. It's along here when you've got your breath back."

It's said without sarcasm so I let her off. I offer her my hand but have to snatch it back afterwards to rub my temple.

The bluebells must be stunning but, through the filter of my sunglasses, seem muted. Jess leads me to the cordon she, or Izzy, has put in place. The body is lying prone, with the face turned towards us, in front of one of those bug houses that kids like to make. Despite the dried blood on her lips and chin, I can see she was an attractive woman. Mid-thirties. Her long, black hair is so straight and silky it has a synthetic quality.

Her right arm is hidden under her body but her left arm has landed by her side, bent at the elbow, palm to the ground. Her pearly pink nail varnish matches what's left of her lipstick and is skilfully applied, but the nails are surprisingly short. I squat down for a closer look. From this distance outside the cordon, there are no obvious snags of skin at the nailbeds – I doubt she was a nibbler – but I'd have expected this woman to have talons. Maybe she's a musician. Or a nurse? Her jacket is tailored linen. The delicate shade of blue is ruined by the swamp of crimson that's covered most of the back and the upper half of the visible sleeve. A pretty floral dress splays over her knees. Thick, toned calves lead to broad feet in navy ballet pumps.

"Her phone is an old Nokia apparently, not locked," Jess says. "Surprising, don't you think?"

The clothes, the shoes and the handbag aren't designer but they're not cheap either. Jess is right. We would expect our well-dressed victim to have a better phone.

"My guess is she was admiring the bluebells when someone, probably hiding behind this thing, climbed up and stabbed her." Jess points at the bug box and then at the knife between the victim's shoulder blades.

It's the first time I've consciously looked at the wound. I'm not squeamish but Forensics will make more of it than I can. It seems an intrusion to gawp where I don't need to. I can allow the victim a final bit of dignity.

"Did Tracey the dog walker see anyone else?" I'm not sure why I'm asking. Izzy will deliver the witness statement later.

"Not a soul," Jess says. "She went into hysterics when it dawned that she could have come face to face with the killer. Izzy calmed her down. It's doubtful anyone else was here that early. I checked the honesty box but it was no help."

"What's that?"

"Out-of-hours visitors are supposed to put the entry fee in the honesty box by the shop, but it only had forty-nine pence in it. Tracey admitted that was hers. First the dog, then that. Regular little rule breaker."

"How much should have been in the box?"

"Fourteen pounds if Tracey the dog walker and our victim Christa had paid full price. I'm guessing we can't expect the killer to have paid."

Damn, it's not a good start. We've no way of knowing how many people came here this morning. Our best chance is that this is a domestic. The time, location and the victim's clothing suggest she was meeting someone. Let's hope it wasn't a blind date. Trawling through Tinder isn't my idea of detective work.

"I take it there's no CCTV?" My back and head are throbbing with the pain of too much squatting. I straighten up slowly; no sense in making myself even dizzier.

"The nearest camera is at the lights in Painswick, but not all vehicles clocked there will come this far. There are plenty of turn offs in between."

I make a mental note to obtain the capture. It'll be pretty useless on its own given the volume of traffic that uses this rat run to and from Stroud, but if we make an arrest, corroborating camera footage from the area might nudge the suspect towards a confession.

I must remind Kevin to include, in his radio appearance, an appeal for other early morning visitors to the garden to come forward. DCI Kevin Richards doesn't know he's going on local radio yet, but something tells me this case will need all the media help it can get.

# CHAPTER THREE

Amy puts down the knife. It's ten a.m. but her mother still hasn't come out of her room. Her pulse speeds up. She should have got the job done quicker, arrived sooner. What if something's...?

The malodorous tang of ageing flesh greets her when she opens the bedroom door. The curtains are closed but it's light enough to make out the mound of duvet. She pauses to listen for snoring, but instead hears a rapid, shallow breathing. A sick taste settles in Amy's throat and she treads closer. A bird's nest of thinning hair rests on the pillow. Amy places two trembling fingers briefly on her mother's forehead. It feels hot and moist. The woman lets out a sigh in her sleep and buries her face in the pillow. She must be running a temperature. There's no telling what a chill could do to someone in her condition. Should Amy wake her and ask if she needs the doctor? But what will that achieve except to give herself cantankerous company for the rest of the day?

Resolving to let her mother sleep for another half hour, Amy creeps back to the kitchen and resumes her flower arranging. Her blouse is sticky and wet at the underarms. After the morning she's had, she could do with a shower. But using this extra time for her pedestal displays means she'll be able to transport them straight to school later and there'll be less to get ready on site tomorrow night.

Picking up the knife, she slices clean through the stem of an orange gerbera at an angle, giving it a pointed end. She lifts three heavy oasis bricks out of the sink and lets another three float in the water. It's a chore doing them in batches and it doesn't work plunging them in quickly. They have to soak up the water at their own pace, otherwise they stay dry in the middle and provide no nourishment for the flower stems. The large Belfast sink was lost to her when her mother sold the family home and came to this tiny bungalow. For weeks Amy tried to persuade her not to move, gently telling her it was too soon after Daddy's death to make big changes. But, given how her mother's health has deteriorated, Amy has come to see her mother's decision as prescient.

She jabs a stem of rhododendron into one of the soaked oasis blocks. A twinge of guilt passes through her when she thinks of where she got the greenery. Until the move, she used to source it from her parents' extensive garden. But for the last six months she's been charging the school for plant materials that aren't hers.

A posh private school like Orchard Prep can afford it. Besides, they don't pay her much as a matron – especially now she's gone part-time to look after her mother. The extra pay from doing the floral displays for their foyer is a welcome addition to her savings. She doesn't know yet how much her inheritance will be. The intestate business since Daddy's death has caused quite a delay.

With all her materials squashed onto the single drainer, it's hard to work. The bungalow doesn't run to extensive kitchen worktops or a utility room. There isn't even a study. All her father's accounts are in the loft. Whenever Amy offers to go through them, her mother doesn't respond. Just another example of how she's changed. At first, after his death, she was brisk and business-like, contacting the solicitor and disposing of stuff in the wood burner when they still had one, but almost overnight her health stalled. The energetic woman who had celebrated her sixty-seventh birthday on a Rhine cruise was confined to a wheelchair within a year.

Amy measures the height of the gerbera against the foliage. Years of practice have taught her accuracy with the knife. But this isn't going to be her best work. If only she had her own apartment with a spacious kitchen table. Even before her father's death – two years before, when she hit forty – she started saving for a one-bed flat in the Bell Tower, but she hadn't factored becoming an unpaid carer into her financial planning.

She hears the bedroom door open and takes a breath, knowing her mother is about to wheel herself – unwashed and partially dressed – slowly and completely into Amy's day. In mere minutes, she'll ask for help with something she was able to do for herself only yesterday, and Amy will see a little less of the person Eileen Ashby used to be.

She loosens her grip on the carnation she's holding, but – too late – she's already snapped the head. Every day her mother grows more like a badly soaked oasis block, crumbling and dry at the core.

# CHAPTER FOUR

DCI Kevin Richards, my boss, perches on a desk, arms folded, looking like a man with the weight of West Gloucestershire on his shoulders. I find out why soon enough.

"Pathologist's initial report," he says, "puts cause of death as single wound, consistent with a knife being thrown from close range. The blade is a common kitchen knife, manufactured by a leading brand and readily available from supermarkets. Victim is..." He points at the board of scenes of crime photographs. The woman is as I remember her. Well dressed, long black hair, dead.

"The victim," Kevin says again, clearing his throat, "is male." He pauses, anticipating the gasps. We don't disappoint. Several colleagues give sharp intakes of breath, others cough. "Initial ID based on ownership of the car left in the Georgian Gardens' car park is Christopher Jason Talbot. His mother, Katrina Talbot, has now made a formal identification."

"So it's a hate crime." A hand waves two rows in front of me. It's Detective Constable Harriet Harris.

"Now, Harriet, let's not jump to conclusions," Kevin says.

"We don't know motive. We can't assume he was attacked for being transgender."

"She, sir," Harriet says. "Christa Talbot identified as female and should be referred to as she."

Kevin Richards nods. "That is true, but we have to keep both identities in mind at this stage. Early enquiries suggest the victim lived his daily life as Christopher, a senior solicitor with Highland and Bosch in Cheltenham. Forty-one-year-old divorced father of two. His ex-wife emigrated to Australia with the children. They've been there seven years."

Blimey, forty-one? Even born into the wrong gender, those male chromosomes have been kind in the ageing process. At the crime scene, I put Christa at mid-thirties.

Kevin unfolds his arms and sits on his hands. "One line of enquiry is the victim's apparent double life. Who knew about it? Who took against it? But let's concentrate most on finding witnesses. Who else was in the Gardens this morning? What will camera footage tell us about cars in the vicinity? Any known thugs with a gripe against the LGBTQ community? Any known relatives or friends of the victim driving in the area early this morning? Let's not rule out the killer being a family member."

We know the score. All enquiries start the same way.

"Is the ex-wife definitely in Oz?" I ask.

"The Queensland police are checking," he replies, but we both know it's doubtful she waited seven years to hop on a plane for a spot of knife throwing.

"What about the mother? What's her attitude to her child's transgender status?" Harriet asks.

"Katrina Talbot? We haven't broached that one yet, so no one breathes a word of it outside this room until the liaison officer has tested the waters."

"Is the mother a suspect?" I ask, hopeful it's a domestic and I can give my aching bones an early bath.

"Unlikely," Kevin says. "Uniform tracked her down to a call centre in Cheltenham. Her colleagues confirmed she'd been there since five this morning."

That sounds solid to me too. The corpse was fresher than three hours dead when I saw it at eight thirty a.m. The mother is out of the frame for first-degree murder but in it for a lifetime of mourning. I rub my forehead as the throbbing goes into overdrive. I make an effort to tune into Kevin again.

"Tracey Chiles, the woman who found the body and phoned it in at..." He glances at his notes. "Call logged at seven fifty-nine. She says she saw no one else. And there was only one vehicle present when she arrived at the car park at approximately seven forty. That's been confirmed as the victim's car. So either the killer was long gone or didn't get there by car."

Harriet taps her pen against her teeth. "That's less than twenty minutes between arriving at the garden and phoning triple nine. Tracey Chiles must have made a beeline for the body."

"It was the dog, apparently," Kevin tells her. "It could smell, or sense, something was wrong and dragged her straight there. Thank God she had it on a lead; forensics would have been even more messed up."

He must be thinking of the dog owner's foray into the victim's handbag that will have compromised forensics. It reminds me of something. "Does the victim have another phone? The one at the scene was vintage."

"Good question. Our liaison officer, Stella P, is on her way with the mother to Christa/Christopher Talbot's place. We expect them to find his main phone and wallet there. The Nokia by the body contained only one stored number – saved

22

under the name of Morag. The same number was the last call, received yesterday."

"Anyone we know?"

"Yep. Morag is our old friend Pay-as-You-Go."

There's a collective sigh of frustration although it's what we were all expecting.

"Right, people, that's all for now." Kevin claps his hands. "Allocations are on the board. I'm off to London Road to record a radio appeal. Harriet, you can catch up with Stella and the mother at the victim's house, get her son's life story – tactfully." He turns to me. "Steph, I'd like your input there, too."

I hesitate. "Yes, boss."

Everyone laughs at my whispered reply as I try to suppress pain in my skull and speak at the same time. I stay seated to fish my sunglasses out of my bag while the others check the board and vacate the room.

Harriet loiters by the door. "I suppose we're in your car." She barely keeps her irritation out of her tone. "I could go on my own, you know. I don't mind."

I shake my head. "Sorry, that's not what the boss said." But when I stand up, the pain in my skull comes back with a vengeance and I have to sit down again. I lean forward, finding a position that takes the acuteness off. No way am I up to interviewing a bereaved mother. Kev said Stella Partridge was the police liaison officer assigned to Katrina Talbot. A safe pair of hands and more than capable of tying DC Harriet Harris's shoelaces.

"All right," I say. "I'll tell Stella you're on your way."

A single ray of joy crosses Harriet's face, but her earnest expression soon returns. "Will you be in the office for a debrief later?"

"Email me the mother's witness statement. In case I'm out and about." *In case I'm in a coma.*

———

Jake's at home, watching Sky Sports with a bucket of microwaved popcorn on his lap. But I can hardly tell him off for skiving when I've sacked work at noon.

"Study leave," he explains. "They let us out after the physics paper. I thought you'd be late tonight because of the murder."

"How do you know about that?"

"Internet."

Naturally. I shrug off my leather jacket and hang it on a hook in the entrance hall.

He doesn't notice me wince with pain and swallows another mouthful of salted polystyrene. "People are saying it was a trans woman in the Georgian Gardens. Is that where we went for Bradley's party one time?"

So much for Kevin's warning to keep schtum. It doesn't mean one of us leaked it, though. There's no telling who Tracey Chiles the dog walker talked to when she got home, or the volunteer woman in the garden shop. Did they twig that the victim was transgender and I didn't?

I need to sit down. I pat Jake's arm as I land beside him on the sofa. "Don't suppose Facebook has announced the killer yet?"

"I can check if you like." He fishes his phone out of his back pocket and for a moment I worry my son has turned as humourless as Harriet Harris. Then – thank God – he grins.

I grin back. "Make me a cup of tea first." I'm not sure I'll drink it, but I need something to help swallow down the extra-strength ibuprofen I picked up on the way home.

When he gets up, I fold the sofa's small handmade throw around my legs. On the TV screen, two thickly thighed rugby players collide. I must be ill; no flicker of libido.

"Do you want another blanket?" Jake asks when he comes in with the tea. "Shall I move this?" He lifts my embroidery frame from the coffee table. It's been days since I've been able to focus on it.

I tell him I might do some stitches later.

"It'll be nice in here when it's finished." His compliment puts stress on 'in here'. My craftwork is banned from his room. Gloucester Rugby official merchandise has replaced the Disney cushions I used to sew for him when he was little.

"Give me a shout if you need anything else. I'll be revising." He kisses the top of my head and leaves the lounge in a trot.

Seeing his energy only serves to sap mine more. "I'll text you," I whisper, not up to shouting.

I lift the remote and switch the TV to a local radio channel.

I must have dozed off, but at some point in my slumber the local chit chat and eighties pop music give way to DCI Kevin Richards's radio appeal. My sleeping brain absorbs the gist: *Anyone in the vicinity... between six and eight this morning...*

When my phone pings, I wake up enough to open an email from Harriet. She's interviewed Christopher Talbot's mother. The mum knew of his transgender status but didn't approve. Believes it was the cause of his divorce – something else she didn't approve of. But she concedes it was an amicable split and can't see ex-wife Samantha bearing a grudge, especially when Christopher was still paying maintenance to the children.

My phone slips out of my hand and I drift into sleep again.

———

A new silence in the room makes me open my eyes. I'm alone apart from young and younger smiling Jakes in the framed photos on the dresser. The telly has switched itself off after a couple of hours of inactivity. I know I should phone work for an update on the case but I'm too exhausted. I snuggle under a blanket that I don't think was there last time I woke.

A phone shrieks under the coffee table. I wake and feel drool on the pillow that Jake must also have brought me. Still lying down, I extend my hand, find the phone and press it to my ear.

"I'm at the meeting," my mother's voice says. "I take it you're not going to make it. You must be stuck on that awful case."

I come to consciousness, but with no idea what she means. "Mum? What time is it?"

"Six thirty. Poor girl getting stabbed like that. A hate crime. Unthinkable."

I sit up. "How do you know...?" My breath's too ragged to finish my question, but she'll have read it on Twitter. She's on social media more than Jake is.

Mum's voice softens. "You've still got that headache, haven't you? I'll come round after the meeting."

———

I can't remember ending the call but I'm dreaming once more. It's a fever dream of cartoon DCI Kevins climbing out of the bell of a trombone, over and over, on a loop. Something brushes the top of my head. Mum again. I dream on until the part of my brain that isn't hallucinating realises that her presence is real. I push myself into a sitting position, clutching my head. She hands me a glass of water.

"You didn't have to rush straight round," I say, proud that I've landed on a rational thought. She could have gone to her meeting, whatever it was.

"We finished at Shire Hall hours ago, a complete farce. I've been here since eight, watching you sleep."

Mum has closed the blinds and switched on my standard lamp. It must be getting dark outside. I can't believe I've slept through the entire evening.

"Can I make you some tomato soup?" she asks. "You need to keep your fluids up."

That's normally my favourite, but the thought of food makes me want to retch. "Tell me about your meeting," I say. If she speaks, I won't have to.

She sits beside me and there's a jolt of pain in my head as the sofa sags. "I don't know why I bothered going. The council man, Steven Baker, called himself a planning officer, although, quite frankly, he must have won the job in a Christmas cracker; he clearly isn't up to it. None of his waffle explained how the roadworks would make the roundabout flow better."

Roundabout. I remember now. It was the consultation meeting about the St Giles roundabout. "Sorry I didn't come with you."

"Glad you didn't waste your time. Baker just kept saying this was the best solution in the given budget."

Budget – we hear that word a lot at work. Kevin Richards shakes his head whenever he utters it. Sometimes I think he's close to tears.

"The meeting ended in a walkout. It would be front page of the *Gloucester Evening News* tomorrow if it wasn't for your murder."

"It's not my murder, Mum." Why do people attribute crime to the poor sods tasked with solving it? "What caused the walkout?"

"Someone asked what would happen to the flowerbeds by the church. Baker ended up admitting he'd only ever driven over the roundabout and hadn't noticed any flowers, or a church."

"What?" A surge of annoyance temporarily quells my nausea. "He's planning a major road project and he hasn't made a site visit?"

"Unless they get enough letters of protest to force another meeting, the works will start in June."

I snatch up my mobile. "I'll fire off my objection now. What's his name again?"

Mum gets out her phone. "I'll send you the link. His name is Steven Baker. We all made a note of that. It was a choice between writing in or lynching him."

After I've sent the email, the phone slips from my hand and I feel Mum touch my forehead for a while longer. At some point I put the radio back on, but whether that's before or after she leaves, my semi-conscious state does not register. I sleep again.

# CHAPTER FIVE

Amy dabs her upper lip with the flannel. The lighting in the bathroom is poor but she can still see the raw pink blotches left by the wax strip. She should have given it twenty-four hours to settle, but yesterday ran away from her somehow. Her mother was agitated all day, needy.

Things seem steadier this morning. Mother was dressed when Amy arrived. Now that she's eaten the breakfast Amy made her, she's left Amy alone for a good twenty minutes. Amy still hurries, though. No time for a leisurely pampering session. She'll have to do the best she can with heavy-duty foundation and thick curl mascara. It's no more than she wears for work; she doesn't want to look too keen on a first date. That's why she's gone for classic jeans and a simple, burnt-orange tunic that covers her bottom.

At the age of forty-two, she's going on her first date in nineteen years. He's supposed to be a fireman, but they all say that, don't they? *I'm a lonely, thirty-something, six foot one fireman looking for love.* She described herself as a thirty-nine-year-old florist, so she doesn't mind if he's embellished the truth. She'll settle for fifty with a steady job and his own teeth. And as long as he's five feet four, he'll be taller than her. Just let him be kind, and fertile. The dating service lady assured her that Second Time Around is for discerning, professional people, looking for long-term relationships.

Does she even count as a second timer? She and Sean never made it down the aisle, even though she was a loyal fiancée and stood by him when... Her mother had been right – she deserved better. But she's not looking for someone to heal her broken heart. A baby is the best she hopes for. She snaps closed her vanity bag. These days she's determined enough to get whatever she needs.

The bathroom door rattles as she slides it open, but there's no movement from the figure in the wheelchair when she peers into the lounge. Mother's head is slumped to her shoulder, the light of the muted TV flickering across her sallow skin.

Amy is almost at the front door when her mother calls out. It's not a discernible word – she stopped bothering with those a while ago – but, when Amy turns round, her mother's wide eyes hold both curiosity and hurt. Has she guessed where she's going? Sometimes her mother's sixth sense works in overdrive to compensate for the decline in the other five.

"I didn't want to wake you," Amy says, twisting the keyring round her fingers. "There's a meeting at school about how to celebrate the Royal Wedding." True, except Amy isn't expected to attend. She's only a part-time matron these days, not management.

Her mother's expression doesn't change. It's harder to lie to her now that she can't answer back. Amy goes over and kisses her forehead. Her mother seems to be sniffing. Surely she can't smell Amy's new perfume?

"Would you like a cup of tea before I go?" Amy asks. If she

shows she's got time to boil the kettle, her mother won't think she's in a hurry – even though she is.

When her mother's head gives a tiny shake, Amy kisses her again, silently thanking the god of first dates that she still has an outside chance to make it on time. Mother's eyes fix on the keys in her hand.

"You don't mind if I take your car, do you? The buses aren't so good at this time." She blinks back tears. Why does she keep on asking when they both know her mother won't need it? Her driving days are long gone.

The old lady's face doesn't move, but Amy dashes out before a new hurt can settle there.

———

St Michael's Square car park is mercifully quiet this morning, even though council workers have cordoned off half of it to prune the beech trees that line the edge of the street. As Amy pays at the meter, she wonders if it's the same workmen who will dig up the flowers in front of St Giles's church when work at the roundabout starts. The pointless consultation meeting last night made her blood boil.

La Patisserie is her blind date's idea and she readily agreed. In a busy coffee shop, no one will gawp at a woman drinking alone. And that's her fear – a table for one because he won't turn up. She trots as best she can, keeping it both ladylike and speedy. It's already ten past and she can't expect a stranger to wait for long, that's if he's waiting at all. The short cut takes her past the new flats where the further education college used to be. She got an estate agent to show her round one once, but she'd rather buy an apartment at the Bell Tower with its semi-rural outlook. She likes to think she's a country girl even though she's always lived in this city.

The ruins of Greyfriars, the medieval monastery, are still pinned in scaffolding. The heel of her slingback catches in the cobbles. She limps over to a pile of builders' stones and perches on the edge to sort her sandal. When the breeze blows take-away boxes and coke cans against a scaffolding pole, she touches her hair. Why didn't she think of hairspray? She emerges onto Southgate Street and turns right. Paving slabs replace the cobbles and she picks up speed, her heart chiming in time with the clock above the jeweller's as it sounds the quarter hour.

Smoothing down her tunic, she completes the last few yards at a walk. It wouldn't do for him to see her running. If he's even there. She pushes open the door.

A man at the first table inside the door stands up to greet her. "Are you Amy?" He holds out his hand. "I'm Matt."

She lays her hand briefly on top of his. It's her first intentional contact with male flesh since... when? There must have been something since the headmaster at the prep school welcomed her to the team, but she can't recall. She cranes her neck, scarcely believing that this handsome man really is as tall as he claimed to be.

He must sense the discomfort in her posture and suggests they sit. "Is this table okay? Can I get you a coffee?"

"Fine." Two answers in one. He's gone to the counter before she can change her order to camomile tea. She doesn't drink caffeine in public; it makes her excited.

He returns with a circular tray. As he unloads the contents onto the table, Amy studies him. Blue and white checked shirt, casual but crisply ironed. And his cheeks and jaw are silky smooth. She doesn't recall ever seeing a man with a closer shave. He plunges the cafetière and asks whether she would like milk.

32

She nods. He pours. They smile and look away. She's grateful when he speaks before awkward silence settles in.

"I'm glad you could take the time off for this. I have to be at the station for twelve. Shift work doesn't lend itself to socialising."

*Station – shift work –* so he really is a fireman. She leans back and tidies her hair. "Mine too," she says, hooking her work pattern to his. "My next shift starts at five."

He frowns. "I didn't know florists worked nights."

Needing thinking time, she sips her coffee. He's put too much milk in and it's cooled down. She tops up her cup from the cafetière. "I do the odd shift as a school matron. I've always done the school's flowers and they asked once if I could help out in the boarding house." In truth, the jobs came to her the other way round, but at least she's almost explained her work status.

"Which school?" he asks. Amy swells with pride to hear the interest in his voice.

"Orchard Prep in Cheltenham."

"Nice." He stirs his coffee. "My ex-wife wants our son to go there, but I can't afford..."

He must be keen if he's mentioned his past already. "How old's your son?" Amy asks, eager to show how interested she is too.

"Charlie's eight."

"What a lovely name and a lovely age." Not too old for a baby brother or sister. "The Orchard would be perfect for him."

"I don't think—"

"Such a rounded education, far better than what the state sector offers." The coffee's kicking in and she warms to her theme, showing she bears his ex no malice. It doesn't matter that The Orchard was the former wife's idea. The three of them can work together to raise Amy's stepson, Charlie. But she's getting a little ahead of herself.

Time to let him talk; men like to talk. "Is it fun being a fireman?"

"Except when there's a fire."

She laughs prettily at his joke and turns her head to smooth the other side of her hair. He's stopped smiling. Maybe it wasn't a joke. She straightens her face. "I expect you've seen some terrible sights."

"It's mostly fire prevention these days. I had to visit a guy with a hoarding problem yesterday. Social Services tipped us off that there was a potential fire risk. They got that right. I had to crawl across newspapers to get into each room. There was only a two-foot gap between the piles and the ceiling. The whole place was a tinder box. I was glad to get out."

"You're so brave." She realises she's swooning and swallows more coffee. "Were you able to help?"

"I advised him to have a clear out and wrote my report, but you can't tell people how to live their lives."

"Your job must be stressful." Empathetic, that's how she sounds. She smooths the front of her tunic below the table.

"A lot of it's hanging about waiting for a shout. Having a good gym helps pass the time."

Her gaze drops to his upper arms. The sleeves are tight across his biceps. Something tugs below her belly. She takes another slug of coffee.

He pushes his cup away without refilling it. She'll be as abstemious next time, or better still go for the camomile. *Next time.* He's looking at his watch and she just knows he's about to make an excuse to go.

"They do a lovely afternoon tea here," she says quickly. "Have you tried it?"

He looks at his watch again. "I'm not sure they'll serve it yet."

"Not now. Tomorrow. Three o'clock. Shall we?" She lowers her head and peers upwards, perfecting her doe eyes. "How about it?"

He hesitates, as if playing out his options in his head. Then he shrugs. "Three o'clock it is."

She gets up to leave. "Sorry, I've got to dash today." A lie but she needs to leave first, keep him keen.

He stands up, arms by his sides. She doesn't expect a kiss, and another handshake would be idiotic. But there's a bubble of disappointment in her nonetheless.

As she retraces her steps along Southgate Street, she wonders if she should have left it an extra day. But this Saturday's no good. She'll be busy all day.

# CHAPTER SIX

"You look like death in a microwave." Kevin gives me his words of welcome as I sit in the seat nearest the door and take off my sunglasses.

"Working half the night." The best comeback I can manage.

"Anyone we know?" DC Tony Smith quips.

"Inappropriate," Harriet Harris says, folding her arms. I forget that sometimes she and I can be on the same side. Resting my forehead against my hand, I give her an awkward thumbs-up.

She gets up to brief us on yesterday. "Katrina Talbot is devastated by her son's murder as you'd expect, but she's conflicted too. From the Philippines originally, she's a staunch Roman Catholic and has struggled to accept Christa's gender issues. I think she still hoped it was a phase her son would grow out of. I didn't have the heart to tell her it wasn't a lifestyle choice."

"Good job you didn't," Kevin interjects. "You're not a counsellor."

36

"Yes, sir." She sounds cowed and sits down.

"How long has she known about Christa?" I ask her.

"She says she found out years ago when her son's marriage broke up, and I believe her," Harriet says. "I talked to Stella P, the liaison officer, after the interview, and Stella says the poor woman was genuinely floored when they broke the news of the murder. Even without the call centre alibi, I'd know she's not our killer."

Kevin nods. "It looks as if we can rule out family altogether. While the murder took place on Wednesday morning here, ex-wife Samantha Talbot – or Samantha Robinson as she is now – was enjoying Wednesday evening at a party for her husband's fiftieth in Brisbane. Both kids were there, and any number of reliable witnesses. Her new husband is a sergeant in the Queensland Police."

"Gold-plated then, boss," Tony says, adding a chuckle. "It looks like an outsider did this one. We're working through the CCTV from the cameras at the traffic lights on Painswick Road, but it's a link road between Gloucester and Stroud, and there are plenty who use it as a rat run to Cheltenham or Ciren at that time in the morning."

"Keep at it, Tony. Good job."

I count several pairs of raised eyebrows, but we all know Kevin's only said that to keep him at it. Tony's work isn't usually noted for being good.

Harriet raises her hand. "Sir, I found out something else." She waits for Kevin to look up from his notes. "The mother told Stella he worked for a law firm in Cheltenham, but when I visited them they said Christopher Talbot left six months ago. They gave me the address of his new employer, a languages agency, also in Cheltenham. He's a tutor of English as a Second Language, working mostly in students' homes or community halls."

"That must be a drop in salary," Kevin says. "What's the story?"

"Jumped before he was pushed, I reckon," Tony says. "The law firm partners must have found out about Christa."

Harriet Harris shifts her weight in her chair. "That's just the kind of outdated discrimination that current legislation is there to protect against. Identifying as a different gender isn't grounds for dismissal."

"We know that, DC Harris." Kevin's annoyed now; he isn't calling her Harriet. "But attitudes take a while to catch up. Did you detect any hostility from his former colleagues?"

"The resignation sounded amicable. The other lawyers were bemused at Talbot's decision to quit, that's all. But it was hard to dig because you told us not to say anything about the gender issue."

Kevin removes his spectacles and rubs the ridge of his nose. "Social media ripped that lid off. The press office and I have been up since five, working on damage limitation. From now on Christopher Talbot's transgender status is an open line of enquiry. We need to find out whether a former colleague held a grudge. And we'll have to speak to his language tutees."

"I've got an idea," Harriet says, curling a few strands of fringe through her index finger. "What if Christopher was planning on becoming Christa permanently? The career change could have been part of the plan." I stop rubbing my temples to listen. The woman has her insightful moments between sermons. "The Morag listed on her Nokia phone could have been some kind of mentor who was going to help Christa with the next stage of her transition."

Kevin nods to recognize her contribution and adds, "We are contacting all the gender advisory centres in Gloucestershire, but so far none has confirmed a client called Christopher or Christa Talbot. But they tell us that people often battle transgender issues alone. It can take years before they seek help, and some never do. We haven't yet found a counsellor called Morag, but we're told it could be an individual, giving advice privately, perhaps transgender themselves."

"Or Morag could be our killer," I say. Christa Talbot hadn't dressed like that for a morning stroll; she was meeting someone. A lover, a friend, a mentor. When a victim's phone has one untraceable number on it, the caller is a person of interest.

# CHAPTER SEVEN

Sean observes Amy from his car as she pulls the wheelchair out of the front door of the bungalow and goes towards the drive. He's been watching on and off for a couple of weeks, ever since he found out her dad had died. That's why he's made the trip from Liverpool to stay in a Bed and Backache on Cathedral Street, spending more than he can afford. Speculate to accumulate.

He almost missed her earlier today. Wasn't expecting her to go out again so soon after arriving at the old duck's place. Creature of habit is Amy-Cakes. Number 94 bus to Cheltenham, a nightshift at the posh school, then home to Mummy. But she broke her routine this morning. He had to put down his newspaper and drive after her. Nearly lost her twice more when she jumped an amber light, and after she'd parked, she practically hurdled the cobble stones as she ran through the city centre. Sean saw her shake hands with a bloke in a coffee shop in Southgate Street. She looked nervous, kept fiddling with her hair. Didn't stay long. Maybe the bloke wasn't right for the job.

Sean's figured it out. He's clever like that. Sweet, dutiful Amy is after a carer to offload her mother onto, but he's not surprised she cut the coffee shop interview short. The candidate looked more like a copper than a nurse. Maybe he was an army guy.

It's a puzzle, though. Unsettling. Twice in two days Amy's done something out of character. Interviewing the carer this morning and attending a council talk last night. Sean took a risk slipping into the back row, but there must have been a hundred people in the meeting room at Shire Hall. No one was looking at him, least of all Amy. All eyes were on the suit at the front as he talked out of his arse. Bloke deserved a thrashing.

He watches now as Old Duck Ashby rests her arms on Amy's shoulders and slowly stands up. Amy pushes the empty wheelchair back with her foot and eases her mother round and down into the passenger seat of her red car. After making sure the old woman's legs are clear of the car door, she shuts it and takes the wheelchair to the boot. Sean slides down in his seat as they drive past, then turns to the back page of his newspaper. He won't bother following. They've probably gone to Sainsbury's, as he hasn't seen Amy with shopping bags for a few days; not that he watches her all the time. A man has needs. And he has the other one to watch. Sean scratches his chest through his T-shirt and smiles.

Maybe he'll bin his surveillance operation altogether. Regardless of whether Amy breaks her routine, he's found out enough. Daddy died and will have left his ill-gotten gains to Amy. A tidy sum, as you'd expect of an accountant, well versed in screwing the tax man. And that's not all he screwed in his time. Amy never knew that about her precious daddy, not while she and Sean were dating anyway. Did she find out in the intervening eighteen years? Unlikely, she was too self-absorbed to know what anyone else was up to.

Sean lets out a bitter laugh, loud in the confines of the car. She was too self-absorbed to know what her own fiancé was up to. Once she'd whined and sobbed his engagement ring onto her finger, she took him for granted. They hadn't even set a date, but that didn't stop her from planning their wedding down to the last sugared almond. Is it any wonder he strayed? He wanted affection and fun, and – okay – lust. And he got it in bucket loads with the other one until she found out he was engaged. She kicked him out, wouldn't hear a word of his side of it. He did the decent thing – no one could blame him – and decided to stay with Amy and make a proper go of it. Amy-Cakes was happy. What she didn't know couldn't hurt her.

And now he's back to rekindle the flame. He's single and broke, and Amy's single and loaded. A match made in alimony.

# CHAPTER EIGHT

By mixing and matching ibuprofen and paracetamol, I manage to last at work until five thirty p.m. After Kevin's briefing, most of us hit the phones, tracking down Christopher Talbot's English language students and speaking to his former colleagues at the law firm. I took notes as best I could but my brain was too full of sludge to let anything get through.

Kevin readily agreed when I offered to work on the traffic data and witness statements at home. I'm known for being good at detail, although the only detail I'll manage tonight, before I lapse into unconsciousness, is the opening credits of *Emmerdale*. I'm hoping a good night's sleep will sort me out.

Pain screams behind my eyes as I shuffle through the lounge. It's still shrieking when I sit on the sofa. I hear a police siren and my natural copper's nosiness drags me achingly to the window though I can't see the road from here. Swaying from hip to hip like I did in early labour, I look out at the cow field. There haven't been any cows in it since kids blinded one by chucking stones. More sirens wail but there's no disturbance that I can see.

Still, I'm lucky to have this outlook only three miles from the city centre. I've fallen on my size fives here, thanks to my parents. When the convalescent hospital closed, developers bought the prettiest building – the one with the bell tower on the roof – and turned it into flats. Dad got his deposit down quick and I moved in when I was still at Debenhams, before I started my beauty therapy training.

In the early days I paid my parents what rent I could, then no rent at all when I was saving to start my salon, and still none when I got pregnant and had to abandon my business plans.

Twenty-two years after moving here, I've bought my parents out and they're pleased but also mildly dismayed that I haven't moved on to a place with a white picket fence. Never felt the need.

Never found the man.

Out of the window I see a teenage girl walking, still in her school uniform. She's leading a Staffordshire bull terrier around the outside of the tennis courts. No one's playing despite it being a sunny late afternoon. The dog squats on a grass verge. To my surprise, the girl flicks out a plastic bag and picks up the mess. Blimey, well done, love. You can date my son. I laugh but wish I hadn't. More pain wallops my head.

My phone goes and I hobble to where I've left my handbag on a hook in the hall.

"Steph, are you at home?" The tone of Kevin's voice says he's about to tell me something I don't want to hear. "There's an incident at the old convalescent hospital building. Can you deal? It's near your place, isn't it?"

Apart from the Bell Tower, only one other building from the hospital remains standing. It's been used for various purposes since the hospital's closure: drop-in centre for the elderly, chiropodist practice, and most recently office space for health service staff. But it shut for good six months ago, padlock on the gate and *development opportunity for sale* board in the car park.

"What's happened?" I ask.

"Suspicious death. I'll tell the PCSO you'll be there in five minutes."

"More like twenty," I say quickly. "Cars can only go left out of here. You have to drive through the new estate, on to Warren Hill and up the back road."

"That's why I thought of you, Steph. It's five minutes if you walk." He ends the call.

I'm almost crying as I put the phone in my bag and grab my jacket. Walking is something retired people do, not forty-three-year-old detectives with an ibuprofen habit. I take the lift to the ground floor, and outside I turn right to embark on the longest five-minute journey of my life. The girl with the Staffy has gone. At the edge of the cow meadow, a couple in grubby track-suits and holding dog leads share a fag. They saunter on when two German shepherds emerge from the meadow, rubbing their back paws on the ground.

The panda in the normally empty hospital car park explains the sirens I heard. The black Range Rover of Siobhan Evans, the pathologist, is also there with three other vehicles I don't recognise. Siobhan is still in the driver's seat and raises a hand in greeting. Police tape cordons off the building and Jess Bolton, the PCSO I met at the murder scene yesterday, is on sentry duty at the gate. She opens it as I approach.

"Sorry, Steph, my patrols aren't usually this eventful."

I shake my head. "To find one corpse may be regarded as misfortune; to find two looks like carelessness."

"Who said that?"

"Oscar Wilde, when he wrote thrillers. What were you doing here?"

"We patrol the estate most evenings. Dealers sit in their

cars over there." She points beyond the path to the remains of the old hospital service road. Grass and thistles split the tarmac and there's a pile of pizza boxes by a burnt-out sofa. "Council erected bollards to keep cars out but kids ripped them up. Same thing happened to the padlock on this car park. I reported it the first few times it got broken, but I guess the council got fed up of replacing it."

"What time?"

"Six fifteen. We noticed the gate was open, and this car parked inside." She points at the green Volvo beside her police vehicle. "It wasn't here when we came past at four thirty."

"You came past twice?"

"We heard a rumour that dealers were setting up straight after school."

I rub my neck as a new ache burns. If I didn't feel ropey, I'd feel ashamed. How can I call myself a police officer and not know what's happening on my own doorstep? Worse still, how can I call myself a mother and let Jake hang out here with his mates?

"We stopped to investigate," Jess continues. "I noticed the door to the building was open, went for a closer look and found him just inside."

"Him?"

"I'd say this one's definitely a him," she says, recalling our last crime scene. "But better brace yourself. It isn't pretty."

Siobhan gets out of her car and the occupants of two of the other cars assemble by her.

"Why the heavy breathing?" she asks as I walk towards her.

"Ran to get here."

"Lay off the fags."

"Got to have a hobby." I laid off fags eighteen years ago, but it suits if she thinks otherwise. It's better than Dr Siobhan Evans knowing I'm struggling to shake off this migraine.

After donning my nitrile gloves, I push open the door to the building and manage not to go arse over victim. The feet and legs rest on the bristly surface of the fitted doormat and the upper body extends to the tiled foyer floor. Matter and blood ooze like lava from the back of the head and merge in colour with the man's rust-coloured hair and beard. I don't dwell there and concentrate on the rest of him, the essence of who he was before this outrage. Black lace-ups, a grey suit, blue shirt cuff below the jacket sleeve.

I make my initial notes as Siobhan and her team begin their work. We discover that the electricity is off so the team prop open the door to get more light on the scene. I stand outside and watch through the opening as Siobhan, two other women and a man – all in masks and coveralls – become active around the corpse, variously dusting powder, collecting samples, taking notes. I spread my feet and put my hands in my jacket pocket.

Eventually Siobhan comes to the door. "I'd say not more than an hour and a half ago. The weapon was probably that rock found in situ." She points as one of her assistants takes photos of a large stone that's lying further into the foyer. It has a regular shape to it – a builder's brick? Its craggy surface colour is a mottled cocktail of claret and honey. "My guess is the killer threw it down after the attack and it skittered on this shiny surface to its current resting place." There's a trail of red scruff marks on the tiles between the victim's head and the brick.

"Any idea where it came from?" I ask.

Siobhan shrugs. "It's possible the killer picked up whatever was handy."

"Unplanned, improvised. Is that what you're saying?" Could the killer be one of PCSO Jess Bolton's juvenile junkies?

Siobhan looks upwards as if pondering the question. "I'll

know more when I've had the stone analysed. It could be that the victim stumbled across something in here he wasn't supposed to see and he had to be shut up quickly. My initial thoughts are that he stepped inside first and the killer came in immediately after him."

"How did the victim get in?" This place must have been locked when they closed it down, or has that padlock gone the way of all the others round here?

"No sign of forced entry, but he's clutching a bunch of keys in his fist. It's highly likely we'll find one that fits the lock. Did you notice the lanyard round his neck?"

"Hard to see his neck." It's covered in blood.

"ID badge says he's a planning officer with the county council. Perhaps he was here on business. His name is Steven Baker."

I make my notes and wait for the rest of my team to arrive, all the while hoping my head will clear enough to remember where I've heard that name.

# CHAPTER NINE

Sean looks across the meadow towards the apartment building. It's been nearly a week since he caught a glimpse of her. Maybe she spent the bank holiday in Ibiza with all the other over-the-hill slappers desperate for a drunken grope and an STD. But how can she still be away with everything that's going on?

A Yorkshire terrier yaps at his ankles until he stamps the ground. It yelps and scurries off, no owner in sight. He's about to abandon his stake-out when he sees her, walking like a granny towards the Bell Tower. Where did she come from? The murder must mean she's been summoned. He throws down his fag end and grinds it into the grass. He never thought she would end up in the Filth. She was a beautician when he was seeing her. There isn't a bargepole long enough he'd poke a copper with.

After tapping in a code at the pedestrian gate into the Bell Tower grounds, she shuffles towards the purple Golf he knows is hers. He can now see that she's proper hobbling. Must have attended a domestic and got caught in the crossfire. He lights another fag and takes a slow drag over his teeth and into his throat, savouring the thought. It happens when you interfere in other people's business. A smoky o-ring leaves his mouth. He should have taught someone else that lesson. If he hadn't lost his bottle all those years ago, maybe he and Amy would still be together.

The woman's stopped walking, both hands resting on her right hip. He rubs the roll of his belly. He's in his prime, but she looks old. No one would believe she's three years younger than him. She used to be a proper firecracker. Up for anything. Then she found out he was engaged and came over all moral.

But she seemed angrier about who his fiancée was rather than the fact that he had one. That's the trouble with women – unpredictable. What was it about Amy that narked Steph so much? Had Amy been one of her clients? That seemed unlikely. Amy didn't have money to burn on beauty treatments in those days. Amy-Cakes was a D-I-Y girl who kept herself tidy. He feels his groin swell and he shifts his weight. Sometimes when he rubbed up against those shins, he could feel bristles. Those were the days: two women, both a turn on.

Now what? He takes another drag on his cigarette to calm himself. Steph is propped against her car, talking to a bloke on a bike. An informant? Coppers have snouts, don't they? A woman like her would have no trouble hooking one. Sean clenches his fists; she hooked him. He's never been sure who he hates more: her or Amy's mother.

She suddenly pecks the bloke on the cheek. The cigarette slips from Sean's mouth. The couple keep on chatting and she touches his arm. After a minute the man walks his bike to the grass verge and she gets into her car. Sean sees her point a remote control at the wrought iron gates and they open. She waves to her fella as she turns left onto the road. Judging by his physique, he can't be more than twenty years old. After she's gone, he wheels his bike round the side of the building. Sean knows from his previous stake-outs that, apart from the bin store that makes a handy step up to a first-floor balcony, there's only a bicycle rack round the back. The lad is making himself at home. So she's moved onto toy boys? Sean always thought there was something desperate there. He almost feels sorry for her, but not quite. She was one of those who messed his life. But he's more than a match now. He'll get his way whatever he has to do.

# CHAPTER TEN

Parents' evening at Parkway Academy. The car park and school field are clogged with 4X4s, as if the parents have arrived from across the Australian Outback instead of the A417.

I hover on double yellows by the main entrance until two women head towards a Honda on the field. As they back their car out, I mount the kerb and wait. The prolonged period of dry weather continues and makes the grass easy to drive over. I slot into the vacated space.

In the foyer, half a dozen smiling teens in school sweat-shirts hand out floor plans and direct parents to the right room. PC Izzy Hutton appears through a door on the right and beckons me.

"We're in here, Steph. The school's given us the library."

We step into a large room where it's eerily quiet after the hubbub outside. The latest teen fiction vies with ancient text-books for space on ugly metal shelves. Desks the size of dining tables fill the floor in regimented rows. By the window on easy chairs, Stella P sits beside a woman who's dabbing her eyes.

Izzy stays at the door to ensure we aren't disturbed. I approach Stella.

"We have to wait for the pathologist before we can really know what happened," she's saying.

"But what about the funeral?" The woman leans forward. "Can I start making arrangements?"

"I know it's hard but leave it for now." Stella sees me and drags over another chair. I catch the look of relief on her face. No interview with the bereaved is easy. She must be glad to see reinforcements.

The woman is late thirties, thick hair. Black trousers, floral blouse, beige jacket. Smart but not quite power-dressing, it's the typical uniform of most secondary school teachers.

"Mrs Baker?" I sit down. "I'm Steph, a detective inspector. I'm sorry for your loss."

Her swollen eyes don't meet mine but she nods her acknowledgement. Her skin is blotchy and I can imagine the sobbing that must have followed Stella's arrival with news of her husband's murder.

"Are you up to answering a few questions?"

She nods again. "He was only forty-one. We should never have moved here. I told him I didn't want to."

"Where were you before?"

"Nottingham. We were both born there. Only came to Gloucestershire a year ago. It wasn't even on promotion. He took a job at the same grade so he could keep a closer eye on his grandfather." She lets out a bitter laugh. "The man's eighty-six, but it looks like he'll outlive us all." Fresh tears flood her eyes but there's anger too.

I keep my expression impassive. Don't family squabbles get set aside at times like this? The woman's resentment surprises me.

"Your husband must have been fond of his grandfather,"

I say.

"They were always close, but since Steven's mother and grandmother died, Steven took it upon himself to look after him. I told him it wasn't his job. The old man needs specialist care. Social Services." She folds her arms. "I told Steven he had other responsibilities."

She must mean children. I'm not warming to Mrs Baker but I don't envy her the task of breaking this news to their kids.

She must read my thoughts. "We've always had a strong marriage – no family of our own, just each other. When Steven was growing up it was him and his mum against the world. Now it's me and him." She bursts into tears. "It *was* me and him."

Stella hands her a box of tissues and we let her cry it out. When she's calmed down, I ask if anything was troubling her husband apart from his elderly relative.

Her eyes flash. "What's his job got to do with anything? It hardly matters now."

Stella and I exchange a glance. "Was there a problem at work?" I ask.

"Work didn't kill him, did it? Not in the end, despite my warnings."

Something pricks in my memory. I try again to recall where I heard the name Steven Baker. Before I can think how to ask, Mrs Baker carries on speaking.

"He got lumbered with a road project he didn't want." Her eyes well with fresh tears. "To think, our last night together and he was late home because of a stupid public meeting. I hadn't seen him so agitated since his mother's death. No one deserves abuse for doing their job, do they?" Her eyes dart between Stella and me. "Do they?"

We nod grimly and don't point out that, for police officers, abuse and job are joined at the hip.

# CHAPTER ELEVEN

INCIDENT ROOM | FRIDAY 11TH MAY, 8 A.M.

Despite the blinds being closed against the spring sunshine, it's hot in the incident room. It's full of live bodies because two dead ones mean no new leave is permitted. Standing room only for many younger detectives in the team, but inspector's perks have got me a seat at the front. That and the fact I look decrepit enough to be their elderly auntie. My eyes are heavy. It was after midnight when I got off duty. Interviews to conduct. Reports to file and several to read. And of course, even then I couldn't sleep, brain wired with facts and theories for both cases.

"Steph?"

I jerk awake. "I'm listening." But I don't even know who is speaking. I make a guess at Kevin. "Sir?"

I'm right. "What have you got for us?" he asks.

I flick through my notes while I manoeuvre my thoughts into gear.

"Come on, Steph," Tony Smith says. "Some of us have worked a full week already. No bank holiday off. What's your excuse?"

"Quality not quantity," I say and raise a titter round the room. Seeing Tony scowl is enough to send a jolt of energy through me. I recount what I found out in my late-evening enquiries. "The victim is Steven Baker. We tracked his wife to her place of work. She's a teacher at Parkway Academy and was in the middle of a parents' evening during the time of the murder, apparently."

"Why apparently?" Kevin asks.

I shrug. "Something and nothing. A funny way of showing her grief, but I think she's legit. Plenty of people saw her at school."

Kevin gets up and paces the room as I carry on. The others turn towards me to listen.

"According to the wife, Steven Baker was forty-one years old, born in Nottingham, but they moved here a year ago so that he could keep a closer eye on his grandfather. Mrs Baker intimated that she would be contacting Social Services to see if they could take the grandfather into a home."

"That's sad." Harriet Harris looks at me wistfully.

Kevin goes back to perching on a desk. "Any threats, enemies, the usual?"

"Everyone loved him. He was a regular Mr Nice Guy – like they all are – but she did mention he'd come home late from work the previous evening and was upset about a public meeting that hadn't gone well. He—"

"Sir, I know what the meeting was." Harriet waves her hand like a ten-year-old answering a times table question. "I managed to get hold of Steven Baker's head of branch at home last night. Baker was involved in a controversial road project. He attended a consultation meeting on Wednesday night and got badly heckled. Some people even jostled him on the way out." She smiles at me, triumph on her thin lips.

I resist the urge to tell her that I remembered who Steven

Baker was halfway through my interview with his wife. My mother mentioned his name when she talked about the disastrous council meeting she attended. Without acknowledging Harriet's interruption, I move the discussion forward from the council meeting to Baker's murder. "His wife had no idea why he was at the old convalescent hospital last night. What did his head of branch say?"

Harriet looks at her notes. "Besides the road project, Baker was managing the portfolio for the sale of the hospital building and the land it's built on, so any potential purchasers would have contacted him. The boss accessed his department's intranet while I was on the line but he found nothing entered on the electronic calendar. He's promised to check Baker's desk diary when he gets in this morning and if necessary ask his colleagues if they know anything."

"Get straight round there after this," Kevin tells her. "Interview the colleagues yourself. Find out what Baker was like to work with. And see if they took a register of everyone who went to that road traffic meeting. Could someone have got sufficiently heated to take their anger further afterwards? We need to talk to those attendees."

I smile to myself. If my mother gets interviewed in a murder enquiry, I'll never hear the end of it. She'll be delighted.

Kevin moves on to give us the main points of Siobhan Evans's initial forensic report. Most of it I know from talking to Siobhan at the crime scene. "A sustained attack, at least five blows, any one of which was enough to kill. This is the weapon." He puts up an image on the screen.

Tony stands up and goes closer. "Looks like a brick to me."

"Takes one to know one," I say.

"What's that, Steph?" He moves towards me.

57

"Sorry, did you say brick? I'm full of hay fever. I must have misheard."

Harriet is the first to laugh. Soon they're all at it except Tony.

"You're full of something, that's for sure," he snaps.

"Weak." Harriet shakes her head, disappointed in his game. Her phone rings and her expression grows serious. "It's Baker's boss. I'd better just take this." She heads to the door.

Kevin waits for Tony to sit down and resumes his briefing on the weapon. "It's Cotswold stone, used – as Tony suggested – in construction. But not on buildings in or around the old hospital. In Gloucester, it's really only used on historic sites in the city centre."

"The killer brought it with them then," Tony says emphatically. "It was premeditated."

"Let's hang fire until Harriet tells us who Steven Baker was meeting. Sorry to be a broken record, but our priority is as per the Christopher Talbot case: find witnesses. Track down anyone in the vicinity of the convalescent hospital yesterday evening. Our killer is likely to have left the scene with blood on their clothing. I recorded an appeal earlier this morning. Radio Gloucestershire has promised to play it every hour. Mids FM will use it, too."

"Did you link the two murders?" Tony asks. For once a sensible question.

But Kevin shakes his head. "Nothing at this stage to say they're connected. We will, of course, be looking into whether Christopher Talbot and Steven Baker knew each other, so we'll keep an open mind. But for now we're treating them as two separate cases."

Harriet returns, pocketing her phone. "Sir, the head of department checked Steven Baker's desk diary. Baker had written down a meeting with Radley Development at five p.m.

No address but presumably at the convalescent hospital. The boss says no one in the planning office has heard of Radley Development. They haven't dealt with them before."

My nose can't help twitching. "Doesn't that suggest a possible link?"

Kev's eyebrows do that annoying thing that says he'll hear you out but thinks you've got it wrong. The others look at me expectantly.

"Two forty-something white collar workers killed," I say. "Both smartly dressed. One meeting a probably bogus company. The other with one untraceable number in their phone. Both lured to an isolated place."

"Interesting theory, Steph. But Christa Talbot had a specific secret. We have to consider that line of enquiry," Kevin says.

"Agreed," I say, listing in my seat, pain throbbing. With supreme effort, I finish my speech. "All I'm saying is that we've got two decisive attacks in two days. Neither victim knew what the hell had hit them."

# CHAPTER TWELVE

At the doctor's surgery, old people – older than her mother – gingerly prod the sign-in screen and creak into the plastic chairs in the waiting room. A young woman, holding a silent, poorly baby on her lap, attempts to occupy an active toddler with a tattered storybook from the plastic crate in the corner.

Amy can't sit here among the sick. There's a restless, almost joyful spirit in her today, thanks to the second date with Matt later. She goes to stand outside the disabled loo, thinks about knocking but decides against it. Her mother won't be able to reply. She paces like a caged tigress, past the doors to the doctors' consulting rooms and the nurses' office, and round a woman with a bandaged ankle, limping along in slippers. At the end of the corridor, Amy turns, dodges the woman again and returns to the disabled loo. It's a good sign, isn't it, that her mother wheeled herself in there and shut Amy out? She bites her lip. She's pleased at the improvement in her mother's mobility but feels like a fraud for booking this emergency appointment.

The doctor they saw last time comes out of his room,

heading towards the waiting area, but stops when he sees Amy outside the loo. "Is your mother in there? She's my next patient." He sounds as impatient as last time.

Amy's mood darkens and she fills with fluster and apology. "I'll go in and get her."

At that moment the door slides open and her mother wheels herself out, giving the doctor a slanting smile. A breath catches in Amy's throat. Has her mother had a stroke? That's not how she used to smile.

The doctor pushes the wheelchair to his room and invites Amy to take a seat.

"How are you feeling today, Mrs Ashby?" he asks, raising his voice slightly.

Amy bristles; her mother's hearing is the one faculty that's undiminished.

"I thought she had a fever," Amy explains. "She was restless in the night. When I went to check on her this morning, her skin was clammy and she seemed unresponsive. It took her a while to wake up."

Ignoring Amy, the doctor turns to the older woman. "Mrs Ashby – Eileen – is it okay if I take your temperature and blood pressure?"

She responds by opening her mouth.

He smiles. "This goes in your ear." He leans over her with his electronic thermometer. It beeps when it's got a reading.

"Nothing to worry about," he says after a few seconds. "Can you roll up your sleeve, please?"

Amy takes charge, pushing up the bobbled sleeve of her mother's grey cardigan and unbuttoning her polyester cuff. Even the clothes seem ill.

The doctor places the rubber sleeve around her mother's thin arm. Her expression doesn't change as it tightens.

"Blood pressure normal," he says. "Is it okay if I listen to your chest?"

"I'm sorry I bothered you," Amy says, twisting her fingers in her lap. "I thought she'd come down with something."

After checking her mother's heart and lungs through her blouse, he lays the stethoscope round his neck. "If it happens again, try an extra dose of paracetamol to bring down the temperature. Do you have enough of everything or shall I write you a prescription?"

Is it her imagination, or is his tone to her far sharper than to her mother? He's annoyed she's wasted his time again.

"We need another bottle of eye drops," she says. She can do sharp too.

He looks up, frowning, then he reads off his screen. "It should be one drop in each eye, twice a day."

"I know that." Amy manages not to snap but it isn't easy. Does he think she's stupid? "Things get dropped sometimes."

He scrutinises her, frowning again. "Are you at home full time?"

Amy isn't sure what he means. "Last night I stayed the night in Mum's spare room." She still can't bring herself to call it her room. A Bell Tower flat is where she'll sleep in her own bed. One day. She feels her skin flush in excitement. One day soon. The decision's made. She's already put the wheels in motion. Nothing can stop her when she puts her mind to something.

With a clipped "thank you", she takes the printed out prescription from him and manoeuvres the wheelchair into the corridor.

## Radio and Social Media Appeal by DCI Kevin Richards

*At approximately six fifteen yesterday evening, in a routine patrol, Police Community Support Officers discovered a man with severe head injuries at a disused office building in the Abbeyfield area of Gloucester. The man was pronounced dead at the scene. He has been identified as Steven Baker, aged forty-one. Mr Baker's next of kin have been informed and are being supported by specialist officers.*

*I want to appeal to anyone in the area who might have seen or heard anything out of the ordinary between four thirty p.m. and six fifteen p.m. yesterday. Did you see anyone close to the office block, formerly a convalescent hospital on Abbey Lane? If you were driving through the Abbeyfield/Warren Hill area, do you have a dashcam? Do you have private CCTV? Any piece of information, however small you think it might be, could be critical in piecing together the circumstances that led to this man's death.*

*This was a vicious and brutal attack. We need to find who is responsible and make sure this doesn't happen to anyone else in our city.*

# CHAPTER THIRTEEN

Sean's car is parked opposite the bungalow. The neighbours have gone to work and the close is deserted. But time is too tight to break in again. Amy took the old duck to the doctor's ages ago and could be back any minute. He followed her and watched her grapple with the wheelchair across the rough, uneven car park because a non-entitled car had taken the last space in the tarmacked disabled bay. No consideration, some people. They lacked... what's the word? Empathy, that's it. Sean has empathy in spades. Look how much he still cares about Amy and how she must have missed him in the empty years of her life since he left. Now she's stuck looking after her awful mother. His knuckles whiten in his lap. *Not for much longer*.

While Amy and her mother were at the surgery, he drove here, using the waiting time for quiet reflection. A chance to get all his ducks in order – one duck in particular. All he needs is another two days – just to be sure.

He hears engine noise and slides behind his newspaper as Amy pulls into the drive in her mother's Toyota Corolla. It's a filthy heap. The task of washing the tyres and wheel arches must be another burden that falls to Amy-Cakes. He grins as he pictures how grateful she'll be when he frees her from all this.

Amy drags the wheelchair out of the boot, scraping it against the paintwork. She's not usually careless, but today her movements are brisk. She pulls the wheels apart to flatten the seat and slips in the cushion. The chair's too close to the passenger door and she has to reverse the chair to give her mother space to get out. Then she steps back, drumming the roof of the car with her fingers while the old duck pulls against the open door to bring herself into a standing position. Amy moves the wheelchair forward so that it nudges the backs of the old woman's legs, causing her to fold into it. Amy closes the door, zaps the key fob and strides to the front door. The chair moves at speed in front of her and there's a determined set to her gait.

Sean slips his hand into the neck of his T-shirt and rubs his chest. Her behaviour has thrown him again. What is it with her this week? Maybe he needs to spend longer on his preparations, just to be sure.

# CHAPTER FOURTEEN

We're making house calls. Harriet Harris managed to get a copy of the handwritten register the council took of those attending the St Giles roundabout meeting. It isn't foolproof. If I'd been planning on murdering the principal speaker, I'd have signed in under a fake name and address, but it's one of the hoops police work has to stumble through.

Harriet offered to drive. Just as well, as my head and neck hurt so much I can only make right turns. We'd have gone via Monmouth if I was at the steering wheel.

Harriet parks outside the home of the next name on the register.

"Do murderers live in bungalows?" I say, eyeing the net curtains. "It's a joke," I add when Harriet sets her expression to sermonising. "Who've we got?"

Harriet peers at the photocopied register. "It looks like Ashby – could be a Mr or Mrs – they wrote down this address."

She rings the bell and we step back from the door to admire the grubby red car in the drive and the pots of plants under the porch. Lilies and carnations, but some of the stalks are cut. The owner must have collected a bunch of flowers for the house.

The door is answered on Harriet's second ring.

A gasp forms in my gut, rises up my chest, squeezes through my throat, bypasses my mouth and explodes in my brain. I don't know what my face is doing, but Harriet throws a puzzled frown between me and the woman on the doorstep. Below her make-up the woman's skin has blanched and her lipsticked mouth has formed an 'O'. But she recovers before I do.

"Steph?"

"Hello, Amy." I manage not to choke.

"Do you two...?" Harriet asks.

Amy and I speak at the same time.

"Used to."

"Not any more."

I brandish my police ID, hating myself for hiding behind it. "Do you mind if we come in? My colleague has some questions."

"Just routine," Harriet adds, picking up my clumsily thrown baton.

Amy studies our identity cards closely. She glances at her watch, bites her lip and peers out from behind her fringe. I stiffen; she always used to do the thing with the lip and the eyes. Never fooled me.

"Please, it won't take long." Harriet moves up to the doorstep.

"I..."Amy checks her watch again. "I've got an appointment and I have to settle my mother before I go."

"You still live with your parents?" If my tone is judgmental, I don't mean it to be, but I'm curious how Mr and Mrs Ashby moved from their big house to here with Amy still in tow.

"This is my mother's place," Amy says tightly. "I'm staying here while she's ill. My father passed away a few months ago."

"I'm sorry for your loss." My voice is croaky and I have to cough. I look at Harriet, my hot face pleading with her to take over. I've clapped eyes on this woman for the first time in forever and history is already repeating. How many times did I used to end up saying sorry to Amy Ashby?

"If you let us come in and ask our questions – about a public meeting you attended on Wednesday – we won't trouble you for longer than necessary." Harriet holds up her hands and gently guides her inside. I'm starting to love Harriet.

The hallway is empty but I can smell talcum powder. Through an open sliding door to a bathroom, I see a zimmer frame inside a shower cubicle. We go past, following Amy. She's wearing designer jeans and a soft pink top. Her waist is still tiny but she carries bulk on her haunches. The opposite of me. When the years caught me up, the weight hit my boobs. Never had a waist, but still got good legs. No arse, though. These hips certainly weren't childbearing on the day and a half it took Jake to pass through them.

Amy's still auburn – natural as far as I can tell – but she wears her hair in a short bob. I tug my hair, beating her on length but knowing the brown needs topping up at the roots.

"You remember my mother?" Amy says when we enter the lounge.

A grey-haired figure with the back of her wheelchair towards us slumps close to a television. It's the quiz show hosted by the actor from *Star Wars*. More familiar than I would like, the programme reminds me how I spent my extra day off, hunched in a blanket in front of daytime TV. Amy mutes the sound and turns the wheelchair. Thin to skeletal, wizened hands, slow-blinking red eyes. Is this the same Mrs Ashby who complained about me to our head teacher on a weekly basis?

Amy folds her arms. "I don't mean to be rude but I can't offer you coffee. I don't have time."

"Your appointment, of course," Harriet says, sitting on the sofa. "We'll be brief."

"It's work. I'll be late for work," Amy says quickly and glances at the old woman.

My gut says she's lying, but for her mother's benefit not ours. I wonder where she's really going. A man? I give myself a mental slap. Why should I care about Amy Ashby's love life, especially if it's better than mine?

I sit beside Harriet, and as she explains why we're here, I take in the fixtures and fittings. No ornaments or photographs, not even the vase of flowers I was expecting. Amy's mother must be renting or fallen on hard times. The coffee table is cluttered with medicine bottles and rolled up bandages. The trappings of old age. I vow to clear my painkillers, water and blanket from the lounge when I get home.

There's one picture on the wall next to me. It's a certificate: *University of Evesham. Presented to the student achieving the highest mark in Child Care Level 3 Diploma: Amy Eileen Ashby.* Does Amy still work in child care? It's doubtful she has her own kids if she's moved in with her mother – no muddy trainers in the hall, no PlayStation plugged into the TV, no crumpled sweatshirt abandoned on the sofa. One thing I've achieved that she hasn't.

"Why do you want to know about that awful meeting?" Amy asks Harriet. "I went because I use that road a lot, but wish I hadn't bothered. It became obvious the council was only paying lip service to the consultation process." The eyes look out from her fringe again.

"Did you speak to Steven Baker, the council officer?" Harriet asks.

"There was nothing worth asking him. Do you know he

hadn't even visited the site? He must have won his town planning qualifications in the lottery."

I grin into my knees. I never thought I'd recall my easygoing mother sounding like Amy Ashby, but Mum said more or less the same thing about Steven Baker.

"Can you remember him being jostled at the end of the meeting?" Harriet asks.

"I left during the questions so that I could get back to my mother."

We all look at Mrs Ashby. She doesn't move, other than the pulse of a vein through her waxen neck.

"The planning officer was getting quite a bit of flak," Amy continues. "Verbal, I mean. People were booing and calling out. I heard them start a slow hand clap after I'd gone into the corridor."

"Did anyone threaten him?"

"He was red in the face and fluffing his answers, but I don't think he was in any physical danger. He must have realised what a fool he was making of himself." She checks her watch again. "I start at three."

"And you spent the rest of the evening with your mother?"

"I had a late duty. At Orchard Prep." She looks at me, letting the name-drop linger. "That's why I wanted to get home quickly to settle her before I went to work."

Harriet makes a note. "Do you work every night?"

"I'm a part-time matron. My shifts vary."

"One on, one off. That sort of thing, is it?" Harriet says. "So last night was a welcome night off?"

Nice one, Harriet. She's working up to the time of Steven Baker's murder.

"I spent last night here but I was at the school earlier in the evening. I do their floral displays. I'm City and Guilds trained." She glances at me.

So what? I have my sewing. I recall her embroidery at school being naff. I'd say we're one-all in handicrafts.

"I've been to Orchard School a few times and always admired their flower arrangements," Harriet says. *Little liar.* No way has this young copper visited a posh prep school. "What time did you do the flowers yesterday?"

"I was out there between five thirty and eight."

"And the school can confirm that?"

Amy cocks her head to the side and bites her lip again. "Why do you want to know? Has something happened?" She puts her hand on her throat and widens her eyes. "Of course, the murder. It was on the radio. A council worker. It's him, isn't it? I'm sorry I said those things about him. You must think me a terrible person. I wouldn't wish that on him. Or anybody." Her eyes linger on me. *With one exception,* they say.

*Feeling's mutual.* Mine are right back at her.

Amy tips her head again. "You've got two murders, haven't you? How awful." Her tone exudes the old Amy condescension I used to know and loathe. I look at Harriet to stop myself biting.

"You've been most helpful." Harriet closes her notebook, stands up and smiles at the mother. "Goodbye, Mrs Ashby." The old woman continues her death stare, hooded eyes blinking.

"I'll show you out," Amy says.

She stays on the doorstep as we step outside. "It's been lovely to see you again, Steph," she says, but has the grace to blush as much as I do.

"I'm sorry about your father," I say. I was never a fan of Amy's mother, but her husband's death can't have helped her condition. How would my mum be without Dad? Doesn't bear thinking.

"These things happen," Amy says, dismissing my efforts at playing nice.

"Thanks again," Harriet says and points her key fob at our car.

As we start to walk away, Amy calls, "How long have you been in the police, Steph?"

I turn round. "Ten years."

"Been promoted yet?"

"I'm an inspector," I say, keeping my tone neutral even though I know she's said it to rattle me. She studied my ID card long enough to know my rank.

She smiles and bites her lip at the same time. "Inspector Lewis. That must be trying at times. All the jokes at your expense."

"Only from the middle-aged. Young people don't watch TV."

Nice one, Steph, I tell myself as we drive away, until I remember Amy Ashby is ten months younger than me.

# CHAPTER FIFTEEN

Amy arrives out of breath. Matt stands up, polite as well as patient. She thought he might have given up waiting for her; she's twenty minutes late. He pulls out her chair and she catches the scent of his aftershave. Her already flushed skin grows warmer.

"Bad traffic?" he asks, taking his seat opposite. It's the same table as yesterday. Does that make it their usual meeting place, like an established couple?

"I got delayed," she explains. "My mother..." She won't mention the police but worries she's made up the wrong excuse. Do men date women with invalid parents?

"Shall we order? The waitress said she'd come across when we're ready." He waves to the young woman at the counter. When she walks over, her smile is a little too wide for Amy's liking and her white blouse and black pencil skirt fit a little too well.

"Do you still want the afternoon tea we talked about?" Matt asks. "Have you got time?"

She's got bags of time – she's not due at school until

tomorrow morning – but the waitress has made her think of Steph. She forces a smile. "Just a toasted teacake and a camomile tea."

She studies Matt's face as he scans the menu. Is he disappointed with her meagre order? She knows she is – she skipped lunch for this. She wants to change what she's asked for to the sandwiches, scones and cream cakes, but she's said it now and she's not in the mood to unsay it.

"I'll have the same but with black coffee, thank you." Matt hands the girl the menu and watches her return to the counter.

Amy clenches her fists below the table. What is it with women who steal other women's partners?

"So how've you been?" Matt says, giving Amy his full attention once a paying customer at the counter blocks his view of the waitress.

"Good. How's Charlie?" Her hands unfurl and rub her thighs as she mentally congratulates herself for remembering his son's name.

His expression clouds. "I haven't seen him since the bank holiday. I was supposed to have him tomorrow but I've got to work the morning shift. Someone's off with 'flu. There's a lot of it about."

Amy narrows her eyes. Steph Lewis looked ill. She'd better not have given her filthy germs to Mother.

He's looking at her and she realises she should say something sympathetic about his son. "I know what you mean. It's hard when you get called into work. Messes up your social life."

The waitress is back with the drinks and he's thanking her again, lingering over his smile. Amy bites her lip. It's hardly surprising his interest has drifted away when she's referred to precious time with his son as social life.

"Actually, cancel my teacake," she calls after the waitress. "I'm not hungry."

There's definitely a flicker of disappointment in his eyes this time. But it's too late to salvage the date. Something she'd looked forward to so much – it wasn't just her mother who couldn't sleep last night – was ruined the moment Steph Lewis stepped back into her life. Amy should have texted Matt and cancelled as soon as Steph and her colleague left. She knew she'd be late and it wasn't fair to dash off and leave her mother to ponder alone the visit from the police.

"Did I do something wrong?" Matt asks, fixing her with his blue eyes. Hers are blue too, like their child's would be. Would have been.

She lets out a sigh. How could Steph have destroyed another chance at love like she did the first?

"Do you believe in having a nemesis?" she asks. "An arch-enemy, a seeker of justice and revenge."

"Revenge?" His eyes do a nervous circuit of the busy café.

Amy forces a laugh. "Don't worry, I'm not psycho." *Not yet.* "A woman came to my house today. I hadn't seen her for eighteen years and hoped I'd never see her again."

"Sounds like the two of you have history." He sips his coffee.

"I'll tell you." She leans across the table towards him. Their relationship's over anyway. It doesn't matter what she says. "Does Charlie get bullied at school?"

Matt chokes on his coffee. "What? I hope not. Why do you ask that?"

"I was bullied," she says, dipping her head and peering through her fringe. "Every single day of my entire school life."

"The woman you saw today?"

Amy allows a tear to fall. He passes her a clean paper napkin from the caddy on the table.

"The constant name calling, setting others against me, taking my coat, damaging my viola, nearly drowning me."

"Drowning?" Matt's eyes widen.

Amy shivers, remembering the cold water dripping down her school skirt.

———

When Amy turns to get her jacket at the end of French, it's gone from her chair back. Terri and Steph grin as they leave their seats in the row behind.

Amy follows them outside. "Where is it?" She keeps her tone light.

Terri's eyes dart to the sky. "Sun's out now. What do you want it for?"

"I'll need it at home time."

"Denim won't keep you dry." Steph grins at Terri and they share a look.

"That's not the point." It's from Top Shop. Her mother bought it as a comfort gift when she had to cancel the music lessons.

The girls stand in front of her, mocking with identical, sneering grimaces. A pair of bitchy gargoyles.

"Haven't seen a jacket, have you, Steph?"

"Not me."

Amy scans the playground and has to shield her eyes as big puddles from the recent downpour shine like mirrors. Everyone else has gone to the next lesson. No witnesses. That's a shame. She bites her lip and blinks. It takes a few seconds but the tears come.

Steph stares. "Crying? Are you serious?"

Amy keeps blinking. Soon there's a cascade down her cheeks. She starts to walk away.

"Wait," Terri calls. "Where are you going?"

"Mrs Hardcastle," she sobs. Not true. Non-uniform clothes such as fashion jackets aren't allowed in school; she'll be in as much trouble as them.

"It'll be like the viola," Steph says to Terri in a low voice. "You'd better give it back."

"All right, you win. Here's your bloody jacket." Terri fetches it out of her bag.

"It's all crumpled," Amy wails. "I'm still telling."

Steph takes the jacket from Terri. "Come here, let me put it on you. I'll smooth it down. Good as new." She holds it up, inviting Amy to slip it on.

Amy hesitates, looking for the trap. But there can't be one now she's threatened to go to the head teacher. She steps forward. Steph smiles, helps her into the jacket and gently tugs out the hem.

Amy flicks a disdainful look at both of them and turns to go. But Steph grips her shoulders. Before Amy can pull away, Terri leaps towards her and lands with both feet in a puddle. Amy gasps as cold, grimy water hits her tights and trickles to her ankles.

"Hope we didn't splash your jacket," Terri says and they run off laughing.

———

"What happened?" Matt asks, breaking into her thoughts.

"Doesn't matter." She shakes her head. "My mother went to the head teacher. It's why I'm there for her now she needs me. Without her, I might have killed myself."

Matt suppresses the flash of alarm in his face and rests his chin on his steepled fingers. "They must have been tough times."

Amy dabs her eyes with the napkin. Some days were tough. Who's to say a weaker person wouldn't have tried to end it all?

"Bet you were glad to leave school," he says. "Why did the nemesis woman visit you today?"

Amy hesitates. "It was the wrong address, but a shock seeing her again."

"Has she gone now, and won't be back?"

"Yes. I won't meet her again." She balls the napkin and her index finger pushes it along the edge of the table. And if she does see her, she'll be ready.

———

Across the street at a smokers' table outside Caffè Nero, Sean watches through The Patisserie window as Amy conducts another interview. It looks like the same candidate. He must have made the shortlist. Amy seems animated. At one point Sean thought she was crying. Hardly surprising if they're discussing the old duck. Being lumbered with that would make anyone weep.

The man gets up, moves round to pull out Amy's chair as she stands, and lifts her jacket onto her shoulders. He's proper grafting for this job. He must be boracic if he wants to bed wash Amy's mother for a living.

Amy lets her cheek touch the man's fingers before he releases the coat. What the hell? What bit of the job description does that come under? She turns to face him and they embrace. As she moves towards the café door, Sean sees a dopey smirk on her pink face.

No way. That will never do. Sean stubs his fag in the ashtray. Time to raise his game.

# CHAPTER SIXTEEN

We spend Saturday morning interviewing other names on the council's list. I'm not at my best, knackered by headache, lack of sleep and fighting off thoughts of Amy Ashby. Harriet does most of the talking. No one she questions seems suspicious. All provide reasonable accounts of their whereabouts at the time of Steven Baker's murder that shouldn't be too hard to check. Most seem more interested in whether the man's death will halt the roundabout project than in the death itself. Oh well, we all have our priorities.

Back at the station we ring round to confirm the alibis of our interviewees. I let Harriet phone Amy's Orchard Prep. As a private school, it is fully open even on a Saturday. Good to know we're not the only beggars at work. By six p.m. we've finished the list and I tell Harriet she can knock off. We're both on earlies tomorrow and it's already proving to be a long week-end. Kevin expects progress despite no sane witnesses so far coming forward from either of his radio appeals.

"Are you staying on a bit, Steph?" Harriet asks as she gathers her jacket and car keys.

"Nope." I decide the second I say it. What's the point when my brain's a mix of agony and Amy Ashby? What I want is my mum.

"You live in Tuffton, don't you?" I say. I remember Harriet having a housewarming for a flat near Charlton High School. To be polite she invited me. To be polite I didn't attend. "Can you drop me off in The Avenue?" I dash out a text to my mum, telling her I'm on my way. I hope she's back from the salon by now.

"Sure, but what about your car?" Harriet says.

"I'll collect it later." After a brain transplant.

———

"What number?" Harriet asks as she drives into the leafy road where my parents live. Aptly named The Avenue, it's lined with lime trees on both sides.

"Where the black Qashqai is in the drive." The act of raising my arm to point makes me wince.

Harriet pulls up outside the house. "I hope you get a good night's sleep."

"Thank you, Granny." I wave to my twenty-four-year-old junior colleague as she drives away.

Mum comes outside to greet me and we hug. Her hair looks and smells amazing. People say good hairdressers have the worst hair, but not when they're the owner of the best salon in town and hire the best staff.

I hold her at arms' length to admire it. Once jet black, her hair is now a gorgeous natural white and styled into layers, flicked back from her still youthful face. "Did Hayley do it?"

"Hayley was fully booked but Travis has done a good job, don't you think? He's next in line for senior stylist when there's a vacancy."

I follow her down the drive past the car.

"Jake came by the salon today," she says. "He was collecting aerosols for a college recycling initiative. He went off with a rucksack full."

"Did he stay for coffee?" Stupid question. Since before he was old enough to drink the stuff, my son has loved the drinks machine at his nan's salon. When he was little and she had him with her at work while I was on my PCSO shift, he'd gaze for ages as the water filtered through the grounds. Since then the machine has been replaced by one that does everything from espresso to babycino. He's still a fan.

"We had a natter," Mum says. "Kelly, the new apprentice, made him a latte. She stayed for a natter too. Jake didn't seem to mind. Pretty girl is Kelly."

That's ma boy. He never did worry when other kids told him it was girly to call into the salon after school. Maybe he foresaw the benefits.

As soon as I breathe in the almond polish of the solid wood hall floor, I know I'm home. My parents have lived in this large nineteen thirties semi since I was two. It was my home for eighteen years, a happy home. Since I moved out, Dad has created a home cinema and installed a hot tub at the bottom of the garden. Two additions that ensure Jake is a frequent visitor here too.

"Let's sit in the garden," Mum says, and leads me through to the back door and onto the patio. It's warm in the evening sun. She's already laid the garden table with a jug of orange juice and two glasses.

"Dad's not still at work, is he?" I ask.

"Even your workaholic father has eased off now he's sixty-four. He's been playing golf all day with Larry."

Do I know Larry? We're a family with a wide circle of friends. I couldn't bear it any other way.

Two ice cubes topple into my glass as Mum pours the juice. She's wearing a candy-pink kaftan and white leggings with leather flip-flops. A fair bit of tanned flesh shows at her neckline as she leans over. Why not? She's got good cleavage. All the women on her side of the family do. My late nan would have given Dolly Parton a run for it.

Mum hands me my glass. I take a sip but struggle to swallow the cold liquid. Mum rubs my back. It's not helping, but it's good to feel her close. Eventually the throbbing in my head subsides.

"You should see a doctor about those headaches," she says, sitting down. "But I've been telling you that all week and I'm sure you haven't come here to hear me say it again."

"I'm fine, Mum," I lie through another cough.

Mum puts down her glass. "So, out with it. To what do I owe the pleasure?"

"Can't I just be here to visit my mother?"

"Two murders in two days. We even made the ITN early evening news. How come you've got time to come here with all that going on?"

I take a long drink. My head still protests. "Do you remember Amy Ashby from school?"

"That's a blast from the past. The Sniveller. I haven't thought of her in years."

The acid taste of orange returns to the back of my throat. "How did you know we called her that?"

"I think Terri Carter's mum and I invented the nickname. She was a sniveller. Snivelled to her mother every time you sneezed within ten feet of her. Do you remember that time when her mum came storming up to see Mrs Hardcastle because you and Terri ran through a puddle? Amy's mother accused you of bullying when it was an accidental splash of rainwater."

I remember the incident. Couldn't have been bullying, could it? All three of us got soaked.

"Then there was that business with her viola. We never did get to the bottom of that."

I sigh, remembering every unjustified hour of those after-school detentions.

"Anyway," Mum says. "What made you mention her?"

"We had to interview her yesterday in connection with something."

"Let me guess: brothel keeping?"

We break into laughter that only stops when I cough again. I've met a few Gloucester madams and Amy Ashby couldn't be a less likely stand-in.

Mum has another drink. "Did you arrest her then?" she says eventually.

"God, no. Eliminated from our enquiries." The Orchard School secretary confirmed to Harriet that Amy was there Thursday evening. "Never a suspect. But it was weird seeing her after eighteen years."

"Sorry, love, I hate to break it to you but you're not thirty-five any more. It's nearer twenty-five years since you left school."

"Oh, yeah. Time flies."

Mum puts down her glass again, giving me her full attention. "Unless you've seen her more recently than your Charlton High years?"

"Of course not." I take another long drink and hope I've obscured my face to hide the lie.

# CHAPTER SEVENTEEN

Nathan J grins through the studio window at Lulu, his producer. "I'm thinking of changing my handle to Love Dude. What d'ya reckon?"

"Thirty seconds." Her eyes don't leave her deck.

Why can't she make an effort once in a while? They're on this graveyard shift together. The radio station's lame enough in the day time, but after dark it's terminal. Just them and the night security guard. Where's the camaraderie? It would be nothing like this at Radio One.

"What about Smooth Mover?" he says, trying to get a reaction.

"Twenty seconds." Sweet Fanny Nada.

"Stud Jockey?"

"There's such a thing as Advertising Standards," she says, but still doesn't look up. "Six seconds. Sound check please."

Following her instruction, he speaks into the microphone. "You know you want me." He alters the sound levels to optimum, increasing the base.

"Three, two, one..." She does that thing with her fingers

like she's on an eighties game show. Nathan winces; she's too young to remember it.

The red lamp on his desk goes green.

"*Evening, night lovers. I'm Nathan J getting it on for the next three hours.*" As he speaks, he touches his spiky hair and checks the wall clock. "*It's just gone ten oh three on Mids FM.*" He fades in the jingle. "*I take the view if you're not in Lisbon tonight, you don't want to listen to out-of-tune Europeans murdering the English language, so this is a guaranteed Eurovision-free zone.*" He scrolls his computer screen to read the script. Wishing he didn't have to stick to it, he grits his teeth. "*Coming up: your wedding nightmares. With Harry and Meghan's big day rapidly approaching, I want to hear how it was for you. Were your nuptials memorable for all the wrong reasons? Tweet hashtag wedding bloopers or give me a call. Details on the Mids FM website. Let's kick this off with a lurve song from the big lover man Barry White.*"

As the music plays, he surveys the room, his mind back on his recurring dilemma: stay or go. Is this enough? It's not badly equipped: two sound decks, computer, various mics and space enough for a studio guest – he's holding out for Cheltenham boy Chris from *Love Island*. There's even a twenty-four-hour news channel mounted on the wall, not that he looks at it much. He's not that kind of presenter. The story currently flicking across the monitor is a stage invasion at Eurovision. People tune into him to escape that kind of bull.

But his latest figures are bleak. Mids FM – famed for gardening tips and cookery recipes – doesn't attract the listeners he needs. Should he jack it? Try out for some reality TV gig? He checks his hair in the shaving mirror he keeps on his desk. Plenty of gel to tame the natural wave. And the bleached colour – his trademark – is holding well. With looks like his, he's a shoo-in for *Celeb BB* if he could just get the break. He's a big fish who needs a larger pool.

As the record finishes, he speaks again. *"Here's Kylie and Jason – the Harry and Meghan of their day. Nineteen million tuned in to watch the* Neighbours *lovebirds say I do. Nineteen million."* He cuts off his mic, unable to keep up the fakery, and they launch into "Especially for You".

"Haven't we got some R&B?" he calls to Lulu.

She looks up long enough to shake her head. "Wrong demographic."

"Speak for yourself." What is it with this shiny-ponytailed, nose-ringed girl? Is she really a decade and a half younger than him? When did kids get so sensible? It's the same in the clubs. The only attention he gets is from the dumped and divorced in leopard print leggings.

Even the chocolates and soft drink that arrived at the studio on Thursday smacked of a fan of a certain age. Who under sixty drinks dandelion and burdock? But at least the truffles got a smile out of Miss Lulu Misery behind the glass when he offered her one.

As Scott and Charlene warble into the sunset, he checks the clock again. *"Coming up to twelve minutes past ten with your night whisperer Nathan J. Here's the latest on the roads with Jamie Cole."*

The pre-recorded bulletin comes on at the press of a button and Nathan glances at his Twitter feed.

**Chaz**@up4a3some
Caught shagging the bridesmaid in the vestry #weddingbloopers

**Elly**@EllyJumbo99
Limo drove bride (me) to wrong hotel #weddingbloopers

**SuperNan**@LindaBench22

Caterers forgot cutlery – main course was curry #wedding-bloopers

"You're not using the first one," Lulu warns as she views her screen.

Before he can answer back in another vain attempt to get banter going, the timer on his monitor counts down to the end of the travel news.

*"And there'll be more from Jamie in twenty minutes. Keep your tweets and calls coming in on your wedding bloopers. I've got some great ones here. Listen to this..."*

Behind the glass, her hand shoots up, her mouth poised in alarm. She must think he's going to air Chaz's tweet. He'd love to keep her dangling but can't risk dead air. He chooses a tame one by a guy called Dave from Pershore.

While he plays the next song, Lulu tells him off for picking a tweet from Worcestershire. "It's out of area," she says, and reminds him patronisingly of the requirement to keep it local.

He's about to protest when her arm goes up, warning him he's due on again.

Talk to the hand? Not bloody likely. Seething, he wheels his chair closer to the mic. *"I've just been talking to my producer, the lovely Lulu, and she says she's never going to get married."*

Daggers through the window.

*"Can I have a collective Aaah across the county for Lulu? Altogether: Aaah. She doesn't think anyone would have her."*

She gives him a middle finger through the glass.

*"But here at Mids FM, we think our Lulu is gorgeous. Is that a playsuit you're wearing, Lulu?"*

A fist now, thrust out of her sweatshirt sleeve.

*"I love the lace trim where it finishes mid-thigh."*

As she stands up to point to her jeans, he ignores her to scroll the playlist. The evening's looking up – not only a rise out of Lulu but at last something decent to play. *"Here's a bit of Oasis for all you true music fans out there."*

But when he grins at the window to resume their spat, he's disappointed to see her attention is elsewhere. The security guard has come into her booth and they're deep in conversation. She's switched off the intercom so Nathan can't hear. After the guard leaves, she turns it back on.

"My name's Louisa. If you're going to ridicule me, at least get it right. And your stalker's brought you more chocolates." She holds up a flat, hexagonal box in shiny purple packaging. The same truffles as last time. "Hope they choke you."

"But not on air, you don't, 'cos then you'd have to cover and find out it's not as easy as it looks." Arms folded, he sends a smug grin her way, proud of his comeback.

As the song ends, he grins at the playlist and says into the mic, *"I think you'll all be with me when I dedicate this next one to Lulu."*

When he fades in "Maneater", he expects her to have a go at him, but she's on the phone. Eventually she looks up. "It's for you."

The phone on his desk rings as she transfers the call. There's something about the smirk in her voice that makes him hesitate. Producers are supposed to filter nutters before they reach the talent. Who the hell has she put through?

"Go on. You know you want to," she mocks. It sounds like something he would say.

Touching his spiky head again, he resolves to take whatever fruitcake caller she's sent his way. He speaks into the phone. "Hi, you're through to Nathan J. What would you like to talk about?"

Silence. Not surprising; callers often get tongue-tied when

they speak to him. "You're not on air. It's just me and you," he says – rather seductively he thinks.

The person on the line finally speaks. "Did you get the truffles?"

Lulu bends over her keyboard. The word STALKER appears in his on-screen script. Her handiwork.

"Who's calling, please?" Nathan asks, trying to keep uncertainty out of his voice, but he's watched *Play Misty for Me*. Clint Eastwood as a late-night DJ who attracts a bunny boiler long before *Fatal Attraction* invented the term.

"A listener who admires your work."

Nathan swivels in his chair, thinking maybe it's an ordinary fan, a woman who appreciates genius. He assumes it's a woman. The voice is indistinct. Is the accent local? He can't tell yet.

"So, did you get them?" the voice says.

"Thank you," he says cautiously, still unsure whether his caller is discerning or crazed. He has an idea to test the water. "I might share them with my producer. She loves truffles. Would that be all right with you?"

"That's nice." No hesitation, no bitterness. Nathan relaxes. Not a stalker; not possessive about who he shares the gift with.

Lulu points at her watch and indicates he's got thirty seconds.

"I'd love to chat longer, but I have to make the next link so..."

"You're wasted in this late slot."

"You're too kind," he says, spinning his chair. He's got himself a superfan. He'll tell Lulu to take the number and get them on live.

"What you need is a scoop."

His bubble of excitement deflates; she's muddled him up with another presenter. He's an entertainer not a reporter. He doesn't do news scoops. Just as well he's going to have to cut her off.

But it's the caller who finishes it. "We'll speak again soon, Nathan. It may be to your advantage." The line goes dead.

Too unsettled to speak the next link, he plays Taylor Swift. Hands behind his head, he leans back in his chair, pondering the call.

Lulu waves the now opened box of truffles, pops one in her mouth and chews it slowly. Her thumbs-up converts smoothly into a V-sign.

# CHAPTER EIGHTEEN

Russell Hill can't sleep. It's not the fault of the deckchair in the kitchen, which has been an adequate bed for more than eight years, ever since the climb to his bedroom began to average forty minutes. Rest deserts him because he can't stop replaying the week in his head. Three visitors in the space of six days when the previous month he had none. Folks know they aren't welcome with their inane and endless nonsense: *would you like to use my chainsaw on your hedges; your recycling's blown into the avenue; you should remove the saucepans from your drive.* Hypocrites, the lot of them. They fall over themselves to visit National Trust collections but baulk when a similar trove is on their doorstep.

The fireman came on Wednesday. Russell thought they were supposed to be fearless sorts, but this one was an absolute wuss about coming into the kitchen. If Russell can vault onto the *Daily Mail*, slither under the top of the doorframe and descend the *Independent* on the other side, how can a fully trained firefighter find it such an obstacle?

Was his house call prompted by the first social worker or the younger one who visited the following day? Typical right hand, left hand. The second one didn't know the first one had been. To think the first one had the cheek to declare his lifestyle chaotic when they can't even run an appointments diary.

"Just a routine inspection, sir. We take our role in fire prevention seriously," the fireman said. Not too seriously, surely, or he'll be out of a job. He completed a home safety checklist, which Russell filed afterwards on the stairs by climbing to the top of *London Review of Books* and enduring a confetti fall of old raffle tickets and sweet wrappers.

Now he's awake, he feels peckish. He takes a tin of tuna from the stack in the sink. The tin opener rests on a tower of aluminium take-away trays above the egg boxes that cover two thirds of the window sill. He likes it that way now that the blind has stopped working. His spare blinds are propped against the wardrobe in the front bedroom, but it's been a while since he could get in there.

He retrieves a teaspoon from the fridge and takes out milk too. It's getting harder to keep space for the carton without risking an avalanche of plastic bags, elastic bands, bag ties, string, old keys, broken coat hangers, cracked saucers and tarnished cutlery. An inventive solution comes to him suddenly and he grins. He resolves to buy long-life milk and dispense with opening the fridge. Ingenious. Not only will the floor in front of the fridge become available for storage, he will also be able to reduce the frequency of his visits to the minimart. He loathes going out since a hideous woman in a tweed coat had a pop at him about personal hygiene. What's he's supposed to do when there are three ironing boards and an electric fan in the shower?

"I was friends with your grandmother," she said. "She kept that house like a new pin."

It's easy to meddle when you know half the story. He grieves for Granny every day – the only parent he ever knew after his mother bolted – but there's no hiding that she was a clean freak. In hindsight it was probably a mental health problem; she never even kept a daily newspaper beyond a couple of days. Her house is far more lived-in now.

He hears a noise. It's hard to tell from where; his archive muffles the sound. Splintering wood? Have foxes got in again? Not much he can do until morning.

Both the fireman and the second social worker suggested he put his archive out for recycling. That's the trouble with the throwaway society: no interest in current affairs or modern history. All he needs is a storage unit, somewhere local, to take the older editions from the lounge – even though it would be a squeeze to get to them. The social worker told him he could access newspapers online. Where exactly does she think he would plug in a computer? He used to entertain thoughts of getting one and stored three printers and a monitor in the airing cupboard in anticipation, but it's a question of priorities.

Another noise. Rustling, snapping, crackling – as if the rolls of bubble wrap on the dining table have started to pop spontaneously. He'd go and look but, with the second mobility scooter in there, reaching the table is too much of a challenge.

What's that smell? The hairs of his beard stand on end and he starts to cough.

Without delay, he scales the *Telegraphs* and scrambles through the gap at the top of the kitchen doorway. Smoke curls into the hall from the direction of the closed dining room door. Adrenaline pumps as he surges along the defunct *Sunday Correspondent*. He dives towards the dining room door handle, but his hand snaps away from the burning hot metal. The acrid taste and smell overwhelm the hall. Tears track down his face. He resolves to save what he can, gathers copies of *The Times* under his arm and swims to the front door. But his panicked lack of care causes his paper ocean to swell and plummet. He slides between two waves and they engulf him. His last conscious sensation is the chemical smell of newsprint.

# CHAPTER NINETEEN

Sirens. I go from asleep to alert in a nanosecond. I'm in a squad car on a shout. Heart pounding, nerves ajangle. God knows what we'll face when we get there.

But I blink and it's dark and everything's soft and lemon fresh. Adrenaline subsides as I become more aware of my surroundings. I'm still at Mum and Dad's. When Jake texted to say he and Bradley were having an all-nighter – pizza and Play-Station masquerading as revision – I stayed over with my parents, sleeping in a pair of Mum's leggings and a T-shirt. I never went back to the station to get my car. Being dragged awake now has done nothing to aid the recuperation a night in my old bed was supposed to bring.

The sirens – two? – are still going, changing pitch as they pass by the house. I creep onto the landing and lift the blind as quietly as I can. Lights are on at upstairs windows across the road and a face at one stares down at something on their far left. With their gaze in the same direction, a middle-aged couple walk along the pavement, arms folded. They're in coats but I can see the woman's nightie below the hem.

A floorboard creaks behind me.

"Can you see anything?" Mum whispers, joining me at the window.

My copper's snout is twitching. "I need to get down there for a proper look."

"My anorak's in the hall, and take the key off the phone stand," she says eagerly before slipping into sensible mum mode. "Don't stay out there too long."

I grab my warrant card, slip on my boots and head downstairs.

The smoke hits me as soon as I open the door. Like the entire city is holding bonfire night in this one street. My eyes and throat itch. A fire engine has stopped about fifty yards up the road, its rotating blue light illuminating the windows of houses on both sides of the road. The man and woman who walked past have come to a halt and seem to be contemplating how much closer to the action they can get. I step round them and find another fire engine further on. Faces press against house windows and some folk have ventured onto their doorsteps in dressing gowns and bare feet. Across the road, Mrs Dougal, an Avenue resident for as long as anyone can remember, leans against her garden gate. She's known affectionately as The Zombie, because whatever time you drive past her house, her lights are on. Insomniac, for sure, but at her age more like the wakeful dead. Her yellow oilskin provides a beacon through the thickening smoke as I cross over to speak to her.

"I called them," she says proudly. "One engine came within fifteen minutes, the other two just now. Ambulance sometime in between."

From this side of the avenue, I can see another fire engine and several firefighters attending to a house across the street.

Although it's a moonless night, floodlights from the fire engines light the blackened façade and warped window sills. I can't see flames but the smoke from all sides is a dense, billowing black. It's the house with the jungle of a front garden I drive past whenever I visit my parents. I recall it looking nice when I was a kid.

"Poor Russell," Mrs Dougal says, shaking her head inside her hood. "He was a difficult boy but he didn't deserve... I've always said Mrs Hill would turn in her grave to see what her grandson has done to the place. If there's an afterlife, she'll be giving him what for now." She lowers her voice. "They carried him out on a stretcher. The bag was zipped."

"How do you know it was him?"

"No one else would go in there. It was a death trap even before this."

"I see." I resolve to get Mum's take on this Russell.

We stand in silence, watching two firefighters hose the upper storey, and we try not to breathe in the thick, pungent cloud that is obscuring our view.

"That one's in charge." Mrs Dougal points at a firefighter in a white helmet as he emerges through the charred front door. "He came in the first engine and directed operations."

The man removes his breathing apparatus and walks up the road to one of the other appliances. Almost immediately it reverses up the avenue. I assume he's stood it down and it's heading for the crescent beyond Mum and Dad's where it can turn round.

Another firefighter crosses to the second appliance and also removes his breathing equipment.

"Go on," Mrs Dougal says. "It looks like they've nearly finished. You're a police officer. Go and have a word."

I have no jurisdiction. They won't talk to me. Their job is

to make this incident safe. The officer in the white helmet, the Fire Incident Commander, will have made the critical communication to the entry control officer when they found the body. The due process of communication to the police will have commenced.

Despite knowing all this, I find myself – police ID in hand – moving towards the yellow-helmeted firefighter by the appliance. The smoky atmosphere would be a challenge for anyone, but my knackered body isn't up to it at all. I can't catch my breath and I double over. In the next moment, the smell intensifies as the fireman in his smoke-saturated fire suit helps me to my feet. My windpipe feels like it's bleeding. My eyes stream.

He looks at my ID. "Stay back, Inspector Lewis. This is still an active fire incident. There may be other casualties."

"Steph," I choke. "Call me Steph." Like a man who has conquered an inferno gives a flying ember about my preferred form of address.

As he leads me back to Mrs Dougal, I feel like a nosy biddy who got too close to the flames and came away scorched.

"Accidental?" I ask, attempting to pull myself together.

I think he shrugs; his padded jacket makes it hard to tell and his shoulders are above my eye line. "We have to wait for the fire investigation officer's report."

————

"You stink, Steph." Mum coughs when I come in. "Use the downstairs shower."

"Dad still asleep?" I ask in a croaky, hurty voice.

"The effects of the nineteenth hole. It would take Armageddon to wake him. What's happened?"

"Fire's out now." My throat aches too much to tell her about the man called Russell. We'll speak about it later.

She fetches a clean towel from the airing cupboard and goes to the kitchen.

Under the shower jet, I shampoo the smoke out of my hair but can't rinse away the embarrassment of the how-to-suck-eggs reprimand from the firefighter. God, I hope it's not arson; I might get assigned. Inspector Lewis, the Swooning Detective. I'm probably the joke of his watch already. I rub myself roughly with the towel. One bad migraine and I'm losing it. My mind hasn't been on the job all week and now I've plummeted to a whole new level. I show pointless curiosity for an accidental death but have done nothing about the two murders I've been tasked with solving.

Giving Mum's offer of an early breakfast a swerve, I'm in a taxi within twenty minutes. My eyes are still smarting from the fire. I'm dog-tired but the scratchiness makes me alert and thinking. When I phone the station, Harriet Harris, disgustingly cheerful and early for her Sunday shift, answers.

I issue my instructions. "Cross-reference the car owners who passed through the traffic lights near the Georgian Gardens on Wednesday morning with everyone who attended the St Giles roundabout meeting that night."

"So there is a connection between Christa Talbot and Steven Baker." She squeals like an excited toddler down the phone.

"Just covering the bases," I reply. And getting off the starting blocks. I should have done this as soon as the planning officer showed up as a murder victim. Kevin's in charge but he expects me to effect lines of enquiry. Two murders – both apparently non-domestic – in two days. *Wake the hell up, Steph.* "Make a start and hand it over to Tony when he gets in."

"I don't mind staying on late tonight. The two of us together should crack it."

I thank her and ring off, my head throbbing again. I'm

supposed to be the one with the work ethic, but, behind me, that young woman is shinning up that greasy pole of ambition. Should I up my game or take two paracetamol and sigh with relief?

# CHAPTER TWENTY

*"A house fire in the Tuffton area of Gloucester has claimed the life of one man. Three fire crews tackled the blaze in the early hours of this morning. The name of the victim has not been released but neighbours told Mids FM News that they believe him to be the home owner. A police spokesman said they are treating the fire as unexplained and enquiries will continue to ascertain the nature and circumstances of the death. We'll have more on this story when..."*

Sean switches off his car radio. Before he started watching Amy, this hour on a Sunday morning didn't exist, but he's got to make the investment if he wants the return. And he wants it like a Rottweiler round a bitch on heat.

The business with the carer guy on Friday rattled him more than it should have. It made him stay away from Amy all of yesterday, day and evening. He rubs his fingers around the steering wheel, recalling how well he occupied his time instead.

Glancing at his watch, he realises he's been parked opposite the bungalow for half an hour with nothing happening.

How does Amy-Cakes spend her Sundays when she isn't working? He followed her to work at the school in Cheltenham last Sunday – messed up his bank holiday weekend in the line of duty – so this week it must be her day off. Does she take the old bird to the park?

Another thought hits him, making his breath so hot that a patch of his windscreen mists. What if she didn't come home last night? Is she with *him*? He wipes the glass with his forearm and forces a lid on his temper. This is the long game; fiery outbursts don't always work.

Leaning against the headrest, he reviews the evidence. There's not much really. When the guy's hand touched Amy's cheek, it could easily have been a clumsy accident and would explain her blushes as she left the café. As for the hug; she must have been upset after describing her mother's illness to a potential new nurse. A sympathetic gesture, that's all. Sean was right not to go after him and make something out of it. Besides, the bloke was at least six foot two and looked like he knew his way around a gym. No sense starting a confrontation you can't finish. That's always been Sean's motto, even after what happened with Amy all that time ago.

The bungalow door opens and Amy appears in an Orchard Prep sweatshirt, black trousers and trainers. Sean slides down in his seat and lets out a pissed-off sigh. Despite spending half the night on his preparations, he's got up at stupid o'clock this morning only to see that she's swapped a shift and is going to work. He watches her put a big holdall on the passenger seat of the Corolla and drive off.

Although there's no point, he sets off half a minute later and catches up to her at the roundabout. Instead of going straight over into Finlay Road towards the A40 and Cheltenham, she signals left and takes the first exit. Where the hell? She drives past Charlton High School, its gates firmly locked on a Sunday. Where then? After another mile, it registers that this is the back way into town.

Taking a punt on where she'll end up, Sean makes a right into the rat run that leads eventually to Lidl. He parks and trots over the swing bridge and through the Quays, emerging by St Michael's sandwich bar just as she's manoeuvring the Corolla into a car park space. He hangs back until he hears her hurried footsteps cross the road towards the library. With the little breath he has left after his run, he sets off after her. To his surprise, she doesn't turn into Greyfriars but carries on past the museum and into the Eastgate Shopping Centre. It's still quiet, so he stops to admire the window of H & M to make sure she doesn't spot him. In the reflection of the glass, he sees her mount the escalator. The only thing on the first floor, apart from a dodgy art display and a closed down cafeteria, is the public loo. Repositioning himself in front of Vision Express, he has a clear view of the down escalator reflected on the shop window. He waits.

But after fifteen minutes, he thinks he must have missed her. The only people he's seen descend are an old couple and a man glued to his mobile. A woman with a pushchair carries it down the steps next to the escalator. Another woman's coming down now but she's wearing turquoise. Quite a looker. He risks turning round for a better look.

*Amy.* She's plumped her hair, changed her top and slung on a pair of high heels. Sean faces the optician's window again and bangs his forehead against the glass. All his preparation has gone to rat shit if she's meeting a bloke. *That* bloke. He taps his pockets to find his fags. *Think, Sean, think.*

At the bottom of the escalator she turns right. He hurries after her.

# CHAPTER TWENTY-ONE

Amy's feet slide on the buffed floor of the shopping centre. Are these shoes too much? What choice does a woman of her petite proportions have when her new boyfriend is over six feet tall? She can't expect Matt to stoop every time they hold hands. She smiles to herself at her audacious thinking. The woman in the Cheltenham Clarks called them killer heels when Amy popped out of school during her lunch hour yesterday. Killer. Does she want that attribute in footwear? Is she ready to be that visible? What if she sees someone she knows and her mother finds out she's lied about where she's going?

She pulls the holdall containing her sweatshirt and trainers close. Did her mother notice she was wearing her best black trousers? Mother's eyes used to be heat-seeking missiles. Nothing got past her. Now she can barely keep them open.

Amy's feet slip, then skip, as she heads towards the exit onto Southgate Street. A third date. Things are moving fast. Same café, same table. After the embrace on Friday, it's bound to be more this time. Pressing her lips together, she feels the waxy sheen of nude pink lipstick and shivers in anticipation of the kiss to come.

A male voice calls her name. Smiling broadly, she twists towards it, expecting to see Matt. But a stocky, middle-aged man with thinning brown hair is walking towards her. She doesn't know him and yet a prickle down her spine says she does. The set of the unshaven jaw, the confident gait, the brown eyes – yellow rimmed but with an echo of someone younger. Her belly contracts and rolls.

"S-Sean?"

"Hi, Amy-Cakes."

The nickname he called her sounds the same as ever on his lips and the years fall away before she can stop them. She knew he'd come back. *Knew* it.

"Say something, Amy-Cakes. Aren't you pleased to see me?"

With all her heart, her days, her life. In this moment, so sudden and unexpected, she's twenty-four again.

———

Beacons are alight on every ridge along the basin that Gloucester nestles in. Amy and Sean jostle with other revellers for space on the veranda of the Spinnaker restaurant for a view of the flames on Wrenswood Hill. Amy links her arm through his and notices how he keeps his hand in his jacket pocket, protecting the box-shaped bulge.

Everyone but Amy looks into the sky. Light flickers across Sean's face and gives his eyes a wild glint. She rests her head on his shoulder and, through a gap in the crowd, glimpses the single red rose and half-drunk bottle of Cava inside. She squeezes his forearm, knowing – just *knowing* – what this millennium will mean.

Her patience has paid off.

New noise erupts. Cheers and applause as the New Year chimes. Sean guides her through the melee to their table.

She gives the air a tiny, triumphant punch.

---

Amy faces her former fiancé and is about to say how she's missed him, when she glimpses the digital clock above the exit. Matt will be waiting. But so what? Maybe her place is here with a man she once thought of as her soul mate.

Sean's gaze lingers on her chest. "You're looking good."

The blush heats her face. "Thank you," she whispers, feeling so wanted.

How can she compliment him in return? There's sweat forming tracks on his forehead and a whiff of stale shirt. An unbidden comparison with Matt clouds her mind.

"Shall we go somewhere?" He grins, teeth not as white as she remembers. Does he still smoke? His eyes stay on her, greedy and bright. Her insides curdle. Suddenly she wants to bolt. This man hasn't been in her life for two decades. Going with him would be like taking off with a stranger.

"I have to go," she says in a quiet voice as her whole body trembles from her lacquered hair to her stiletto heels.

"What?" The grin evaporates and anger flashes in his eyes.

She presses her nails into the flesh of her palms. "It's a shock, that's all. I need time." At least a lifetime, if not more.

"Is that it then?" His voice is taut, like he's on the edge of something. "I've made plans. Got things ready. You've no idea what I've done for you."

Amy's skin is gooseflesh. What is he talking about? Her eyes search the marble effect of the floor. She can't look up in case he has more to say.

"Give me your phone." He thrusts his hand towards her.

Too flummoxed to argue, she jumps back and fumbles her phone out of the holdall. Fingers in uncontrollable tremor, she hands it over.

"Here's my number. I'll wait until tomorrow." He lays the phone on her palm and squeezes his clammy hand over hers, composed again. He smiles at her. "Call me at noon." He stalks away.

On legs of jelly, she watches him go, loses him as he turns into the indoor market. The piped music of the shopping centre fades behind the thump of her heart as she ponders the enormity of what she's done. Should she go after him and rekindle everything that was right in her life? A chance after all these years to make herself complete?

But... she checks the clock... Matt is waiting.

Out on Southgate Street, the fresh air clears her head and she hurries towards La Patisserie. She'll phone Sean tomorrow and explain she's not that girl any more. If he won't take no for an answer, she'll find a way to rid herself of his attention. A shadow crosses her eyes. A few ideas come to mind.

The man who accosted her is not the gorgeous delivery driver who brought supplies to the day-care nursery she managed and wooed her with flowers and champagne. She's not the romantic girl, deeply disappointed they didn't get engaged on her twenty-fourth birthday. Not the patient woman who, nevertheless, put him first in her life, assuming it was for keeps and expecting them both to work at it. Not the one whose persistence paid off with the millennium night proposal. Not the pathetic wreck who sobbed herself senseless a few months later when she heard the truth. And she's not the disbelieving fool who followed him to see with her own eyes, and will wish to the end of her days that she hadn't.

No, Amy is not that girl any more.

# CHAPTER TWENTY-TWO

When Matt stands to greet her, Amy kisses his cheek. It's so smooth, with an apple-fresh tang. There's a pause before he smiles, maybe taken aback by her forwardness. She hopes it's a pleasant surprise.

"Sorry I kept you waiting." Her breath is still racing from her encounter with Sean. "I had to run." Should she tell Matt? It might keep him on his toes if he knows he has a rival, but, no, she's not that sort. Besides, he doesn't seem to be waiting for an explanation. He's studying the menu.

"Don't you know it off by heart by now?" she teases.

He looks up. "Sorry?"

"We've been here so often, I thought you'd know the menu by now."

"I see." He tries a chuckle, but Amy realises it wasn't a good joke.

His face is paler than she remembered and there are shadows under his eyes. His ex-wife must be making demands. This date will be a welcome interlude, especially if Amy brings some levity to the proceedings.

"So what's been happening with you since we met on Friday?" she asks.

He drops the menu and seems to retreat into his thoughts.

Then Amy remembers. It's an opportunity to show her compassionate side.

She lowers her voice. "Were you there, at the fire? In the night?"

He runs his fingertips along the laminated edge of the menu. Eventually he nods.

Taking her chance, she lays her hand lightly on his. "I'm sorry," she whispers. When she leans back, he snatches his hands off the table and sits on them.

Touchy subject, she concludes, and moves to safer ground. "Work was busy for me yesterday, too. I got the girls in the boarding house to make flags of all the countries in Eurovision and we let them stay up to watch. My shift finished before the end but I heard who won. Such a shame for the British singer, wasn't it? She kept going though. I admired her pluck. Did you watch it?"

He's looking at the menu again and probably doesn't hear her question.

"Of course you didn't," she adds quickly. "You had work to do."

He stares at her, and for a moment she thinks she's said something wrong.

"We got the shout at three a.m.," he says, now staring into the distance as if she isn't there. "It was well ablaze by then. Nothing we could do."

"I'm sure you did your best." If only he'd put his hands back on the table, she could give them a comforting pat.

"Did I?" His eyes narrow. "Did I do my best?"

What can she say? He must be suffering from that condition soldiers get. Post traumatic something. At least it's not hereditary so won't affect their plans for a family.

"All firemen must think that sometimes," she says, spreading her palms on the table and hoping he'll take the hint and touch her.

"I met the victim on Wednesday." He's still not looking at her. "One of the householders on my fire prevention round. I should have intervened, but I had no right."

"I think we all feel like that at work." She speaks rapidly, leading the way to lighter ground. "Only last week I tried to get the Year Four boys to eat at least one vegetable with their lunch, but most went no further than potatoes. I did my best, that's all any of us can do. I'll try them with courgette next time. I'm sure..."

His attention is lost completely and he's watching something through the window. She follows his gaze to two women emerging with takeaway drinks from Caffè Nero across the pedestrianised street. Her hands curl into fists. Flanked on one side by an Amazonian is the short but brassy figure of Steph Lewis.

"Do you know them?" Amy asks lightly. It might be the tall blonde he's acquainted with. Not quite what Amy wants but better than the alternative. She watches as they reach the Cross and disappear into Eastgate Street.

"The dark-haired one looked familiar," he says. "I think I met her at the fire—"

"You met *her*," Amy snarls. Customers at other tables glance her way. Matt has opened his mouth but says nothing.

Amy picks up a napkin and twists it in her hands. "Well, let me tell you something. I was engaged once. He proposed on millennium night. The end of 1999. It was so romantic – the ring, the champagne, the beacons."

"Sounds amazing," Matt says cautiously.

"But you've no idea how much it hurts to find out the love of your life is cheating."

"I might."

"The pain invades every bone," she continues, ignoring the anguish in his face. "It's with you when you wake, when you sleep, wherever you go."

Matt looks at the shredded napkin in her hand. She scrunches it into a ball and drops it on the table. "I'm over it now, of course, long since." She quietens down but there's no less fury in her tone. "Where did you meet her?" She flicks her wrist towards the window to indicate who she means.

Matt's bewildered eyes scan the street. Eventually he replies, "I can't say. It's a police case now."

She laughs. A delicate chuckle. "Having secrets isn't the best way to start a relationship." She'll flirt the truth out of him, whatever it takes. Steph Lewis isn't a match for her, never has been.

Rubbing his face with the heel of his hand, Matt leans back from the table. He takes a breath. "You're a nice lady, Amy. Beautiful, intelligent, and I've enjoyed our time together, but my head is all over the place right now. I don't think I'm ready for... this."

Amy stands up, knocking her chair over. There's silence all around but she doesn't care. She kept quiet last time but she's not that person any more. "I won't let her win." She gathers up her holdall, tears streaming. "You can tell her that."

# CHAPTER TWENTY-THREE

Christina Aguilera's "Beautiful" plays to Gloucestershire as Nathan J mouths into a microphone and gesticulates to Lulu that it's not working.

"Switch it on then," she says on her side of the glass, not yet sounding worried enough for his purposes.

On his side, he gives theatrical shrugs and hand gestures worthy of a French onion seller.

"Try it again," she tells him. "I've turned up the volume."

"Lalala," he mouths, making no sound.

"Right, this is as loud as it'll go. You'll have to segue into the next song if it doesn't work and I'll bring in my mic."

*Gotcha*. He takes a big swig of dandelion and burdock – God, the stuff is rank – leans over his mic and belches big time.

"Creep!" Lulu throws down her headphones and stands up. "Why would you do that? You're such a pig."

"You shouldn't have given me the drink."

"Your stalker brought that, not me."

He'd been surprised to see the security guard deliver the package and been even more surprised when Lulu brought it straight into the booth while Britney's "Toxic" was playing. Maybe the clue was in the song. No truffles today, only the foul-tasting soft drink.

Lulu leaves her work station, but instead of coming through the connecting door to belt him for burping at full volume in her earphones, she heads to the door into the corridor.

"Where are you going?" he asks.

"To stick my head down the toilet; it'll be more pleasurable than listening to you."

A flurry of panic goes through him. He hates it when she leaves the room while they're on air. If his kit fails, there'll be dead air. It's every DJ's nightmare and the one that has him waking up and screaming.

As Christina sings her last lines, he fades out the song and speaks. *"Good to hear that one again. Don't forget to call the show if you've got something to share. In our build-up to the big day this Saturday, we've come over all matrimonial. Today's Twitterthon is: Have you ever been a bridesmaid or pageboy? If so, what's the worst outfit you've had to wear? Hashtag Knickerbockers or phone the usual number."*

He reads the script on his screen, then glances through the glass. While the cat's away. Time for a deviation. *"With all this talk of marriage, I feel a Bee Gees song coming on."* He cues "Tragedy" and beats his fist on the desk, loving his own wit.

The Twitter feed has started:

**Chaz**@up4a3some
Tartan jockstrap #knickerbockers

**Mandy**@AmandaJanes99
Apricot puff ball dress. It was 1987. #knickerbockers

**Alison**@AllyRoberts90
Medieval maiden garb – bride and groom were Arthurian re-enactors #knickerbockers

The top line is a familiar handle. Nathan might have to block him if he keeps on. He's the kind of lad Nathan would willingly have a drink with, but not the kind of listener the station hierarchy wishes to attract.

What the hell is an Arthurian re-enactor?

Lulu's chair is still empty. To quell his nerves, he turns his attention to the TV news screen. Arsène Wenger's last match with Arsenal, after twenty-four years as manager. Nathan can't imagine staying anywhere that long. Two years is his limit. Time for his itchy feet to climb the ladder. Question is, which ladder? It's like the caller said last night: he's wasted here.

The TV programme switches to local news and to a photograph of a dark-haired man in a suit and tie. It's the kind of image you get in a corporate brochure. The ticker tape runs across the bottom of the screen: *Police appeal again for witnesses in the hunt for the killer of Christopher Talbot, also known as Christa.* Nathan walks over for a closer look but can't see much better because the monitor is mounted high on the wall. He visualises the pleasant, slightly South-Asian features in a wig and false eyelashes, trying to recall whether they've ever met. Knowing his luck, they probably snogged at a club. He'll take whatever.

Lulu is back and answering her phone. That's another reason she shouldn't leave her desk; dozens of calls could come through. Well, one or two.

"It's the dandelion and burdock donor," she says through her mic, waving the phone at him. "Do you want to speak?"

"What, I'm getting a choice?"

"You're not exactly fighting off other fans, are you? And I know your fragile ego needs a boost."

The call is transferred before he can respond. He picks up his handset. "You're through to Nathan J. What would you like to talk about?"

"Did you get the drink?" No hesitation tonight.

"Delicious, thirst-quenching. In a job like this, I have to protect my voice." But send truffles next time, he adds silently.

"Do you protect your sources too?"

Nathan rolls his eyes at Lulu, winding his finger in a circle close to his head to indicate the caller has a screw loose. They've still got him confused with someone else. Investigative journalists guard their sources – not late-night DJs with a Twitter feed. Much as he enjoys truffles, he doesn't want to get backed into this conversation every night. He's going to have to disillusion her – or him. The voice sounds as if it's inside a duvet.

"I don't have many sources," he laughs. "Not really my thing."

"You only need one if they're reliable. Look at Watergate."

He's vaguely heard of the Watergate scandal that brought down a US president. But there's never been politics on the Nathan J Show and there never will be. If the caller mentions Trump or Brexit, Nathan's hanging up. The timer on his screen is on twenty seconds.

"It's been lovely to chat but—"

The voice cuts him off. "The fire victim, Russell Hill – it was murder. No one knows yet. Announce it on air. It can be your scoop."

In that moment Nathan sees the call for what it is – a crank or a troll, someone out to get him to make a career-ending blunder. Who would do...? Through the glass, Lulu, head low, concentrates on her deck. *You would, wouldn't you?* She's got the technical know-how to rig up a fake call. He drops the phone in its cradle and plays Dire Straits. He's got thinking to do. Revenge is a dish best served live.

# CHAPTER TWENTY-FOUR

I tell myself I'm feeling better. I managed five hours sleep. My skull still feels like Tyson Fury's had a go, but severe migraines take their time to diffuse, don't they?

"What's this about, Steph? Has Kevin got an update?" Tony Smith's got his feet on an empty chair in the row in front and turns his head towards me. "I've got calls to make. I might catch the people from the St Giles roundabout meeting before they go to work, the ones you failed to visit yesterday."

"Unlike you, not everyone's at home on a Sunday afternoon," I retort. Harriet and I wasted a good two hours in the city centre, chasing up more attendees from the heated meeting. None were at home, but I doubt any would have had a personal grudge against the town planner. They lived nowhere near the disputed roundabout and probably only went to the meeting because they were within walking distance of Shire Hall and fancied a free cup of Tetley's and a custard cream on the council. Yesterday got us nowhere with either case. I'd have achieved more at home in bed and could have avoided the dizziness that kept coming and going. At one point I hallucinated that Amy Ashby was in a coffee shop window with a man.

Tony's feet hit the floor as Kevin walks in.

"Sorry for the early start." Kevin parks his files on a desk at the front and perches beside them. "But we've got news from the fire investigation officer. The fire that killed Russell Hill in the early hours of Sunday morning was definitely arson. Smashed window, petrol thrown, followed by a lighted match. The room – a dining room – was stacked to the ceiling with newspaper. A lovely way to burn."

"Bugger." Tony leans forward in his chair. "Three in one week. Even I don't want that much overtime." Since his recent and unfathomable engagement to an apparently sane woman called Nikki, Tony's been saving hard for a house deposit.

Kevin puts another photo on the crime board. It shows a young man in an oversized white shirt with downcast eyes beside a smartly dressed older woman. "The victim with his grandmother, taken at a late cousin's wedding years ago. We haven't found any more recent photos so far, and if there were any in the house, they'd have burnt. We've released his name to the press. Sadly no next of kin to notify." He returns to his perch on the desk. "The victim was already known to the fire service. Social Services requested a home safety visit, which was carried out last week. The fire officer who attended submitted his findings to Social Services." Kevin crosses his legs at the ankles. "I've been onto them this morning. It may interest you to know that social workers do even longer hours than us and without the aid of a warrant card and a stab vest." Flicking through his notebook, he continues, "I got hold of the case worker, Clare Burgess, who was handling Mr Hill. I say handling but there wasn't much she could do. He wasn't an obvious danger to others despite neighbours' frequent complaints about the state of his garden."

Would my parents have complained if they'd lived closer to him? At their end of The Avenue, they were barely aware of Russell Hill. I'd like to think they'd be the live-and-let-live types even if they were next door. Maybe they would have empathised as they're clearing my late nan's cottage at the moment, a small house with Aladdin's Cave proportions of stuff.

"Russell Hill was a recluse," Kevin says, "and a serious hoarder, broadsheet newspapers his eccentricity of choice. Aged forty-one, he was deemed mentally unfit for work and on benefits. He inherited the large property from his late grandmother, who died eight years ago. She'd brought him up since he was a baby. Neighbours told Clare Burgess that her death triggered a deterioration in his mental health, and a long-term interest in archiving newspapers became an obsession to never discard anything."

"Poor sod." Tony shakes his head and adds, "And no, Steph, he's not a kindred spirit. I get my daily news online."

Nodding, I give him a thumbs up, too groggy to joke that those websites he visits might be an outlet for something but it isn't news.

"Uniform are already on the house to house, canvassing on Russell's road," Kevin tells us. "Apparently it's taking a while, as residents have plenty to say about their late neighbour. None of it good. We need to establish his movements in the last week. Was he as much of a recluse as the social worker thinks or was he seen out and about?"

Mum will think all her birthdays have come at once; first questioned about attending the St Giles roundabout meeting, now for living near Russell Hill.

"The most likely culprit is an irate neighbour who couldn't stand the eyesore of the Hill residence any more. They might not have intended murder, but they weren't going round with a pot luck supper either."

Let's hope the house-to-houses go tactfully. The last thing we need is a street of neighbours, including my mum and dad, who think there's a killer among them.

Kevin returns to the crime board. "Meanwhile, back to Tony's mortgage repayment plan: our other two murder cases.

"Christopher Talbot, also known as Christa, killed at the Georgian Gardens near Painswick between six and eight on Wednesday morning." He points at the grim scene of crime photo of the prone body. "No forensics, and a knife too common to trace its origin. Also, there's nothing emerging on the hate crime angle. We can't find any gender counselling service in Gloucestershire or neighbouring counties that was contacted by Christopher – or Christa. And no one knows an advisor called Morag, the mystery number on the pay-as-you-go phone found with the body. The idea of her being an advisor could well be a blind alley." He looks at Harriet. "Anything on the phone we found at Christopher's home?"

"Still going through the saved numbers," she says. "It seems to be the main phone that Christa used for work and family. Nothing out of the ordinary so far." She glances at another female DC in the front row. "Also, Cally and I visited LGBTQ clubs on Saturday night..."

"Don't plant images like that in my head; I'm an old man with a weak heart." Tony puts his hands over his eyes.

Harriet ignores him superbly. "A few recognised Christa's photo, but they said she kept herself to herself and wasn't part of the scene. They'd never heard of a Morag. No one reported an increased level of aggression towards the community, nothing beyond the usual unacceptable level of intolerance."

Tony sits up and flicks through his notebook. "We're still interviewing Christopher Talbot's English language students, but no one seems suspicious so far. They're an amorous lot – most alibis involve being in bed with someone at the time of the murder."

In the front row, Cally raises her hand. "I still have a few part-time paralegals to interview at Highland and Bosch, Christopher's former employer, but the ones I've spoken to so far were sorry he quit and even sorrier he's dead."

"Keep at it, team. I'm making another appeal later today." Kevin turns his attention to the bloodied and battered image of the other victim. "Steven Baker was killed between four thirty and six fifteen on Thursday evening at the old convalescent hospital building. No witnesses have come forward, even though it was broad daylight and the killer was likely to be wearing a good smattering of Steven Baker's bodily fluids after availing themselves of a piece of Cotswold stone that they probably brought with them. We need to widen the house to house. Someone must have seen something. There's a swanky apartment block around the corner; try that."

He doesn't look at me as he speaks, even though he knows I live there. He knows it's not swanky either.

"I'm following up with the people who were at the St Giles meeting that we haven't been able to contact so far," Tony says.

Kevin thanks him and adds, "And, as we suspected, Radley Development, the firm that Steven Baker wrote on the calendar for a meeting at the time he was later killed, is bogus. There is no such firm registered with Companies House."

He shuts his notebook. "Any questions before we go back out?"

Harriet's hand goes up. "Are we still treating this as three separate killers?"

"Open mind, Harriet, I've said that. But the most likely motive for the Russell Hill attack is a neighbourhood dispute."

"Funny though, isn't it?" Tony says, putting his pen behind his ear. "All three victims were forty-one years old."

"But does that make for a likely motive?" I ask, not because I particularly object to Tony's observation but because Kevin's looking at me expecting something intelligent from his inspector. "Why would anyone bump off a load of random people when they reach the Over the Hill club?"

Tony grins. "Does it make you nervous?"

I laugh along with everyone else. Got to let him have that one. "I'm thirty-eight, same as you," I say. We've both been thirty-eight for five years.

Harriet, always the first to sack a joke, raises her hand. "Two of them have one other thing in common: they were meeting someone we can't trace. Although we don't know for sure that Christa was meeting Morag, she was dressed to meet someone, and Steven Baker was supposed to be with Radley Developments."

A mutter of agreement spreads through the room. Kevin waves his hand for quiet. "But that doesn't give us a solid link between our two victims. Is there one?"

"Not that we've found so far," I say. "Steven's only been in Gloucestershire for a year, although his mother and grandparents were from Gloucester. Only the grandfather is still alive, and barely that, according to Steven's widow."

Harriet looks at me. "Tony and I did what you said and cross-referenced the car registrations caught on camera at the traffic lights near the Georgian Gardens on Wednesday morning and the car registrations of those who parked in the Shire Hall car park for the St Giles roundabout meeting that evening. We found four matches."

"Not quite the jackpot, but better than three oranges and a banana." Tony quips. He sees Harriet's stony face. "Sorry, carry on."

"One match turned out to be Steven Baker himself. He lived in Stroud."

"Interesting. Did he know Christopher Talbot?" Kevin asks.

"I don't think so," Harriet says, "but I asked his wife what time he left for work on Wednesday. It was twenty-five minutes before his ID was swiped at Shire Hall. He wouldn't have had time to meet Christa at the Georgian Gardens."

"Who are the other three matches?" I ask.

"Two people who live near the St Giles roundabout," Harriet says. "I need to get confirmation that they work in the Painswick area and had legitimate reasons and timings to be out there that morning."

Something is tickling at the back of my mind. "And the other?"

"I didn't find a precise match. The car at the lights on Wednesday morning is registered to someone in Tuffton. Someone with the same surname and also in Tuffton, but at a different address, attended the roundabout meeting. Could be totally unconnected. The name Ashby is common enough."

# CHAPTER TWENTY-FIVE

"Do you want me to take it?" Harriet asks as we drift out of the incident room.

I want to say yes and duck the follow-up interview with Amy Ashby, but, as a likely attendee of the council meeting, she has inexplicably moved up the potential suspect list. She's at the very top of it, in fact, as we don't actually have a list. Three victims and no suspects – not our finest week.

"We'll go together," I tell her. "But let's get a coffee first. Miss the school rush." Prevarication: first rule of policing.

Unlike every police canteen joke you've ever heard, the cafeteria at our police HQ serves decent coffee in pleasant surroundings.

"Have I time for a granola bar, with rooibos tea?" Harriet asks.

"There's always time for rolled oats." I smile, wondering how she stomachs rooibos. I pay for her order and get a black coffee, my drug of choice after an early start. Migraine or no migraine.

"Thanks, Steph," she says, taking her things off the tray

when I return to the table. "Do you think Amy Ashby is mixed up in this?"

"That's what our next interview should find out." I can't believe I'm even considering it. The Amy I knew is more likely to frame someone for murder than to commit one herself.

Harriet opens her cereal bar and takes a dainty nibble. My belly rumbles and I could snaffle something that size in two bites, but I wouldn't be able to keep it down, headache making me queasy.

After she's chewed and swallowed, she asks me how I know Amy Ashby. There's a long and a short answer.

I keep it short. And bendy. "We knew each other slightly at school but didn't mix much. Different circles – you know how it is."

Harriet nods, unaware of the line I'm spinning. "So not close friends, but not sworn enemies either." She pops the rest of the snack in her mouth.

*If only.*

Tony Smith queues at the counter while the canteen assistant loads half a pig into a white bap and puts it on his plate. Thankfully he doesn't give us a glance and joins a table of uniformed male officers.

"Do you think he has a point with that forty-one thing?" Harriet asks quietly, glancing at Tony.

It takes me a moment to work out what she means. A slug of coffee helps open the synapses. "Like I said, it's the weirdest motive. Why would a killer seek out victims of the same age?"

"Maybe it's one of those reunion things. Someone bumping off their classmates, except Steven Baker didn't go to school in Gloucester. I'll check what schools Christa and Russell went to." She looks up. "I wonder if it was the same one as you and Amy."

"Not a chance," I say. "We went to Charlton High."

"You went to the girls-only grammar school?" Harriet's eyes widen. "Did you go to uni? Were you fast-tracked?"

I choke on my coffee. "Not unless I suffered a derailment since, and, no, I didn't go to uni. Did you?"

Shaking her head, she lowers her eyes. "Messed up my GCSEs."

"We've all been there," I say, even though my results were pretty good.

She puts down her cup. "Why did you join the police, if you don't mind me asking?"

My mate Terri's idea. She became a PCSO, said the hours worked with grandparent childcare, so, having given up my dream of owning a beauty salon when Jake was born, I took a challenging job that paid a steady wage. Turned out I was good at it. When our kids got older and Terri's hearing deteriorated, she went into teaching and I joined the police proper.

I shrug. "Seemed like a good idea at the time. What about you?"

"I always wanted to be a police officer, like my dad." Her eyes drop to her drink and she takes a sip.

Oh crap. Next she's going to tell me her father's a retired chief super. Note to self: always treat a baby detective constable with kid gloves; you don't know who they might be related to. "Is he still in the job?" I ask.

"He was off duty and intervened in a stabbing at a super-market. Got a posthumous commendation."

Her eyes fill with tears and I feel myself welling up. I remember the case from when I was still a constable. Harriet must be the sixteen-year-old daughter the press talked about. No wonder she messed up her GCSEs.

"Sergeant Michael Harris," I say solemnly. "I didn't realise he was your father. A brave man. A credit to the Force." I cringe, sounding as trite as a chief constable.

"Thank you for remembering him." Her voice quivers.

We're both going to bawl if I don't force a change of gear. I stand up and sling my handbag over my shoulder. "You've been in the job long enough to know we don't forget our own. Are you ready to go?"

She pushes away her half-drunk tea and wipes her face with her hand. "Born ready. Can I drive?"

———

The dirty red car is parked in the Ashby's drive.

"Same registration clocked in Painswick and Shire Hall car park," Harriet confirms as we park outside the bungalow. "But that car is not registered to this address."

Taking a deep breath, I step ahead of her and ring the bell. Like last time, it's answered on the second ring. Unlike last time, Amy Ashby looks a wreck. Her auburn hair hangs in greasy hanks around her face, and her grimy apple-green housecoat does her blotchy skin no favours. At least she'll be a captive audience; she can't claim she's about to go out.

"We'd like to ask you more questions. Can we come in, please?" It's a standard opener that I normally punctuate with "madam" or the witness's name, but I can't call her Miss Ashby, not with our history.

Tutting, she leads us into the house. The bathroom door is closed but I hear running water. The mother must be in there as she isn't in the lounge. Amy mutes the TV and we sit in the same seats as before.

My body decides it's a good moment to have a dizzy spell. It starts with a tremor in my hands as I get out my notebook, but soon all I see is furry black dots. "DC Harris, can you explain?"

Harriet gets the hint and asks Amy where she was between four thirty p.m. and seven p.m. on Thursday.

After a big sigh, she answers the question. "I already told you. The flowers at my school, Orchard Prep in Cheltenham, needed replacing. I completed eight displays for the foyer and the great hall. I used orange gerbera as the focal flower."

My dizziness passes and I'm on it like an exocet. She's given us detail. Liars elaborate. Burglars out on a job will swear they were home, eating their mum's Sunday roast. They give you the cut of beef, how they had their potatoes and the number of Yorkshire puddings that came their way. *Detail*.

"Did you know Steven Baker?" I ask.

At the sound of my voice, she recoils and a twist of anger settles on her mouth. "We went through this last time. I attended the meeting that he chaired on Wednesday."

"Did you go to Shire Hall by car?" Harriet has her pen poised. "Where did you park?" Clever girl, asking what we already know.

But Amy isn't caught out in a lie. "The council car park. Why?"

"In your own car?" I ask.

Again my voice makes her scowl. "At the moment I'm using my mother's car. It was pointless keeping two cars taxed when only one of us can drive. My mother's car had lower mileage so we sold mine."

Sounds reasonable, but she's doing that detail thing again. "When your mother moved to this bungalow, did she notify the DVLA of her change of address?"

With her eyes boring into mine, Amy shakes her head slowly and snarls, "At school, you used to say *I* was petty-minded."

Thrown off my questions by the unexpected aggression, I

turn to Harriet. She points out that it's a legal requirement to keep a vehicle registered to the current address.

Amy gets up and closes the lounge door. "Have you any idea what state my mother was in when my father died? If you'd ever lost someone, you'd know that form-filling isn't high on priorities."

Holding my breath, I look at Harriet and think of her late father. Has Amy touched a nerve? Does my colleague need me to intervene?

But she gets up and leads Amy back to her chair. "It must have been an awful time. We don't want to make things difficult. Do you think you can get your paperwork sorted this week? And we won't pursue it."

Got to admire her professionalism. Empathy without giving away her personal circumstances. And she makes it sound like we're doing Amy a favour, even though police officers with three unsolved murders seldom have time to dob sick, elderly women into the DVLA. Sitting forward, I add my own sympathetic nod and get back to business.

"Had you ever met Steven Baker before the meeting?"

"Never." Body language is defensive. Another lie? Or just peeved that I'm in her house, breathing the same air?

"Are you sure? He was about our age. Perhaps you met him socially?"

Her face moulds into another sneer. "Between work and looking after my mother, there isn't much time for socially."

Pretty sure that's a whopper. I recall how dolled up she was last time we called – that wasn't for work or her mother. A flickering light goes on in my head and I picture Amy in a coffee shop window with a man. Another headache-induced hallucination or something I actually saw when I was in town yesterday? What else is she lying about? The house is hot, no doubt the central heating on for her mother, but I shiver. I haven't seen Amy Ashby for years, but maybe the school cry-baby has grown into something more sinister. I'm meant to be probing her for a link to Steven Baker and Christa Talbot, but I try something else. "Is the name Russell Hill familiar to you?" Maybe she's linked to our third victim, too. Nothing like using the clutching-at-straws style of policing when all else fails.

"Everyone in Gloucester knows that name." She turns to Harriet as her voice grows breathy. "The poor soul who perished in a fire in his home. It makes me ill just thinking about him."

A typical Amy attempt to sound like the injured party. It feels like only yesterday I last heard her try that one on our head teacher. Unfazed, I ask, "Had you ever met him?"

"He was a recluse, wasn't he?"

The pitch of her voice takes me to Mrs Hardcastle's office. That bloody viola all over again. Me and Terri versus Amy and her affronted indignation. It's the way she raises her voice just before she bursts into tears and convinces Mrs H that Terri and I are devils incarnate. I don't want that today; my head's not robust enough for battle. I retreat to my Christa Talbot questions.

"Were you at work on Wednesday morning?"

"I worked the previous nightshift." Her voice has returned to the middle of its range. Apparently safe ground, so probably the truth.

"What time did you get back here?"

"About nine."

"And you came directly from Cheltenham, along the A40?" I dangle the trap; we've got her car on camera at Painswick.

She doesn't bite. "I never go that way after a nightshift; it would mean I'd hit the morning rush hour in Cheltenham town centre. I go along Stroud Road, the A46."

I straighten in my seat and sense Harriet doing the same. Amy would have turned onto the Gloucester Road in Painswick. As per the evidence from traffic light camera, she's just confirmed being in the area at the time of Christa's murder. I jot a note.

"That's if I went by car," Amy adds suddenly. "If I was on the bus, it takes the A40. I don't drive every time."

"What about Wednesday morning?"

Amy shrugs. "One day is much like another."

I catch Harriet's eye. What's Amy playing at?

"Do you keep your bus tickets?" Harriet asks.

"I have a monthly MegaRider. Don't think the driver keeps a record of when I use it. Is it important?" Amy gives Harriet a dainty smile.

"We'll check with the bus company," I say, knowing it's a dead end and wondering why she's being vague about her travel arrangements. To piss me off? Or because she's attempting to fake an alibi for murder, not knowing we have the car on candid camera?

"Can anyone vouch for what time you got home?" I ask.

"My mother was still asleep." Her eyes narrow to what-you-gonna-do-about-it. My grogginess floods back, sapping my energy. The last thing I need is another *she said, she said* war with Amy Ashby. I had enough of those in the old days.

Standing up, I tell her she's been most helpful.

But she stays in her seat. "You know the way out."

Harriet raises her eyebrows and we head into the hall. That's a side of Amy I haven't seen before. She was always charming in front of witnesses. The bathroom door is still closed, but the water's no longer running.

As Harriet pulls the front door open, Amy appears behind us. "Actually," she says, "I had heard of Russell Hill before he died." She comes up close to me. "Matt mentioned him on Thursday, our first date. Told me about the state of his house."

Harriet and I exchange a glance. Is there a witness statement from a Matt?

"What's Matt's full name?" Harriet gets out her notebook again.

Amy glares at me. "Ask her; she knows him better than I do. That's the only reason for these questions, isn't it? A trumped-up excuse for you to gloat." Amy nudges me in the back and I stumble down the front step.

Harriet grabs my arm to steady me and the door slams behind us. She reaches up to the doorbell. "I don't think so, madam. You can't assault a police officer."

I catch her hand. "Leave it." I walk on and Harriet follows with a puzzled expression.

Back in the car, I tell her to get in touch with Amy's employer to check her shift timings. I still can't believe she's guilty of murder, despite her new-found stroppiness, but it gives me something to think about other than who the hell Matt is.

# CHAPTER TWENTY-SIX

In the car I get dizzy again and this time I can't hide it from Harriet.

"I've seen more colour at post mortems," she says. "I'm driving you home."

I don't argue.

When we get to the Bell Tower, she offers to come in and make me lunch, but I say I'll eat after I've caught up on some paperwork. Making a supreme effort to stand up straight so Harriet can stop worrying, I cross the car park, wave her off and enter the main door. Mercifully the lift is there. I take it to the first floor, fumble along the wall to my flat and crash on the sofa. There's a glass of water on the coffee table left over from yesterday and I use it to see off three paracetamol. Not sure how long I've dozed, I jump awake thinking Amy Ashby has nudged me in the back again.

Who is Matt? Why would he know about the state of reclusive Russell Hill's house and tell Amy about it on a date? And what does she think he has to do with me? Then I remember that Russell Hill had at least one official visitor last week. Could there be a connection? I phone the office and catch Harriet before she heads out again. I request the phone numbers for Social Services and the fire service HQ, which she duly supplies. She tells me I still sound rough and I tell her I'll see her in the morning.

I phone the fire service and ask to speak to the fire investigation officer for The Avenue blaze. I get told he's out on another case but can ring me back.

"He's not called Matt by any chance, is he?" I ask.

"His name is Neil Morris," the man on the line tells me. "We do have a firefighter called Matthew Ward. Is it him you want? Ironically, he'd only just completed a fire prevention visit to The Avenue property."

My heart pumps faster, sensing I'm on to something. "Can I speak to him?"

"He's not on shift but he's here tomorrow from six."

I say I'll call back tomorrow. I'm relieved he isn't there. My head isn't up to conducting a telephone interrogation right now, even though it's highly likely this is the Matt that Amy was squawking about. Amy Ashby is dating a fireman! I want to laugh but my body can't take the vibration. Lying on the sofa, I close my eyes. I'll get hold of the social worker dealing with Russell Hill tomorrow too.

———

The doorbell rings.

*Jake. Work. Amy.*

My thoughts jumble at the rude interruption to my sleep. My phone says it's three p.m. I could ignore it, but it might be Harriet back to check on me and with news of Amy's shift times. If I don't answer, she'll send in a battering ram and an armed response unit.

But it turns out to be Mum at the door. With a Thermos flask. "Tomato soup."

"How did you know I'd be here?" I lead her into the lounge, fold up my blanket and put the blister packs of painkillers away.

"A nice police woman came round enquiring about poor Russell Hill. I couldn't tell her anything, but when I asked her if you were going door-to-door too, she said you were working from home."

"So you've come to interrupt police business." I give what I hope is a wry smile.

"You've worked from home twice in one week." She takes the flask into the kitchen. "Knowing you, that's code for *I can barely get out of bed*," she calls out. She returns with a steaming mug and a table mat and puts them on the coffee table.

"Thanks, Mum."

"You need to let someone else take the lead for a couple of days," she says, sitting beside me and feeling my forehead. "No job's worth this."

Her hand clasps mine and I love the warmth, but she spoils it by pointing out my fingers are stone cold. She rubs my hand between hers. Her nails are a nude pink. Exquisitely done, but all I see is Amy Ashby's lipstick from the first time we visited her.

"That doesn't hurt, does it?" Mum loosens her grasp. "You're pulling a face."

"It's not you, it's the case. I saw Amy Ashby again today."

She takes both my hands and squeezes them. "Gloucester's a small city. You've done well to avoid her this long." She grins. "Was she snivelling?"

Retrieving my hands to cover my mouth, I splutter as I try

135

to laugh. "Actually she was," I say, but wish I hadn't. I don't want to talk about Amy's odd outburst. No telling where that might lead. "She's got much to snivel about," I say instead. "Her mother's in a bad way."

Mum passes me the soup. "I never liked the woman, but I wouldn't wish ill health on her." Sitting back on the sofa, she launches into a reminiscence I'd forgotten. "Remember the parents' race at sports' day when she went round the sporty parents suggesting it would be funny if they ran backwards and didn't take it seriously? When the race started, she ran forwards. She was running against the overweight ones and the grandmas that she hadn't told to run backwards. There was a smirk on her face a mile wide when she won."

"Did you run backwards?" I ask, vaguely remembering the day. In the spectating area, Amy's smile at her mother's triumph had been equally broad, until Terri knocked it off.

"With these puppies, what do you think? I stood on the finish line and videoed Dad. There must have been five of them running in reverse. They linked arms and crossed the line together. Someone took a photo and it made the school newsletter. Bet Eileen Ashby hadn't expected that. But it was the same slyness when she complained about you and Terri to the head teacher. The pair of you wouldn't hurt a fly, even one buzzing round a limp lettuce like Amy."

I put my head in my hands, trying not to laugh as she makes light of my misdemeanours. Mum's hilarious when she wants to be. My brain just wishes it wasn't today.

Mum stops smiling. "You need a doctor. A migraine shouldn't last like this. They have that Access place on Eastgate Street. You don't need an appointment."

"I'll see how I feel after a rest."

"You said that yesterday, and the day before." She gets up to leave.

"You don't have to rush off, do you?" I know Monday is her day off and suddenly I want her fussy, bossy presence to stay.

"Model night at the salon. Someone's coming to take photos and we'll have fizz and nibbles. I'd invite you along but the soup will do you more good." She kisses my forehead and I smell her comforting perfume. "Make sure you drink it."

# CHAPTER TWENTY-SEVEN

Even with the bedroom curtains drawn, Amy can see the rise and fall of her mother's chest. She perches on the wheelchair – the only place to sit apart from the bed – and watches. The breathing is steady, not ragged like it was yesterday. Mother is on top of the sheets, fully clothed. Brown slacks, beige cardigan. The worn, grey slippers on her feet have dropped apart in a lopsided vee. Her mouth is slightly open, releasing a trickle of saliva onto her chin.

Seeing Steph again has stirred up her feelings. When did Amy stop hating her mother? When she first had to use the wheelchair? When she reversed into the coffee table and sent her medication scattering to the floor? When she became a crumbling, desiccating husk that no longer resembled the mother Amy grew up with?

———

"I don't have to listen to this." Amy gathers her coat and bag, and slams the front door behind her.

Now where? The spring night chills her fury and she wants to return to the warmth of her parents' house. But she must find Sean first and quell the whispers her mother has planted in her head. Even though it's rubbish. No proof needed. She trusts him completely.

She finds herself driving to the city centre and walks to The Whittington, where Sean said he'd be with his friends.

The pub's busy, there's a pool competition. Doesn't that prove he's telling the truth? It's Sean's regular Tuesday thing. His night away from her. And on Thursdays. Sometimes a Monday too.

Amy spots Lenny and the other one – Mark? – at the bar. Clears her throat. "Whereabouts are you sitting? Thought I'd tag along."

Is that alarm in the look that passes between them?

Lenny finds a smile. "Amy, right? Sean's running late."

"Problem at work. Could be ages." That's Mark, adjusting his elbows on the bar.

Amy folds her arms. "Maybe I'll watch the pool while I wait."

Another silent exchange of something. Amy feels her colour rising.

"We'll tell him to call you, when he gets here." Lenny waves cash at the barman as he turns away from her. No more to say.

Embarrassed, Amy cuts along Quay Street, the quickest way back to her car. Her steps are brisk, keeping ahead of the doubts. What's delaying him at work? He's a delivery driver, doesn't work evenings. The men must have made it up to protect their territory from female invasion. Sean won't like it when he finds out they gave her the brush off.

Sean's car is parked up by the river. He must have just arrived. She darts under a tree, away from the streetlamps, and studies the silhouette in the driver's seat. Just sitting. No movement at all. She's about to go over, surprise him, when another figure pulls up into sitting position in the passenger seat. Long hair. A woman. Sean leans over and wipes her mouth with his hanky.

Bile scorches Amy's throat and she clutches her belly. Her mother was right. Through her tears she sees the heads come together in a kiss. On and on. The longer they kiss, the more Amy's dizziness grows. She knows she should act. Hurl open Sean's door, snatch his keys from the ignition and lob them into the Severn. No man – even one she thought she loved – gets to sully her.

A car drives by and its headlights illuminate the couple in their sordidness. Amy collapses on her haunches, gasping, sobbing. The shock constricts her windpipe. She'll never breathe again. Her life is over. The woman's is a face she hasn't seen for seven years, but she knows it instantly.

Then rolling, pulsing balls of rage burn their way through her veins. She stands up, keeping herself hidden in the shadows. As she thinks it over, her anger subsides. Patience is her virtue. Something as grubby as a fling with Steph Lewis will scrub itself out.

This isn't school. The bully won't win.

———

The wheelchair is hard against Amy's legs as she sits in it. She shifts her weight. On the bed, her mother sighs, blinks open her eyes. Closes them; her head drops to the side. Does she know what Amy is thinking? Amy called her a witch behind her back often enough. Perhaps she really is one.

———

Amy kicks up just enough fuss about wanting more time together to make Sean drop his Thursday and Monday assignations. So as not to arouse the suspicion that she's rumbled him, she lets him keep his Tuesdays. Steph is consigned to a weekly screw. Only a matter of time until the slut shrivels in his affections. With Amy, he's more loving than ever; she makes sure of that. The only cloud is his reluctance to set a date. "Let's save for another year, Amy-Cakes. We want our wedding to be special, don't we?" And his smile almost convinces her.

———

Amy idly counts the medicine bottles on the bedside locker. Four. What would happen if one got lost? She tucks the question to the back of her mind, knowing she'll always do the right thing. Hasn't she always, especially recently?

———

Weeks later, Amy arrives home from another wedding fair, weighed down with the catering and photography business cards in her bag. It's a happy weight. A bride-to-be's badge of honour.

Her mother greets her in the hall, eyes shining with tears. She holds out a handwritten note.

*Amy-Cakes,*
*I'm leaving Gloucester. Forget me.*
*Sean.*

"I'm so sorry, darling," her mother says and hugs her tight.

———

Amy grips the arms of the wheelchair as she recalls how she screamed at her mother, accusing her of faking the note even though she'd know Sean's spider-writing anywhere. She followed Steph on and off for a month but never caught her with Sean. He really had left. The only good thing to come out of the trauma was that she got to know Steph's haunts and has avoided them ever since, managing not to clap eyes on her until this week.

The shabby figure on the bed turns and sighs again in her sleep. Amy knows her mother never grew to like Sean. Did he sense it? Is that why he left? Surely they could have brought her round in time.

But they never really worked, did they? Amy breathes out sharply. If she really thought there'd been a chance, she'd have made the call to Sean at noon today. Her mother was right all along. Amy will leave things as they are.

Amy grips the spokes of the wheelchair. But things have changed. There's Matt to think of. *Matt*. Did he and Steph go on a date? Is that why Matt recognised her through the café window? It's taken Steph eighteen years, but again she's come between Amy and a man.

But Amy's a grown-up now. If Matt prefers a tart, he's welcome to her. The wheelchair rolls backwards as she presses her feet into the floor, and she snatches her fingers away from the spokes. She can't leave things like this. She remembers telling Matt that Steph wouldn't win. There must be a way of showing Steph that she has stepped out of the race.

*Sean*. Wouldn't that be the ultimate victory? They almost married once. What if it was meant to be after all? That would show Steph. Amy would win the long game.

The old woman lies still, her breathing almost silent. Amy creeps out of the room. In the kitchen, where her mother won't be able to hear if she wakes, Amy gets out her phone. It's three fifteen – more than three hours after the deadline Sean gave her. Is she too late? Her fingers tremble as she gets up the number he pressed into her phone.

It's answered on the fourth ring.

"Sean?" Her voice quivers.

"Amy-Cakes. Amazing to hear you." He sounds like he's smiling, and there's a touch of Liverpool in his dropped g. Perhaps he returned to his home town when he left. "When can we meet?"

The urgency of the question throws her. She should have thought this through. She isn't ready.

"You haven't gone shy on me, have you? You don't need to, not with me. The Spinnaker at six thirty."

"Tonight?" Her shaking increases. Too fast. All too fast.

"Come on, Amy-Cakes, it's just a drink."

The Spinnaker restaurant is where he proposed. Flames on the surrounding hills. Her happiest day ever. "Okay," she says. Why not? Who's to say she – they – couldn't be that happy again?

"Great. It always used to be cocktail hour on Mondays. Maybe we'll get lucky."

Something catches in Amy's throat. He's talking about cocktails, isn't he? Get lucky means so many things. "Actually," she says slowly, "I'm not sure tonight's going to work. I look after my elderly mother. She's a bit unsettled today."

"She came between us last time." His voice has changed, more snarl than charm.

"She didn't." Steph did that, but Amy doesn't want to say her name.

"You can't let your mother control you."

"I don't. She doesn't." Amy feels helpless against the fury coming into her ear.

"So what's it to be?"

"There could be other nights." Amy hears the lack of enthusiasm in her voice. There won't be others, not with this man. "Mum's calling. I'll have to go."

"It's time you stuck up for yourself." He rings off.

Nearly dropping the phone in her trembling hands, she blocks his number and deletes it from her contacts. She perches on a kitchen stool and puts her head in her hands as tears run down her face. She sobs harder when she realises Steph has won again.

# CHAPTER TWENTY-EIGHT

It's late afternoon and Amy Ashby is snuggling under the blanket on the sofa with me; I can't seem to empty my mind of her and go to sleep. I grab my phone and search Facebook. In as far as anyone puts their true self on social media, I might as well fill my head with facts rather than speculation. Amy has set her privacy so I can't see her posts, only her photos. Fifty friends – not many by my son Jake's 1800 standards – but in Amy's case they'll be people she's met in real life. Many might be school friends; she was popular in her own way. We both were, although our circles didn't intersect – not at school anyway.

No selfies with hunky firemen on her profile, but she did say she'd heard about Russell Hill on a *first* date, so she and Matt probably haven't reached the joint selfie stage. There's a picture of her with her parents. Amy looks tall beside her mother but is dwarfed by her father. Clicking on the photo to enlarge it, I see how healthy Mrs Ashby looks. Steel grey, well-cut hair – exuding older woman chic like Honor Blackman. Mr A's complexion is florid, maybe a sign of the heart trouble to come, or it could be a touch of sunburn.

His hair was sandy, so he probably had skin that didn't tan. Amy stands between them, smiling into the camera, neat in a white t-shirt and black leggings, an orange scarf tied at her neck.

As I look, I feel the old anger rising. I click through her other pictures. Most are of flower arrangements, presumably ones she's done herself. I'm no expert, but I can see that they're good – full-bodied, balanced, with excellent use of contrasting and complementary colours. The earliest photos show genealogy charts. The Ashby line going back a few generations. No doubt she thought she'd find a link to royalty. But she hasn't posted any similar photos in the last year, so it's unlikely she found an Ashby maiden who made it to a king's bedchamber. She must have lost interest in the hobby, now she has to look after her mother.

Amy's shove from earlier burns my back. I wrap the blanket tighter around me and I feel a prickle of shame. She had every right. Not for the shove – I could have let Harriet caution her for that. But for...

My phone goes.

"You sound terrible, Steph," Harriet says.

"Hay fever."

For the first month afterwards I showered twice, three times a day. Eighteen years later, I'm not sure I've washed off the shame.

"Steph, are you listening?" Harriet says down the phone. "You've got it bad, haven't you?"

I pull myself together. "Sorry, my phone went funny. Say all that again."

"I checked with the bus company whether Amy Ashby was on the bus on Wednesday morning, but they don't scan Mega-Rider tickets on that route. New equipment hasn't been installed yet. But why are we bothering anyway? We know she used the car. We've got it on CCTV in the vicinity of the Georgian Gardens."

"At the traffic lights in Painswick," I correct her. Amy wasn't caught as near to the Christa Talbot murder scene as we'd all like. But if we can prove she wasn't on the bus, we can find out why she muddied the waters by saying she might have been. Typical Amy, always liked her smoke and mirrors. Her hue and cry. *Her bit of rough.* I wince and force my thoughts back to Harriet. "Have you checked her alibi for the Steven Baker murder?"

"I've asked the head teacher at Orchard Prep for a copy of Amy's shift rota. He's put a minion onto it. I forgot to double-check with the secretary about Amy doing the flowers on Thursday night. I'll phone back tomorrow."

Harriet's voice fades in and out as I feel dizzy again. I try to ring off but she has more to say.

"There's no school connection between Christa Talbot and Russell Hill. Katrina Talbot says her son was privately educated at The Guild School. And according to a Mrs Dougal, one of Russell's neighbours, he attended the boys' grammar school. But she says it was a criminal waste of a place for a more deserving boy – if you're interested."

I'm not. I thank her and end the call.

Phone still in my hand, I think of my best friend Terri and send her a text.

She picks up the text immediately. *How's it going?*

I text back. *Fine. How are you?*

I wait, seeing a longer text on its way. *Pissed off. They had Inspiration Day in assembly and applauded me.*

Terri is the same up-for-a-laugh girl I went to school with and worked alongside as a PCSO. Even the gun blast that shattered her hearing didn't change her, but there are two things people say that drive her mad. One is how well she's overcome her disability.

She's typing again. *If the kids don't care, why does the head? My story is so fecking uplifting.*

*At least he doesn't think you're faking,* I type and add a laughing emoji. Her other pet hate. An ex-colleague once declared he'd caught her out because she didn't 'sound' deaf, whatever that means.

She replies with a devil emoji. *Only thing worse is a real faker. How's the headache?*

I have to reread. Does she think I'm making up my migraine? She types more. *You should get checked. That's advice from an NHS fan.*

I text *ok.* She can interpret my non-commitment as agreement if she wants.

*Got to go. At checkout. Jake okay with pepperoni again?*

*Yeah thanks for having him over,* I reply, and suppress my regret that he won't be home for a while.

*Our turn next. Night out, murder enquiries permitting?* She adds a champagne glass emoji. *Don't work too hard.*

I type *ok* again and put away my phone. I lie down to sleep, but my head throbs.

---

"What you need is a night out," Terri suggests when she finds me sobbing over my bank statements.

I shake my head. "I'm at least another year away." My evenings and weekends are booked solid with private clients, but the dream of owning my own salon is beyond my saving power.

"You'll get there." She squeezes my shoulder. "In the meantime stop living like a spray-tanned Scrooge."

I have to laugh as I blow my nose.

"Singles night at Taboo," Terri says. "Half-price cocktails. What do you say?"

She buys the first round. Doubles. It is weeks since I've had a drink – part of my economy drive. In no time, my brain's thumping faster than the drum and bass.

Over Terri's shoulder I make eye contact with a guy at the bar. He's average height but tall from my short-house perspective. Open-necked white shirt, good skin. Brown eyes – reckless, brown eyes.

The moment Terri goes to the loo, he takes her seat, and another double appears in front of me.

"Sean."

"Steph."

Is it the alcohol? The release after months in purgatory? Or just that I fancy the bones of him? We leave before Terri comes back.

No strings, we agree from the first hot kiss. A bit of fun. His car, mine, hotels, a caravan in Weston. A shared lust for fags, Merlot and enclosed spaces.

———

The pain goes into a frenzy and I clutch my forehead. Still dizzy, I stagger to my jacket and car keys. There's something I'm going to have to do.

# CHAPTER TWENTY-NINE

Evil cow. Goading, letting him think one thing but all the time knowing it's something else. Now he knows, too.

Sean strides towards The Bell Tower. Two girls on the tennis court turn his way. He slows his pace until they get bored and go back to their game. He keeps it slow; it wouldn't be wise to attract more attention. When a car drives through the automatic gates, he slips in behind. Pausing to pretend-tie his laces, he waits until the driver has parked and entered the building.

His gait feels awkward. It's hard to walk when every muscle is tense with schemes of revenge. Women – he hates them. A coven of witches, twisted to the core. One of them should have been sorted for good today, but when he tried, an express train of shock crashed that out of his head.

*A boy.*

That young guy on the bike he saw around here on Thursday could have been him. He was about the right age and good-looking enough. So, he's been denied access all these years, but not for much longer. The witches have conjured the devil in him. They'll all pay. Starting with *her*.

When no more cars come up the drive to the gate, he moves briskly across the car park and around the building to the dustbins at the back. This is his tried and tested route to her flat. The general waste skip moves easily on its wheels. As he lines it up underneath a first floor balcony, an idea occurs to him.

He opens the bin and hoists out a bulky bin bag. He puts the bag on top of the lid and pushes up beside it. Sweating at the effort, he hoists himself up the balcony railings and clasps the bin bag between his feet. He tosses it over and clambers onto the balcony.

He takes out his flat blade knife and levers it in the door catch. After a couple of jinks, he hears the click and steps into the communal lounge that no one ever seems to use. He crosses the room, opens the unlocked door into the corridor and heads towards her flat.

To be on the safe side, he rings the doorbell and waits. His belly flutters in case the boy answers the door. But after he rings a second time, still no one comes. The lock is as easy to release as the one from the balcony. Whenever he's got this far before, he's lost his nerve. This is the first time he's actually going inside. The hall smells of almonds... or rose petals? He's not sure, but it's good, just like he remembers her.

Nice lounge – tasteful throw and cushions. She still has an eye for design. His mouth curls as he approaches the photographs on the dresser. There she is in a hospital gown, cradling a new-born baby. On a beach, in shorts – still all legs and tits – swinging a toddler in the air. Another taken outside this building: proud schoolboy with a fresh haircut and a pristine school uniform. *The years he's missed*. He should be in these pictures, part of the boy's life. He lifts a four-by-six-inch glass-fronted photo of a worse-for-wear teenager in a grass-stained rugby strip. The eyes, the smile, say it all. *His* boy. He puts it face-down on the dresser and balls his fists, hating himself for not breaking in sooner. These photos would have tipped him a warning and maybe spared him the vindictive, hammering shock he's endured today.

Time to take what's his. But he has to do it slowly. First wear her down. This is the long game. She's played it for eighteen years. He'll take his time. He's never been a stalker – a bit of light-touch surveillance doesn't count – but she's about to find out what he's capable of. In a variation on the three-cup conjuring trick, he shuffles the photos around the dresser, leaving scratch marks in the polished top. When he's satisfied he's moved them all, he knocks each one on its face.

He picks up the bin bag and goes into the kitchen. An exam timetable is stuck to a magnetic board. Sean takes a photo on his phone. Responsible parenting – always good to know where the nipper is. Shame there's no print-out of her shift roster. He'd need to hack into her laptop; not his style. He looks around for where he can make maximum impact. A pair of Marigolds and a dishcloth folded over the mixer tap; draining board and work surfaces clutter free; floor spotless. *Not for long*. He rips open the bin bag, braces himself for the pong and tips the contents into the sink. Bits of plastic, broken coat hangers, nail clippings, tin lids, used tissues. Mank.

But he's disappointed there's no smell. That's the trouble with all this recycling. You can't rely on it. He needs food waste: tea bags, coffee grounds, eggs shells, potato peelings – the mouldier the better. Someone must have lobbed a bag of stuff into the food skip. He'll go back down and fetch one. It will be disgusting to hoik out but worth the effort to smear crap over her cooker hob and bathroom floor. He takes the washing up gloves. She's bought large; they fit him. He feels his groin swell. She always did know where to put her big hands. Leaving the front door on the latch, he retraces his steps through the communal lounge, climbs over the balcony railings and drops to the skips.

# CHAPTER THIRTY

Tests. I sat in the Access Centre waiting room for two and a half hours to be told they couldn't diagnose without more tests. The doctor – shiny smile and odd socks – was a bigger drama queen than Jake or Mum. After shining his murderous light in my eyes and measuring my blood pressure, temperature and heart rate – with *hmmm* muttered under his breath – he announced, "This might require more investigation," and added cheerfully, "I'll input your data to see where you are on the scale."

Eventually the computer drew a pie chart that looked like crime figures. It decreed I was below the threshold for immediate incarceration and let the doctor prescribe me the painkillers I came for in the first place. In a tone way too solemn for my liking, he said I would get a letter, inviting me for a brain scan.

Not bloody likely.

As I take the elevator to my flat, I open the white paper bag I got after another thirty-minute wait at the Access pharmacy and read the multisyllabic labels. If they don't give my headache a seeing to, nothing will. No need for scans. Stupid idea. Waste of NHS money. I'll be doing them a favour by cancelling when the appointment comes through.

My phone rings as I exit the lift, and I balance my chemicals in the top of my handbag as I answer it.

"Hello, Jake."

"You sound awful."

"I love you too."

"Seriously, Mum. Are you okay?"

"Stop worrying. I went to the doctor's and have the default dose of painkillers. I'm on the mend already."

"Do you need me to come home tonight?"

"Where else would you be?" The mock outrage in my voice is faked; my disappointment is real. I miss him when he's away.

"Brad and I have come up with a good revision regime. Terri says I can stay the night again."

I move the bag to my other shoulder and search for my house key. "So all that concern for my health is really for whether you can stay over for seconds of Terri's pizza."

As he makes his protestations, I laugh and unlock the door. Something prickles at the back of my neck. The hallway carries an alien smell.

"Jake, have you started smoking again?"

"No way, Mum. I'd get kicked off the team. What made you say that?"

"Nothing. I thought I could smell... Doesn't matter. Good luck for Maths tomorrow."

"Bye, Mum. Hope the drugs work."

Me too. This migraine business must have affected my nasal cavities if I think I can smell cigarettes. I hang my bag and jacket in the hall and take the prescription boxes to the kitchen.

There's a pile of stuff in the sink. I put the tablets down and peer. Why's Jake done this? What did he want an unspooled video of *Top Gear* for? And a pair of old slippers? Tissues? I consider calling Jake back and making him come home to clean up.

*If it was him.* I grow cold at the thought. Has someone else been in here? A police matter? I imagine how I'd have handled a report like that when I was a bobby. *You see, officer, there's an old make-up compact in my sink and I don't think my son put it there.*

I take a roll of bin liners out of a kitchen drawer and tear one off. Best thing is to scoop the crap away and speak to Jake about it tomorrow night. I go back to the drawer and open a new packet of rubber gloves. I thought I had an open pair already, but maybe they're at the bottom of this pile of junk. Gloves on, I fill the bag and tie it closed. Jake always takes out our bin bags so I'll leave it on the kitchen floor until he gets back. It's his mess anyway, *hopefully*. I lay the gloves on the draining board.

One box of painkillers contains enough tablets to stun a hippo. The blister packaging in the other box reminds me of the warehouse flats in the Quays – rooms on a giant scale with not much more furniture than a sofa and a glass-topped coffee table. Each sheet contains only one tablet. After filling a glass of water, I pop out one of each type of tablet and swallow them. Although I've removed the debris, the sink looks grimy, so I don the Marigolds again and get out the cleaner.

The effort of cleaning depletes my energy, and I recuperate on a kitchen chair. The bin bag smirks at me as if it's a turd on my polished tiles. When the painkillers have kicked in, I snatch it up and march out of my flat to the bin store at the back of the Bell Tower, dreaming up the bollocking I'm going to give Jake when I see him.

A shambolic array of receptacles greets me and I don't know which one to stick the bin bag in. I've left my phone in the flat, so I can't phone Jake to ask. Do they always look like this, pushed together in a line, some tipped over like outsize dominoes? Oh, what the hell. It's all rubbish, isn't it? There's a brown skip in the middle of the line-up. That'll do.

*Fuck.* My heart spews into my throat. There's a body on the ground.

*Jake? It can't be; we've only just spoken. He's at Terri's. It can't be. Please, God, no.*

My blood pulses and I see it isn't Jake. The man is heavier, middle-aged – but there's something familiar about the shape of the head – what's left of it. The body is slumped in a lake of blood, with more gore congealed on an upturned skip beside it. As a police officer I'm trained in first aid, but I don't need to be a pathologist to see it's too late. I'll do this guy more good by leaving him in situ so forensics have a better chance of getting his killer. It's the Steven Baker crime scene all over again, but worse. It's not just his skull caved in, there's crushing, irreparable damage to the torso and legs. Only his arms still seem intact. He's wearing Marigold gloves.

Hurriedly I check the area for other bodies and even look inside the skips. Taking my bin bag with me so as not to confuse the crime scene, I return to my flat for my phone and warrant card. Adrenaline triumphs over headache and I manage to make a coherent call on the way back to the body. In front of the refuse area, I form a one woman police cordon. As I wait for my colleagues, I try not to think of that agonising moment I thought the victim was my son.

# CHAPTER THIRTY-ONE

"The Controller won't like it," Lulu warns. She takes off her headphones and stares at Nathan through the glass.

"Relax, it's topical." Why can't she be on his side for once? Some presenters take their producers with them when they move stations. Not Nathan J. When the call comes, he'll ditch this school ma'am and fly solo. "The listeners will love it."

"Not the ones who—"

He cuts her off so he can speak over the end of the record. "*That was the sound of the Buzzcocks. 'Ever Fallen in Love.' Remember that one? We've all been there. Time for tonight's Tweetalong. There could only be one topic after news surfaced today that Meghan Markle's dad will not be attending the Royal Wedding. We want to hear from you if you'd like to volunteer for that special vacancy. Give us a call tonight and let us know why you should walk Meghan down the aisle.*"

Lulu shakes her head vigorously.

He ignores her. "*Or you can tweet. Here's Wham to tell you the hashtag.*"

George Michael bursts into "I'm Your Man".

Lulu's on his case the second he releases the two-way mic. "Our tweetalongs are supposed to be inclusive. Ever heard of gender equality?"

His Twitter feed moves:
**Chaz**@up4a3some
I'd see her nice. Know what I mean? #Imyourman

**Alison**@AllyRoberts90
Meghan's mum should do it #Imyourwoman

**David**@DavidBadders99
Daughter's wedding last week and I still have the suit. #Imyourman

**Louisa**@OnTheDecks10
Sexist Pig #Imyourwoman

Nathan looks across at Lulu. "You sent that one."

Before she can protest, the phone rings. Her face grows serious as she listens to the caller. After putting them on hold, she speaks to Nathan through her mic. "It's the stalker. Shall I say you're on another call?"

Nathan's pulse quickens. He's tempted to accept Lulu's suggestion. Get her to put the phone down. What if the mystery caller has another so-called tip? He'd rather chew the fat with Chaz@up4a3some.

He narrows his eyes. Is Lulu grinning? What if his gut instinct was right last time and she's behind this to get him sacked? Does she really think he's stupid enough to make a comment on air about a police investigation? *Two can play that one.* He draws his fingers through his spiky hair. "I'll take it." He glares at her defiantly.

Lulu loses a bit of colour. "Are you sure you want to do this? After that creepy stuff about arson before it was announced. We should have told the police."

He studies her through the glass. She looks genuinely anxious. Maybe she didn't make the call about the fire, and she can't be the person on the other end of the line now. Suppose it wasn't a hoax, and this caller did have inside information. What else might they know? If Nathan was favoured with one news exposé, others could follow. Not usually his thing, but this could be the break he needs. The big time.

"I expect it was a lucky guess." He shrugs, feigning a lack of interest. "Fifty-fifty chance on a blaze like that." He can't help flexing his fingers, eager to grasp the handset when she transfers the call.

"Your funeral," Lulu whispers and puts through the connection.

He gabbles his line. "You're through to Nathan J. What would you like to talk about?"

"Why didn't you use the scoop I gave you?" The tone is neutral but Nathan worries that the caller is angry. It won't do to piss him off, or her (he still isn't sure).

"I'm sorry about that. We get a lot of crank callers. I, well, we..." He shifts the blame, keeping his eyes away from Lulu's window. "My producer wasn't sure your call was genuine."

"But you know now."

"I regret that my producer didn't take you seriously. It was bad advice."

Silence.

The anticipation is exhausting. Nathan sweats and grows short of breath as he thinks of what to say.

The caller takes the lead. "I have something else for you."

"About the fire? About the hoarder?" He sounds squeaky, like a little boy waiting for a treat.

"Russell Hill is *one* victim," the voice says.

Nathan's gut plummets; he's being lied to. Everyone says the hoarder lived alone. The only casualty. If other people were in the blaze, it would have been in the news by now.

The voice continues even paced as if reading the shipping forecast. "Christopher Talbot, Steven Baker, Russell Hill – all connected."

Through the glass, Lulu crosses her eyes and puts her arms out like the walking dead. Nathan might not like it, but she's got a point. The caller is cuckoo. The police would have said if there was a link between the hoarder's death and the two murders. Nathan decides to bail out.

"It's been great to chat, but..."

"A senior detective with West Gloucestershire Police is involved."

With his hand over the phone cradle, he pauses. It doesn't sound like a lie, or a script. It's said in the same way that the caller told him the blaze was arson.

"How involved?" he asks.

"You want to move on, don't you? To greater opportunities? So move on in your thinking, Nathan."

Lulu shakes her head and shrugs, making it clear he's on his own.

"So this isn't just about Russell Hill?" he asks. "A police officer is connected to all three deaths?"

"Why stop at three?"

Nathan's heart races, the sweat beading on his forehead. Play this right and he's sitting on an eighteen carat route to Radio One. "I need more information."

"Next time."

"Don't go. At least tell me your name."

"You can call me Morag."

The line clicks dead.

# CHAPTER THIRTY-TWO

"Full P.M. later today," Kevin tells us, "but Siobhan Evans says she'd bet her pension that he was run over."

"A hit and run?" Harriet asks, sounding surprised. She's signed up to the serial killer theory too. I could tell her this one's different. Christopher Talbot and Steven Baker were law abiding, Russell Hill was eccentric but harmless, but this one – whoever he is... Someone went into my flat last night and it wasn't Jake; I phoned him. The junk in the sink wasn't his.

"He was facing towards the dustbins and the vehicle was driven at speed straight into the back of him. Driver then reversed and drove at the prone body a second time." Kevin looks at Harriet. "Does that sound like an accident to you?"

We all shake our heads.

"Time of death: between five and seven p.m. There's every likelihood he'd been lying there a good hour – if not longer – when Steph found him."

All turn briefly to commiserate with me for being the poor sod who clocked him. I nod and wait for Kevin to continue.

The pills are working but I'm still dizzy with lack of sleep and shock.

"So, lots of knocking on doors this early morn. Catch some of the Bell Tower residents before they head to work. Did they see him? Did they know him? Did they put their bins out and, if so, at what time? And most importantly, what cars do they drive? Ask to see them. Siobhan hasn't ruled out damage to the vehicle."

"Have we got an ID?" Tony asks.

"This one is forty-four years old so misses your serial killer profile by three years. A wallet was found on the victim. Driving licence in the name of Sean Farrell. Home address Liverpool."

*Sean Farrell.*

*Sean Farrell.*

*Sean Farrell.*

The name clangs in my head like a death knell. My dizziness goes into a fast, swirling, whooshing spin. I sit forward, elbows on my knees, head in hands. The sweat seeps from my scalp.

"Harriet, your job is to track down next of kin." Somewhere in outer space, Kevin is still speaking. "We need a formal identification. Find out whether he had an address in Gloucester or whether he was just visiting and why."

What was it the doctor said about tests? A new illness invades me. I float in a fever above the incident room, not fully registering the briefing. My only thought clamours: *Sean Farrell.*

"Now," Kevin says. "Any more on Steven Baker?"

Harriet stands. Her voice competes with the thrumming in my ears. I make out some of it. "...Baker received hate mail and complaint letters about the roundabout scheme." She seems to be smiling at me. "Even you sent him one."

My head whirls. She must mean the protest email Mum asked me to send after the planning meeting. To Steven Baker? My mind is on Sean Farrell.

Tony Smith stands, points both arms at me. "Ladies and Gentleman, we have our serial killer."

In and out of focus, a carousel of faces. Loud and quiet, applause and laughter.

I stand up. I feel my colour draining.

"Here comes the defence." Tony folds his arms. "It was an accident, your honour. I didn't notice I had the rock in my hand."

Mirth dances around me. The beat is *Sean Farrell, Sean Farrell*. I turn to Kevin. "I need to speak to you in private."

# CHAPTER THIRTY-THREE

We eye each other across his desk.

Tell the truth, and nothing but. I'll manage that, but the part about the *whole* truth is the deal breaker.

"This better be good, Steph, to break up a briefing when we have four murders on the table." Kevin scratches his elbow through his sleeve.

The office dances to the beat of my dizziness. Standard beechwood desk, overflowing in-tray, Kevin in a black swivel chair. Linda and the kids in a silver frame on the filing cabinet. Police Dogs calendar on the wall, still on April. Computer cables trailing from the desk to a tagliatelle heap on the floor.

"Has something happened?" Kevin speaks in a gentler tone, one I can't ignore.

I launch into a speech and don't stop. "Get Forensics over to my place. I think the victim was in my flat yesterday afternoon. I found a load of junk in my sink and blamed Jake, but something was off about it. I found the body when I took the junk down to the bins. When I eventually got back to my flat – after I'd talked to Siobhan at the crime scene and given my statement – I found some photographs had been knocked about."

"A burglar? Was anything taken?" A shadow of concern crosses his face and he opens up his computer. "Sorry, Steph. I'll ask Forensics to take good care." He reads his screen. "Nothing here about other residents reporting an intruder. We'd better check with Uniform that things haven't got mixed up in the excitement. He hasn't got a record, if Sean Farrell is his real name. But if he's turned to burglary, his murder could be a falling out amongst thieves or a hopeless getaway driver who ploughed into an accomplice. Or a vigilante householder who caught him breaking in." He rubs his eyes. "God, I hope not. We'll have the *Sun* ringing up every five minutes, offering to take up their cause."

I could leave it there. Any of Kevin's theories could be right, but there's another theory – the nail in my coffin.

"I knew him," I whisper.

Kevin hesitates, giving me his full attention. "An informant? I knew that Liverpool address was bogus."

"He's from Liverpool originally." The gift of the Scouse gab that caused my trouble all those years ago. "But he lived in Gloucester in the late nineties, early noughties. He left. May well have gone back to Liverpool." I admire the weave of my jeans. "Not an informant. A friend, once. We haven't seen each other for eighteen years."

"Why was he in your flat?"

"Not a clue. Didn't know he was in Gloucester."

"What's the history?" Kevin bores into me with his copper's eyes. No wonder his clean-up rate is the best in the county.

"We were close once."

"How close?"

There's a knock at the door. Harriet enters. "Sir, I thought you'd like to know straight away. Forensics have finished with Sean Farrell's phone. He took a photo of a college exam timetable within his final hour. And the last call received was from a name that's come up in the Steven Baker enquiry, someone at the roundabout meeting: Amy Ashby." She looks at me, before closing the door on her way out.

My head spins again. How can Amy be mixed up in this? Why is my life imploding under the weight of its past? It's too surreal.

"She was his fiancée," I blurt out in shock. "Years ago. They split. He did a bunk."

Kevin is still staring at me. "Another woman?"

Crap, he's good. I nod.

He gets up from his desk and looks out of the window. I'm in trouble. He only looks out when he's about to make an unshakeable deduction. "Your lad's doing exams this week, isn't he? Could it be his timetable that Farrell photographed, inside your flat?"

"I don't know." I shiver as the terrifying thought dawns that Sean broke into my home because he'd found out about Jake. If so, whoever mowed him down may have saved my family.

Kevin eyes me quizzically. "How's your lad getting on?"

"Fine," I whisper. I see the trap and know I'll fall.

"GCSEs or A levels? I've lost track."

"Mock A levels." My voice is quiet but clear.

"Lower sixth? Seventeen?"

I thought I was the mathematician. I say nothing.

Still looking out of the window, he asks, "Just for the record, where were you before you found Farrell's body?"

If I tell him I was at the doctor's, he'll send me home, take me off the case. I'm too invested to let that happen. If police are going to dig into Sean's background, I need to be in charge.

"On enquiries, I think. Can't remember where." *Lame.* "I'll check my files and get back to you." *Never.*

He straightens up and returns to his seat. "Steph, I've noticed you've been under the weather lately." He looks straight at me, his eyes kind but unnerving. "I'd like you to take the rest of the week off."

"Sir, you can't do that. I've done nothing wrong."

"You need to put yourself as far away from this case as possible. Amy Ashby is a person of interest and now her ex-fiancé has turned up dead outside your flat. I don't want to find any more links between you and Amy Ashby."

# CHAPTER THIRTY-FOUR

*"Evening, night lovers, I'm Nathan J. Before we get it on, let's go over to the newsroom for the latest from Dale Green."*

*"Good evening. Police have not yet named the man found dead outside an apartment block on the edge of Gloucester yesterday evening. Emergency services were called to the Abbeyfield area just after seven p.m., but the victim was pronounced dead at the scene. A police spokesman confirmed that the death is being treated as suspicious and a murder investigation has been launched. This is the fourth murder in the city in the last week."*

Amy turns down the car radio; she's heard enough. Doesn't sound like the police have a clue. Again. Steph Lewis is floundering. Amy smiles.

Watching the shoppers push trolleys across the supermarket car park, she sits in her car for another minute. What do they all do for a living? Must be shift work if they're here at this time. She spots one woman in a nurse's tunic loading her boot. White bread and ready meals. Amy smiles to herself again. She makes sure she and her mother have fresh food and wholemeal.

There's a twinge of guilt when she thinks of her mother. She promised she'd take her to Sainsbury's tomorrow. It's one of the few pleasures the old lady has left. But there's no joy in it for Amy. Back-breaking lifts, wheelchair caught on the bottom shelves and the pity of others, many doing about-turns into other aisles. Coming to this late-night Tesco on her own is far easier. Amy just wishes she hadn't lied to her mother that she was doing an extra night duty at work. She's going to have to hide the shopping and creep back into the bungalow like a teenager.

When the news has finished, she turns up the volume.

*"Nathan J here with something very special. From now on, Tuesday night will be Smooch Night. Sit back, relax and enjoy some non-stop music. Segue to segue of great tracks for lovers. While you snuggle up with the one you love, Lulu and I will have our own private party right here in the studio.*

*"What's that, Lulu? Have I got that wrong? I thought you wore the leather hot pants especially for me."*

The presenter's innuendo disappears behind the intro to "Unchained Melody". Amy gathers her shopping bags and cardigan, but pauses when his voice cuts in again.

*"And when you're all loved up, I'll be back with a little something that may shock you awake. A piece of news we all need to know. Morag, I'm waiting for your call."*

Amy hits the off button, gets out and locks the car.

# CHAPTER THIRTY-FIVE

The presenter jabbers. Alexandra doesn't like him, but it's the only station she can find with a clear signal. Maybe it's the price she pays for having the radio poolside against her stepfather's express wishes. But why is there even a socket out here if it's so dangerous? The floor is dry and the cable won't reach anywhere near the pool.

Alexandra lights the last of the candles, puts the matches on the floor by the radio and dims the ceiling lights. The water shimmers dark blue. Perfect. She's been looking forward to this since she drove her parents to the airport. She has the house and this indoor pool in the garden to herself. She can recreate the backdrop of flickering candlelight and soft music that she used to enjoy in Barlow's pool when she lived at his place.

Piling her hair onto her head and securing it with a clip, she wonders whether she ought to fetch her mother's bathing cap. Her hair extensions are new and she's unsure how they will react to chlorine. But the swimming hat will be in her parents' bedroom somewhere, and Alexandra doesn't want to tramp across the garden in the dark and slog up to the master suite on the second floor. She'll stick to breaststroke with her head up.

The built-in steps sweep into the shallow end and, as the radio plays "Unchained Melody", she descends like a movie star on an MGM stage. The designer bikini shows off her new figure, hiding the tummy tuck scar. White goes well with her fresh spray tan.

The water is like a warm bath. She turned up the temperature as soon as she got back from dropping off her parents. She must remember to turn it down next week; her stepfather always moans about heating costs. She's far too old to be beholden to him again, but she had to move back home. Nowhere else to go.

The little waves she makes ripple off the pool walls and caress her arms and legs, breasts and hips. She remembers how seductive she found Barlow's pool. They never swam for long, always ended up in the sauna. As her fingers scoop the water in front of her, she admires her new manicure. It's a trial run for next week. She'll make sure she looks a knockout when she collects her parents, in case they've got Barlow on the return flight with them.

When she reaches the end of the ten-metre pool, she holds the gulley and gently kicks her legs behind her. Will they find him? Denny, her stepfather, is confident he knows all the bars between Marbella and Lloret de Mar that a suspected fraudster would frequent. Alexandra doesn't doubt it. Denny must have done his share of creative accounting over the years.

Keeping her head and shoulders out of the water, she places her feet on the wall and pushes off on her back, her body assuming the shape of an armchair.

*We'll find him, Alex, I promise.* Denny's parting words as he gripped her in a bear hug at the check-in desk. And behind him, her mother's face, *say thank you to your father* pleading

172

in her eyes. But she didn't oblige. They both know he's showing this interest in tracking down Barlow because of the investment she made in Barlow's company. Denny cares more about her trust fund than he does about her. It's all about the money.

Why can't her parents just leave them alone to work out their own problems? As soon as Barlow sees how she's worked on her body and the new wardrobe she bought following her surgery, he'll take her back. She can move out of her parents' place for good.

A splash of water hits her eyes, and, squinting to keep the sting at bay, she heads for her towel on the side. Barlow – her other Barlow – has curled up in the thick, fluffy cloth. She gently lifts him away and wipes her face on the corner of the towel.

"You can have it back now," she tells him. But he's taken umbrage at her wet hands and stalked off out of sight, probably through the slightly open door into the garden.

*I can see why you call it Barlow*, her mother said soon after Alexandra turned up with her cat cage and suitcases. *That cat does whatever the hell it pleases and shits on its own doorstep.*

Her mum never let Alexandra have a pet as a child when they lived in the council flat, arguing it would be cruel in the cramped space. But in this big house, she can't use that excuse. She never wanted Alexandra to have a boyfriend either and turned her nose up at several over the years, which is why Alexandra was still single at thirty-nine. Barlow changed that – two years of bliss. But her mum disliked him most of all. *He's after your dad's money.*

Pot and kettle. What made Mum fall in love with short, round, bad-breathed Denny – his scintillating wit or his business portfolio? But the marriage has somehow worked. They've been together sixteen years. Alexandra's mother finally living

173

the life she only dreamed of as a single parent, able to give her daughter the finer things.

So what if Barlow appreciated Alexandra's finances before he appreciated her? Why shouldn't a successful man want a solvent woman?

There's a clatter and a waft of cool air across her shoulders. Barlow trots in, mewling. He rubs his ears against the towel, continuing to miaow. Strange, he normally slips in without her noticing. The cat must have pushed the door into a more open position to cause the breeze. She smiles. Is the little kitty cat after her attention? Still smiling, she swims off. He can't have it all his own way. That's what she should have made clear to her other Barlow. Maybe if she'd played hard to get with both money and sex...

The music has stopped. Did the cat nudge the radio on his way in? Keeping swimming, she continues to ignore him and decides not to investigate the radio until she's done another length. But the music returns, filling the steamy air with Michael Bublé. Must have been a glitch. Alexandra feels romantic again and yearns for Barlow.

As she turns in the water, she sees a figure – clad in black – pick up the radio. The cat stretches and wraps himself around the intruder's legs. Before Alexandra can react, the figure launches the radio at her. Somehow it's still playing when it hits the water. A burning sensation snaps through her limbs, her tissues, her heart. The last thing she sees is poor Barlow shivering before complete paralysis sinks her below the surface.

# CHAPTER THIRTY-SIX

I'm finally in bed, and the tightness across my scalp has loosened. The painkillers must be working, but I can't sleep. My whole body is an angry argument of everything I should have said to Kevin this morning, even though, in his shoes, I might have sent me home too. The more I recall the stuff he said, the more I detect well-meant advice.

My family – me, Jake, Mum and Dad – don't need a Sean Farrell-shaped chasm blasting through our perfect unit. When I think of him, there's a hard taste in my mouth, like biting on a walnut shell. Despite what he did, I haven't thought about him for years. He's been neither alive nor dead. What he did erased the right to have an existence in my life at all. I should have suspected something was off when he wouldn't meet Mum and Dad in the four months we were together, but fun and lust are blind bedfellows. I was the other woman and didn't even bloody know it. Didn't know what kind of man he was until...

My skin freezes. Does Jake have to find out? He's missed out on nothing. My dad saw to that. But if despite Kevin's efforts to protect me, this gets out, my son will hate me.

Throwing the duvet over my head, I banish that nightmare and think of the case.

Have they interviewed Amy? Arrested her? It's bollocks, it must be. She never so much as broke a fingernail in a physical spat at school. Her weapons were of the emotional kind. I turn on the bedside radio and tune to a local channel. If anyone's been taken in for questioning, it will be the top story on the next news segment.

*"You're listening to Nathan J on Mids FM. Hope you enjoyed the Tuesday Smooch. Keep your tweets and calls coming in. There was such a great response to last night's tweet-along that we're keeping it going tonight. Get in touch if you think you're the man, or woman, to walk Meghan Markle down the aisle.*

*"Lauren in Longlevens has nominated her grandad Geoff. No one could do it better, she says. So here's a bit of Carly Simon. Who said this show was thrown together?*

*"And Morag, if you're listening..."* The presenter's voice drops lower and deeper like a priest at confessional. *"Please get back in touch. I know what you told me tonight is true. Our news desk has confirmed it. I'm here to listen."*

I sit up in bed but not sure why. Something in his babble, maybe? But I've lost the thought, if it was ever really there.

The Bond theme kicks in and Carly assures me "Nobody Does It Better". Maybe we'll all be singing it to Kev in the incident room. If he can prove Amy Ashby murdered four people, he'll get a medal. For services to fiction.

The figures on my clock radio roll to the hour and I turn up the volume.

*"It's eleven o'clock and time to link to our newsroom with Dale Green. Dale, what have you got for us?"*

*"Thanks, Nathan. News just in. West Gloucestershire Police have launched a fifth murder enquiry following the*

discovery of a woman's body in a swimming pool in the Wrenswood area of the city. Police were called to the private home within the last hour. They and forensic teams are still attending. Cause of death has not been announced."

I get dressed and grab my car keys.

"Welcome back to the Nathan J Show. As you heard on the news: another day, another murder. But spare a thought for the police. They've got no chance of catching this serial killer if one of their own is in on it. What if a senior officer knows more than she's letting on? That's right: she. I've a feeling in my water about this one. But enough of that doom and gloom, here's some S Club 7."

# CHAPTER THIRTY-SEVEN

Blood pumping – too loud for me to even try listening to the radio – I drive across the south side of the city towards Wrenswood. Parked cars and trade vans clog the main roads and grass verges, but I don't have to dodge and weave; there's no oncoming traffic in the dead of night.

A fifth murder. What the hell? My heart's pounding as if I'm the next victim. It feels like a personal attack. On me, on my job. West Gloucestershire Police are better than this.

I'm driving by houses with wide driveways now; fewer vehicles have to park on the streets. Welcome to Wrenswood.

Is it a middle-class thing? A serial killer with a grudge against the privileged? A woman found in a private pool smacks of money. Christa Talbot was an ex-lawyer. Steven Baker a senior council official. Russell Hill educated and living in a big house. I must suggest it to Kevin.

My heart rate dips. What if he tells me to get lost and go back to bed? But Kev's not like that. He knows when he needs help. He'll be pleased to see me, won't he?

It's been ages since I've been down here. Wrenswood is relatively crime-free, although the tax man might disagree. Under streetlights, one sweeping cul-de-sac of double garages looks like another and I have to stop to put Holly Gardens in the sat nav. The news report didn't give the address, but it's the only road in Gloucester I know with gardens big enough to have private swimming pools.

The voice of the GPS tells me to turn back and take the next left. Easy for her to say. Bet she couldn't manage a one eighty in a lead helmet of headache. I'm tempted to carry on to Waitrose, pick up the outer ring road and beggar off home. But not my style, too nosy. I do as Auntie Satnav says.

Holly Gardens is wide and long, but the moment I turn in I know which house. Lights at every window splay through the trees in the big front garden, like beacons of misfortune. There's a gaggle of coated figures. A bank of civilian cars on the kerb. Various pandas in the road, badly parked – drivers who've come over all TV cop and have bolted into the action.

I switch off and walk the last hundred yards. A couple of cameras flash and a bloke with a microphone asks me something. Journalists are here already. Bystanders murmur. I don't react. Years of experience keep my eyes on the do-not-cross tape across the imposing gateway. I show my warrant card to the constable. He lifts the tape and directs me down the side of the house. The place is modern, nineties vintage I'd say, but they've gone for an ornate double side-gate the likes of which I associate with the National Trust. The gate's open and leads to a courtyard tastefully decorated with flowers in container pots. I head through a stone arch to the back garden, lit stadium-bright with police floodlights. Activity is centred on an odd-shaped brick building in the centre of the lawn. It reminds me of an art gallery and seems incongruous in the suburban garden, even one of this size. As I walk towards it, Tony steps out and removes his mask.

"Steph," he shouts before I reach him. "We've got him this time."

# CHAPTER THIRTY-EIGHT

"Forensics found saliva," Tony says. "He's made his first mistake."

There are so many fundamental flaws in that statement that I don't know where to start. I ask him to explain the scene. "Facts only. No supposition."

"Don't be tetchy," he says. With his protective hood up, he looks like a grubby baby. "Without gut work we might never get near this one. How many more are we going to let him kill before we stop him?"

I nod and shrug. He's got a point. We now have five unsolved murders. Whether they're connected or not, we could do with an inspired guess.

"Siobhan Evans is jogging on in there." Tony unzips his suit. His hair is matted and sweaty. "Not easy conditions. We're boiling on poolside in these things. She couldn't do much to start with. Had to wait for the electricity people to reconnect the power."

"Was the woman swimming in the dark?" Maybe I'm the

one making assumptions. The victim might not be a woman; never believe what you hear on the local radio.

"It looks like she went for a candlelit swim. Place is decked out with tea lights. Most have burnt out now. Neighbours reported a power surge around ten. It knocked out their electrics. They'd had problems with this pool before and reckon the builders crossed the cables. Good to know even mansions get built by cowboys. Both houses trip whenever a light blows in the pool. The homeowner – the victim's father..." He fishes out his notebook. "Denny Simpson – usually flicks a switch in the fuse box and the lights come back on. The neighbours knew the family had gone away – Spain apparently – so thought they'd see if they could get into the pool building themselves and try the fuse box." He gives a hard chuckle. "Got more than they bargained for."

"Where are the neighbours now?" I ask.

He points to the high hedge on the far side of the garden. "Kevin's interviewing them in their place. It's taking a while. They're in shock, if you'll pardon the pun." He gives another chuckle, just as hard.

I cotton on. "So cause of death was..."

"Someone dropped a radio into the water while she was swimming. It was on a ruddy great extension lead to the mains. Before he lost the power of coherent speech, the man from next door said he thought it was the lead the owner's gardener uses to mow the lawn, but apparently the owner keeps the lead in the shed, well away from the pool."

He points down the garden to where a team have spotlights trained on a wooden building. Shed is an understatement. It's bigger than my parents' double garage.

"They're checking for prints," Tony continues. "According to the neighbours, the owners are always throwing pool parties with barbecues on the lawn. But they never have music inside the pool building. Denny Simpson..." He pauses. "I've heard the father's name before."

"What do we know about the girl?" I ask.

Tony narrows his eyes, a look of mirth on his face. "The woman, please. Show some respect for the mature victim."

I bite my tongue. Tony has perfected the habit of saying the right thing and making it sound insulting.

"How old was she?"

"Neighbours say around forty, but she'd had some plastic surgery lately so it's hard to tell. And as a corpse, well, not pretty." He flinches, apparently remembering what he's seen. "My money's on her being forty-one."

"Does she live here?" I move him swiftly on from his serial victim theory. I still think sticking to the facts is key.

"Mrs Neighbour said Alexandra moved out a couple of years ago but seems to have been staying here again recently. A bit of an ageing princess. Parents spoil her."

Jess Bolton, the PCSO, steps round the pool house, carrying a bundle of fur. "He's alive," she says, her voice anxious. "But terrified. I'm meeting my vet at his surgery."

"Is it really worth the bill for a midnight callout?" Tony says. "The cat's not going to give us an ID on the killer."

Jess turns the trembling animal away from him. "Don't be cruel. You said yourself this cat's provided our first clue." She looks at me. "I'll let Tony explain. This little thing needs help." She hurries away.

Tony watches her go, shaking his head. He turns back to me. "Siobhan Evans's lot found spittle on the floor near the socket the radio was plugged into. My theory is the killer fixed up the radio on the extension lead. While he was sorting it, the cat came over to say hello. He hissed it away and left his spit at the scene."

It seems too flimsy a scenario to me and I rein in his enthusiasm. "Let's wait for DNA. The saliva is more likely to be from the victim."

"Posh girls don't spit," he says.

"Posh women, Tony," I quip but my smile dies on my mouth as Kevin joins us. His expression is thunderous.

"A word, Steph."

Tony's eyes shine in the spotlights as I follow Kevin beyond the swimming pool to a darker place. Kevin stops at a wooden arbour encased in clematis and climbing roses. Petals not at their fullest, yet the scent still penetrates. It hasn't rained for days, but the seat is damp in the night air. We both stand.

"You need to go, Steph. You can't be seen here."

Can't blame him for being concerned about my prior relationship with Sean Farrell, but I assure him I don't know this latest victim. "I haven't even driven down here for years."

"Go!"

His tone sends my voice into a croak. "You need me. You're no closer to solving—"

"You still haven't told me where you were between five and eight last night." He looks over my shoulder, can't meet my gaze.

"You're asking me for an alibi for Sean's murder? You think I'm capable of killing someone?"

"Just routine. Where were you?" He's still not looking at me. Do I even know this man?

"I told you I was on enquiries."

But, even in dim light, it's clear Kevin's face says that isn't good enough.

"I was at home. No, out for a drive," I falter. "I found Sean Farrell when I came back." True in its way. I drove back from the doctor's.

"You've been working from home a lot recently."

"I wasn't meeting him, or killing..." I lower my voice. Tony

Smith stands on the lawn. He's got his back to us, but I can feel the draught from his flapping ears. "...or killing people."

Kevin lowers his voice too. "Look, Steph, we'll continue our enquiries, but it's going to be tough if rumours about you muddy the waters."

"What rumours?"

"In the last twenty minutes, a presenter on Mids FM has claimed a female police officer is involved in the serial killer case. Harriet's gone to the station to interview him."

"And you think he means me? Are you serious?" I splutter. "Most local radio DJs burble bullshit. You can't..."

Kevin shakes his head. "It might be trouble. Anyone in the council's planning department could have phoned the radio station and told them about your letter of protest to Steven Baker." He holds out his fingers and counts off a version of the facts. "Less than twenty-four hours later, Baker is found dead a hundred yards from where you live."

"At a disused hospital building that is nothing to do with my Bell Tower apartment. My email was a legitimate complaint about traffic proposals, not a threat."

But Kevin's still counting. "Russell Hill died in a house fire on the same avenue where you are a frequent visitor."

"My parents live there. Of course I visit. But I didn't know Christa Talbot and I don't know this latest woman." I feel myself getting hotter. "If you're questioning all officers with a connection to more than one victim, why don't you start with Jess Bolton?"

"Who's that?"

I lower my head, feeling guilty for landing the young PCSO in it. "Doesn't matter." Jess was the first on the Christa Talbot murder scene at the Georgian Gardens after the dog walker's emergency call and she discovered Steven Baker in a routine patrol, but it doesn't make her a suspect. She's a cat lover and here tonight, but I don't bother mentioning it as Kevin continues to count.

"And you found the body of your ex at your apartment block."

"Keep your voice down." I glance around. Two officers are by the shed. "Don't call him that."

"I'm sorry, Steph. I know you didn't do any of this, but things are... awkward." He rubs his neck. "It would help if you'd tell me where you were."

"I was out. Nowhere near my apartment when he was killed."

"But that's not much of an alibi. If the radio people dig into this..."

Fury surges through me. How dare he? "I'll give you an alibi," I scream. Tony has turned towards us but I'm past caring. "Check with the receptionists, the doctor, the pharmacist, the NHS Access Centre CCTV. That's my alibi and my reason for everything. Taking an extra day's leave at bank holiday. Going home early. Working from home. Mind not on the job. Call yourself a detective, Kevin. Call yourself a caring boss. I need a fucking brain scan."

I try to leave the garden gracefully with my head high, but my headache sends me staggering through the courtyard.

# CHAPTER THIRTY-NINE

Nathan's heart's in his bowels the second he sees the visitor through the glass. No one ever comes to the studio during his show, but right now Lulu is standing up and facing a tall figure. He could be in danger; the visitor only has to get past Lulu. But when he looks closer, he relaxes and spikes up his hair in the mirror on his desk. It's a woman – young, blonde, *fit*. Morag? He dismisses the flutter of unease the name conjures. If all stalkers are built like this one, he'll take a busload.

But the grin on his face freezes when Lulu and the visitor turn towards him. *Oh crap.* He knows that expression on a woman: he's in trouble.

Lulu speaks into her mic. "This is Detective Constable Harris. I'm letting her in." The studio door buzzes as she releases it.

"Not while I'm on air," Nathan calls, but Harris has already entered his space, filling it with a fragrance that speaks of morning runs and soapy cold showers rather than seductive perfume.

"Cue another record, Mr Jackson, then we can talk," she says.

It crosses his mind it's a practical joke. Lulu's roped in one of her drama mates to put on the frighteners. But when the woman waves her West Gloucestershire Police ID, he loads KC and the Sunshine Band.

"What seems to be the trouble, officer?" he says, and cringes at his own crassness.

"At just after eleven tonight you broadcast an allegation against a police officer."

Nathan lifts his palms towards her. "It was hardly that. Come on."

"Let me quote you..." She retrieves a notebook from her pocket. "'They've got no chance of catching this serial killer if one of their own is in on it.'"

He winces at every word she recites. *Bloody Morag. He shouldn't have listened to a crazed fan.* "It was meant to be a joke. I'm an entertainer, that's what I do. You know?"

"I'd have to take your word on programme content as I've never listened to your show."

Nathan rolls his eyes. Wound a man, why don't you?

"However, your producer has just told me you've never commented on a serious news item before."

"Look, Lulu's as much to blame as I am. She puts the calls through. It's her job to filter." He leans forward in his chair. "I'd never have said what I said if she'd done her job."

Through the glass, Lulu kills him with her eyes. He's left the speakers on.

"I've heard your producer's version of events," the police officer says. "Perhaps I could hear yours?"

When he sits back in his chair, there's a cracking sound as something inside breaks. Even the furniture's against him. He interlocks his fingers behind his head and recounts the conversations he's had with Morag. As he speaks, he realises how dumb he was to be taken in. "She phoned soon after I went on air at ten. Said there had been another murder and claimed again that a female police officer was involved. She'd said that before but I didn't believe her. Then tonight the newsroom confirmed a woman had been killed in a swimming pool so I thought I'd say it for a laugh. I never really believed the police were involved." He looks her in the eye. "You all do a fine job. Get Lulu to give you some signed photos on the way out. Put them into a Police Benevolent Fund raffle or something."

"Did you recognise the caller's voice?" she says.

He shakes his head. She's ignored his charm. That's happening more and more these days. God, he feels old.

"Do you think you've met her before?" she asks.

The thought sends a shiver down his spine. "I hope not."

"Can you describe the voice? An accent? Old? Young?"

"Bland, muffled," he shrugs. "I wasn't even sure it was a woman until she said her name was Morag. Maybe Lulu has a better idea; she talked to her for longer." He glances through the glass as Lulu looks away.

The police officer fixes him with her blue eyes. He squirms under her gaze, feeling guilty even though he's not sure for what.

"One more question," she says. "What did you do during the..." She reads from her notebook. "Tuesday Smooch?"

"Do? I didn't do anything. Well, I mean, I prepped the rest of the show. Technical stuff."

"So you didn't leave your turntables for any length of time during the first hour of your show?"

"Of course not. I never do. Lulu will tell you."

# CHAPTER FORTY

I chuck down more painkillers and throw myself into bed. The shock of my landing judders my skull. Is this my new permanent state? Before the brain scan shows... A physical wreck, with my reputation shredded, too. Why would some third-rate radio presenter have it in for me? Of course I'm connected to all the murders; I'm the lucky sod assigned to investigate. We all are – Kevin, Tony, Harriet and the rest of the team. Kevin said himself he doesn't know for sure which officer had been targeted. He must think it's me because of my history with Sean. But no one knows that except Kevin and he's only just found out.

What if Sean tipped off the radio presenter before his death? He broke into my flat, so what's to say he didn't make other trouble too? But why now? What he did was eighteen years ago. He'd have no reason to mess me up now. *Unless he found out.* I start to sweat, cold and shivery. How? No one even knows about Jake except Terri.

*Could Amy know? If I saw her that day in the florist's, she could have seen me elsewhere. With Sean.*

———

I go to a flower shop in my lunch break. A posy would be nice for Mum. My mood plummets. The customer ahead of me is that annoying girl from school. Amy Ashby, flicking through a wedding flowers catalogue with an attentive assistant. This is going to take ages.

It's been seven years since I've heard that grating show-off voice.

"Usually I do my own arrangements," Amy is saying to the assistant, "but I won't have time on my big day. I'll be in your hands."

I duck behind a display of roses, hoping she won't see me. I don't want the awkward exchange. We never had anything to say to each other at school. Even less now.

After enduring several minutes of her stupid plans for silver service, lace trains and string quartets, I'm about to forget Mum's flowers and sneak out when someone knocks on the window. I can't see but the shop assistant has a clear view.

"Is that your fiancé?" she asks. "Would you like him to look through the floral choices too? What's the date, by the way?"

"We haven't actually gone firm on a... I'd better go," Amy says hurriedly. "Thank you for your time."

I hear her tottering, silly steps and then the shop door open and close. Curiosity kills me. I look through the window and see Amy plant a kiss on his cheek. Her man. Her fiancé.

Sean.

———

What if Amy has seen me with Jake and done the maths? She must have told Sean. That would explain why the vindictive bitch's number is on his phone. My nails scrape the mattress.

She must be the one who called the radio station. But would she really do that after all these years?

I think of the viola, no doubt decomposing on a rubbish tip somewhere. Of course she bloody would. I kick off my covers. She's not getting away with it. No one messes with my family.

The phone goes. Although I'm wired with anger, it still makes me jump. Kevin.

"Now what?" I snap. He's already grounded me; not much more he can do if I give him lip.

"I want to apologise." He's got his kind voice on. "I should have known you'd have a good reason for your whereabouts."

"Well, yes. There you are." I'm going for affronted but my tone softens.

"The Access Centre doctor has confirmed you were there."

"You still checked. My word not good enough? Thanks a lot, Kev." What a nerve. I get out of bed. I'm not getting to sleep after this. Then I think of something. "Hang on, it's one o'clock in the morning. The Access Centre closes at ten."

Hesitation. "Well, when I ask the doctor in the morning, I've no doubt that's what he'll say. You're sound, Steph. I never doubted you but I know how these things can go. I have to get proof of your whereabouts in case the media get hold of your connection to Farrell, or worse, the chief super gets wind of it. I hope you can see that."

"Fair enough," I mutter. I get his point but I'm still pissed off. What about my previous ten years of impeccable service? Don't they count? I've never gone rogue. Hardly ever.

The silence on the line lengthens until I hear him clear his throat. "About the brain scan, is everything...?"

"Fine," I say quickly. "Just routine. Not even needed now I'm on new painkillers."

"What do they think it is?"

192

"Migraine," I snap. "Just a migraine."

"So not a t—"

"Of course not!"

He takes a breath. "Sorry, I shouldn't have..." He takes another breath. "I'll let you get some sleep. If you're well enough, you're back on duty."

"Fit as a fiddle."

"But steer clear of Amy Ashby. She's a person of interest, and we don't want a link to you compromising enquiries."

"Yes, boss."

My fingers are still crossed as I put my phone on the bedside. Like I said; hardly ever rogue. Hardly ever lie. Except when I have to.

———

My car windows mist with fury as I shriek every insult in the book when we meet that evening.

"What's it to you?" Sean says, running his hand through his hair. "We never said exclusive."

"But you're engaged to *her*. Get out. Out!" I scream so hard it hurts my throat.

He grips the back of my head, laces his fingers through my hair. "You're such a turn on, you know."

Using all of his bulk, he manoeuvres me as easily as he's done many times before. I try to form my hands into fists – try so hard – but I've no hope of landing a punch. To him, this time is no different. To me, it changes everything.

Afterwards he shrugs, he actually bloody shrugs. He lifts his shoulders, climbs out of my car and strolls away.

Shaking with fear and shame and rage, I go home and tell no one. I shower for hours. The water stream is so hot it hurts, then freezing cold until it burns some more. I never see him again, but the sickness of what happened soon becomes a daily nausea.

# CHAPTER FORTY-ONE

The Romanians wave their wet sponges as Amy pulls off the garage forecourt. She should come more often; it's as good a tonic as going to the hairdresser's. Her car is not the only thing they made gleam. She heads through the city towards her mother's bungalow, refusing to allow her good humour to dip. Sean. Matt. Neither were right for her. They brought her nothing but misery. That's not what a boyfriend should do. Cliff Richard is on the car radio and she hums along.

When she turns into her mother's close, her mood plummets to her feet and makes her slam on the brake. Steph's purple Golf is parked outside the bungalow so close to the driveway it's going to be a squeeze for Amy to park. Amy's torn between fleeing the scene and turning so sharply that she clips the Golf's headlight. But she gets to do neither. Steph climbs out, leans against her car roof and watches Amy manoeuvre onto the drive. Amy grows warm under her scrutiny and has to jiggle the car several times to line it up.

After she's turned off the engine, she sits gathering her nerve. Is she ready to hold her own against Steph Lewis when she can no longer run to her mother or report her behaviour to Mrs Hardcastle? Looking at her reflection in the rear-view mirror, she sees a coldness in her blue eyes that she rather likes. She's ready.

Still taking her time even though Steph has moved to wait at the back of the car, she collects her bag and jacket and heads for the boot without acknowledging her.

"Sorry, didn't I leave you enough room?" Steph says, pointing at Amy's driver-side back wheel.

Damn, she's driven over the lawn. She ignores the comment and retrieves her flowers from the boot.

"Can I help with those?" Steph asks.

Amy shakes her head. She shifts the cellophane-wrapped bunches higher up her arm so that she can lock the car with her other hand.

"I phoned your school. They said you finished at eight thirty this morning."

Amy tilts her wrist, taking care not to crush the flowers. Her watch says nine forty a.m. Anger grinds in her belly. Does she have to account for every second now? Without replying, she heads towards the house.

Steph moves round Amy's car and squats by the front wheels. "Have you washed your car?"

Amy feels herself reddening, insulted at the suggestion she would engage in manual labour.

Steph is staring, waiting for an answer.

"That's where I was this morning if you must know, getting the car washed."

"And buying those." Steph looks at the flowers.

Amy's blush lingers. She stopped in the Golden Valley layby on the A40. They always have a good stock on a Wednesday morning. She pays her money and doesn't ask for provenance.

"You must be gasping after your shift," Steph says as Amy unlocks the front door. "Are you making a brew?"

*Of all the nerve.* "I have to see to my mother." She watches Steph lower her eyes and savours her embarrassment. Sometimes an invalid parent is a trump card. She tells Steph to wait in the lounge and goes to the kitchen to fill the sink with water and stand the flowers in it. Her mother's bedroom is empty when she checks and the bathroom door is locked. For once irritated that her mother doesn't need her help, she returns to the lounge to face Steph, but her visitor has gone into the kitchen.

"I'd rather you didn't touch those," she snaps, and is pleased when a startled Steph drops a carnation into the sink.

"I was admiring the colours. You've always had a good eye. Orange and blue were your favourites at school too, weren't they?"

Amy's skin freezes.

———

Art class, Year 8, her alien landscape with watercolours, one of her best. Steph, working in black and white beside her, tips over her ink pot. Not onto Amy's work – Steph's too clever for that. The blue-black liquid trickles off the desk onto Amy's skirt, leg and white sock.

By the time she's cleaned herself up in the girls' loo and changed into her P.E. skirt, the art lesson is over. The next week they move onto still life and Amy never gets to finish her landscape.

———

Amy makes a point of rearranging the flowers in the sink, marking her territory.

Steph stands aside. "You put a lot into your arrangements, don't you? I've seen the photos. The one with the dark red roses and lemon chrysanthemums had a clinical chill. Inventive, striking."

A carnation stem snaps in Amy's hand. Steph must have looked at her Facebook page. Clinical chill, how dare she? While she thinks of a suitable admonishment for the barefaced intrusion into her private life, Steph digs deeper.

"How's the genealogy going?"

Amy's face must betray the venom she's feeling, because Steph raises her hands and takes a step backwards. "I always fancied tracking down my grandad's war record. You'll have to give me some tips on where to start."

"No can do," Amy tells the liar. There will be no war record. She knows Steph's grandfather was a Forest of Dean free miner. Reserved occupation in World War Two. "I don't work on my family tree these days. My files were lost months ago."

"Lost? How?"

Amy sighs. This woman has become a PC Plod. "These things happen." Not a police matter. "One day they were on my laptop, the next day they were gone. I had made printouts of the important stuff but I kind of lost interest." Behind her the kettle clicks. Amy looks round to see it steaming. "Did *you* switch it on?"

"While you were checking on your mum. I hope you don't mind. I thought you – we – could do with a drink." Her voice peters out and she has the grace to look embarrassed.

The last thing Amy wants is to drink tea with this woman, but she doesn't see how she can refuse.

They hear the toilet flush and the bathroom door unlocks.

The slow, squeaky turn of wheels follows. When her mother rolls into the kitchen, something in Amy dies. The old woman looks worse than ever. Her hair is unkempt. Only two blouse buttons are fastened, a yellowing vest showing below. Toothpaste is stuck to her chin and there are dribbled stains on her brown trousers. Amy can barely look Steph in the eye until she realises Steph has grown flushed and dropped her gaze to the floor. Immediately Amy feels she has the upper hand.

"As you can see, I've no time to stop for tea."

Looking at Steph with vacant eyes, Amy's mother wheels further into the kitchen.

Steph brings her gaze up to Amy's. "I have to ask you more questions."

"About flower arranging?" Amy adds a neat smile now that Steph is on the back foot.

"It's a delicate matter." Steph glances at the wheelchair. "Perhaps we could talk outside?"

"Anything you want to say you can say in front of my mother."

"But..."

"Say it."

Amy's mother closes her eyes and her neck slumps to the side. The effort of reaching the kitchen must have made her doze off.

"Okay." Steph lowers her voice. "When was the last time you saw Sean Farrell?"

Amy's eyes shoot to her mother but she's still sleeping. She pushes past Steph into the lounge. Steph follows. Amy closes the door and admires the patch of carpet where her mother dropped her hot chocolate months ago. One of the early signs that something was wrong. That and the first time she knocked over her eye drops. Amy scrubbed and scrubbed but can't quite get it clean.

"About the same time you saw him, I should think," she says eventually, pleased with her evasion.

"That's not what I asked."

Amy fights back. "Your police status doesn't give you the right to disconnect our joint history. If you want to talk about me and Sean, it has to be you and Sean as well."

Steph studies her for a moment, then sighs. "There's something you need to know. The body at the Bell Tower. You must have heard about it on the news."

Amy's heartbeat clangs in her ears. She senses what's coming and wants to sit down, but more than that she wants this vile woman to go. This is one half of the duo who terrorised her with their bullying. Not again, not again.

"We'll be announcing the name today. I'm afraid it's Sean."

Amy collapses on the sofa. What else can she do?

"My colleagues will be along later today to check your whereabouts on Monday night. I thought it best to warn you."

"Thank you." She keeps her voice formal, hiding the hate.

"One more question."

Amy puts her head in her hands. Get on with it and go.

"Did you tell him about Jake?"

The door opens and the wheelchair squeaks into the room. Her mother has managed to fasten her buttons and wipe her mouth.

Amy frowns. Who is Jake? The question must be a trap. "How could I tell him anything if I haven't seen him for years?" She sticks to the lie; no choice now her mother is listening.

Steph stands between Amy and her mother, her back to the wheelchair. "Tests have confirmed that Sean Farrell broke into my flat shortly before his death." Her voice is low, but Amy doesn't know why she's bothering; her mother isn't deaf. "And I can't help wondering why he would do that?"

"Search me." The petulance rises in Amy's throat. Still a

two-timer then; Sean came back and was after seeing Steph too. She's glad she's rid of him. "You knew him better than I did. Why don't you ask yourself that question?"

"Don't play dumb," Steph says, her skin darkening. "Did you tell him about my son?"

Amy takes a moment to digest the question, then a vacuum sucks the life from every part of her. Her mouth opens but nothing comes out. No sound, no air. The wheelchair creeps towards her, and a million miles away she senses her mother's icy hand on her arm.

Steph's florid face switches her glance between Amy and her mother. She blinks away a tear. "I'm sorry, I shouldn't have asked that. I'll see myself out."

Some of the feeling comes back into Amy's limbs but she's sure she's marble white. Even after the front door has opened and then closed, even after a car starts and drives away, even after her mother rubs her arm again, Amy doesn't move. The world has shifted on its axis and there's no place for her to go. Steph Lewis and Sean Farrell had a son.

Her mother raises both arms towards her. Amy crumples by the chair. Her mother strokes her hair as she sobs.

# CHAPTER FORTY-TWO

INCIDENT ROOM | WEDNESDAY 16TH MAY,
10.30 A.M.

The general discussion, in full swing, cuts to silence when I walk in. Harriet examines her notebook. Tony and most of the others stare at me.

I stare back, daring any one of them to mention the scan word. "I'm better now, thanks for asking," I say defiantly.

Tony stands up and offers me his chair. "Course you are." He pats my shoulder, his expression sympathetic.

I mouth *thanks* and we hold each other's gaze for a moment. Then his face changes and he grins. "Bloke on the radio said you'd been suspended."

For a second he's got me, and my first, panicked thought is that I need to warn Jake and my parents. Tell them it isn't true. Then I see Tony's grin.

"Harriet's set him right," he says. "He won't be spouting more of his bullshit on his so-called radio show unless he wants to broadcast from Leyhill. But, seriously, where have you been this morning?"

"I was asked to rest." Warmth of the evasion spreads up my neck. "Now I'm back."

The door bangs open and Kevin appears with a tray of coffees. "Caffeine for the mind." He puts the drinks on the front desk. "Help yourselves. Sugar sachets on the side." He spots me. "Good to see you, Steph. What would you like?" he asks, his face not betraying any of our recent history. He's a good boss, discreet. Cappuccinos in the open office and bollocking behind closed doors.

"Just had one thanks," I lie. I couldn't swallow a thing after I left Amy's. Judging by the way colour leeched from her face, she had no idea Jake existed. What the hell have I done?

Kevin looks at Harriet. "For Steph's benefit, can you repeat what you told us about the radio station?"

Harriet turns round in her seat. "A presenter on Mids FM announced on air last night that a senior detective was implicated in serial killings. I got round to the radio station while he was still on air. Once I'd negotiated my way past the zealous security guard and the producer, Nathan Jackson – the presenter – deigned to speak to me between soundbites. He said a caller phoned in after ten saying a police officer was involved. Second night in a row – same caller, same claim. Jackson said airing it was meant to be 'a joke'." Harriet makes inverted commas in the air. "He didn't believe the story and wasn't given a police officer's name but he decided to repeat live on air what the caller said. For the 'craic'." More inverted commas. "I spoke to the producer, Louisa Brady. No love lost between the two. She said there's been an increase in crank calls recently and Nathan has played along with them, probably to wind her up. Pushing it further on air is just the kind of idiotic thing he does."

"But you educated him?" I ask.

"He acted the big I am – offered me his autograph – but I made him see the error of his ways."

I bet she did. I feel almost sorry for him. "How do you mean there's no love lost with his producer?" I ask.

"Although Louisa Brady more or less confirmed what he said about the caller, she told me something else. She said Nathan had launched a new feature – all his idea, not much consultation with her. For most of the first hour of his show he played back-to-back love songs. He says he stayed in the studio while the music played, but she had an extended call of nature and can't confirm it."

"What's your point, Harriet?" Tony asks.

"Oldest alibi in the book: commit a crime while you're live on air. Alexandra Simpson probably died during his show."

"He'd have had to fly like Superman to get to Wrenswood in time. And why would a radio presenter do that?"

Harriet shrugs. "I just thought I'd mention it. Something and nothing, probably."

"Okay, if there's nothing else to report from your brief delve into show business, let's park the sideshow," Kevin says. "Thanks, Harriet." He draws our attention to the picture board. Not a pretty sight, and I have to swallow. "Our victim, Alexandra Simpson, was indeed forty-one years old."

"Knew it." All eyes are on Tony as he punches the air. Another notch on his serial killer theory belt.

"However..." Kev waits for everyone to simmer down. "We have a motive for this one and a likely suspect who I'll come back to in a minute. Siobhan Evans says death was between nine and ten thirty. The live electricity in the water from the radio caused fibrillation leading to cardiac arrest. Alexandra also suffered extensive tissue damage." Kevin pauses and we bow our heads. It's the nano-second of respect we can devote to our victim before we plough on with finding her killer.

"The neighbours' electricity was knocked out at just after ten, so that's the likely time of death," Kevin continues. "Killer left no fingerprints either in the pool building or the shed where we believe the extension lead came from. Nor are there footprints. Clever sod kept to a dry bit of floor."

"Must have watched *CSI*," Harriet mutters.

"In other news, Alexandra's parents caught the first flight from Alicante." Kevin's eyes drop, as they do whenever he mentions grieving relatives. It's the tell behind the world-weary facade. "Her stepfather is Denny Simpson."

"I've remembered why the name rings a bell. He's Mr Moneybags the Mobile Phone Magnate," Tony says.

"Retired. Sold the business three years ago. So these days he's Mr Moneybags With Time On His Hands. They were in Spain to track down John Barlow, fraudster of this parish."

"The Stroud Meadows con man? I know that name, too." Tony rubs his chin. "Surely a shrewd cookie like Denny Simpson didn't invest?"

"Stepdaughter, Alexandra, did. She lived with Barlow for a while. He wined her, wooed her and parted her from several hundred thousand. After he sold the last of the non-existent flats, he did a runner. Bank foreclosed on his Cotswold mansion and Alexandra had to move back in with Mummy and Stepdaddy."

"I reckon I interviewed Barlow before he legged it," Tony says. "Slippery beggar. Could charm the birds out of the night-clubs and into his bed. But why kill her when he's already spending her money on the Costa Plonka? And doesn't being out of the country rule him out?"

"I'm waiting for a call back from the Spanish police. UK Immigration has no record of him returning." Kevin looks at Tony. "But the reason he's a suspect is that Denny Simpson believes Alexandra took out a life insurance policy with Barlow named as the beneficiary. We're waiting for confirmation."

Tony puts his head in his hands. "So Barlow's DNA will match the saliva at the crime scene."

"Cheer up, Tony," I say. "We've still got four other unsolved cases to be getting on with. Besides, as a female, Alexandra doesn't fit your serial killer pattern."

"Christa Talbot identified as a woman," Harriet pipes up.

Kevin points out that the killer might not be as enlightened as her with regard to gender and adds, "At this stage John Barlow is as elusive and unproven as any other suspect. We still have five victims."

"Maybe six," Harriet says sadly. "Jess Bolton says the cat's not eating."

An idea occurs to me. "Where is the cat?"

"Jess has taken him home."

"I wonder how close the cat got to the killer. If we collar a suspect, could we get a forensic match for cat hair on clothes or shoes?"

"I'll ask Jess to bring the cat in for testing." Harriet sighs. "If the poor thing lives."

"Right, people." Kevin claps his hands. "Let's talk timelines for these cases that may or may not be linked." He puts up a PowerPoint slide and talks us through each line.

*Christa Talbot – Wednesday 6–8 a.m. – Georgian Gardens – stabbed*

*Steven Baker – Thursday 4.30–6.15 p.m. – Old Hospital – bludgeoned*

*Russell Hill – Sunday 1–3 a.m. – own home, The Avenue – arson*

*Sean Farrell – Monday 5–7 p.m. – Bell Tower – run over*

*Alexandra Simpson – Tuesday 10 p.m. – own home, Holly Gardens – electrocuted*

"As I said, although we have a suspect in mind for the last one, I've put her on the list for completion."

I wince. Completion seems an unfortunate word. If all of this is down to one killer, I doubt he's finished. Or she.

Harriet peers at the list. "When you see it like this, the last killing seems to fit. Another murder in quick succession, a different method again."

"Unless John Barlow has read his Agatha Christie and knows that the best place to hide a murder is among a bunch of others."

"You might be right, Tony, but setting Barlow aside, what other suspects do we have?" Abandoning the PowerPoint, Kevin takes a marker pen to the white board. He scribbles the first name and underlines it: *Christa Talbot*. "Who have we looked at for this?"

Harriet flicks through her notes. "The mystery name in her pay-as-you-go phone."

Kevin writes *Morag* under Christa's name. Something nags at the back of my mind.

"We ruled out his mother, the ex-wife, former law firm colleagues and current language pupils," Harriet continues. "All we've got are random car registrations from the traffic lights in Painswick that morning that also turned up at the Shire Hall car park where Steven Baker spoke the next evening."

Kevin writes *Car Regs (incl. Amy Ashby)* and puts *Steven Baker* on the next line and underlines the name.

"There's the untraced rep from the bogus company – Radley Development – who had arranged to meet him at the old hospital site," Tony says.

Kevin writes *Bogus Rep.*

Harriet offers her suggestion. "Disgruntled residents angry about the roundabout development, Amy Ashby among them."

*Roundabout Protestors* and *Amy Ashby* go on Kevin's list. When he writes and underlines *Russell Hill*, he adds *Angry Neighbour* as Harriet calls it out.

My throat goes dry as he writes the next name: *Sean Farrell*. Although he was years out of my world, it's the first time my personal life has crossed with work. And I've made that entanglement worse by seeing Amy today.

Kevin looks straight at me. "Any ideas?"

Bastard. I shrug. Not that many hours ago he would have put my name on the list. No one offers anything, so he writes *Amy Ashby*, reminding us she was the last person to call Sean's phone.

He clears his throat. "We've released his name. Next of kin have been informed." Who does he mean? I don't even know if Sean had parents. We never discussed family things. We weren't that sort of couple. Not a couple at all, except in snatched moments.

Kevin moves onto *Alexandra Simpson* and adds *John Barlow* below. "Have I missed anyone?"

Colleagues look to each other but everyone shakes their heads. I see Amy's name against three of the victims and know, but don't say, that she was also aware of Russell Hill because of her conversation on a date with fireman Matt Ward. But she can't be involved, can she? Could someone I knew well from the age of five to eighteen change that much? I think of Sean. I got him wrong, allowed myself to be taken in. Maybe I'm a poor judge. But Amy? All I know for sure is that until I blundered in this morning, Amy Ashby was unaware that her fiancé left me pregnant.

# CHAPTER FORTY-THREE

You can tell from their first touch when a hairdressing apprentice is going to make the grade. Firm but gentle when they're shampooing, they'll progress to nifty scissor work when their time comes. Plenty of kids have come and gone in Mum's salon over the years and I'm nearly as good at picking winners as she is.

Kelly has a future. As she massages my scalp, the knots of worry about work and Amy untangle. The new painkillers are working a treat and my headache has gone completely. I relax as she lets lukewarm water trickle past my ears. Finally she sits me up with a towel turbaned on my head and hands me a coffee. Pretty girl – she's resisted the temptation to experiment on her own hair, and I can see why Jake has taken to calling on his nan at work more often.

Mum appears and leads me to a styling chair. A feeling of pure contentment comes over me as she combs my wet hair from root to tip in a slow, confident rhythm. I close my eyes and take in the scents of hair product and the buzz of chatter and hairdryers.

"Are you sure I can't put in some more layers?"

At the sound of her voice, I return to planet caseload. "I've got to get back to work."

She scoops the damp length into loose bunches at the side of my face. "Choppy would suit you."

I look like a hamster. "Just a trim if you have time," I say. I've booked for a colour next week – time to fight off the grey again. I'm only here now so that I can talk to someone outside work. My colleagues seem convinced Amy Ashby is West Gloucestershire's answer to Aileen Wuornos.

Mum clips the top layer of hair over my crown and cuts the ends of the layer below. It's bliss, the pleasant tug at the roots and the sound of snipping. I feel guilty, though. With five unsolved murders even Tony won't see the inside of the police canteen, and I'm here skiving and being pampered. I tell Mum there's no need to blow dry afterwards.

"No client leaves here with wet hair, especially not one prone to migraines. If I had my way, you'd be signed off sick for seven days."

"I'm recovered, Mum." The pain's gone, but I'm bloody knackered. "I don't think the good people of Gloucestershire would appreciate me taking a week's leave right now."

Mum lowers the scissors. "Did you hear what they were saying on the radio?"

"A crank call," I say quickly. "The radio station fell for it. No truth in any rumours."

"Good. I thought for a minute... Nah, I figured it was media lies to up the ratings." She squats level with the bottom of my hair so I can't see her face.

Did she actually contemplate that the radio was talking about me? Was there a chime of recognition when the Bell Tower victim was named? My parents never met Sean, but I must have mentioned his first name. Hopefully that's all. My handbag's on my knee. Reaching under my salon robe, I feel for my mobile and pull it out to check the time.

"I should be going soon."

"Nearly finished. Have you seen any more of your school pal?" She continues cutting but glances at me in the mirror.

It's a question asked without naming names. We both know salons have elephant ears. How often have I heard clients divulge intimate details to their hairdresser, oblivious to the rest of the salon listening in?

"I'm giving her a wide berth." The woman next to me is under a drying hood, an old *OK!* magazine open on her lap. Katie Price is getting married. I hate lying to my mother but hope I've shut the conversation down.

I haven't. "I'm sorry her mum's ill," she says, tugging harder as she cuts. I'd tell her to stop, but she's speeded up and I'll be able to leave sooner. "But I always resented the way that woman complained to Mrs Hardcastle about you and Terri bullying her precious daughter. I suspect the girl gave as good as she got but still managed to get the pair of you marked as troublemakers."

My hands retreat inside the robe's voluminous sleeves and I cross my fingers.

Brandishing the scissors, Mum looks at my reflection. "I was never a fan of that girl. That business with the viola..."

"Amy's dad died," I say quickly before she delves into the incident I've tried to forget.

She drops the curl of hair she's holding and lowers her voice. "Sorry to hear that. I didn't like him either, but I shouldn't speak ill of the dead, even if he was a sleaze."

I twist round. "I didn't think you even knew him."

Holding my chin, she turns me back to the mirror. "I didn't, not really, thank God. Your dad said he caught him ogling my boobs at a carol concert once."

"Gross," I say and can't help wishing I'd known that at the time. More ammo against Amy.

She rests the handle of the scissors against her chin as she changes tack. "That's something I noticed about all these murder victims: no dads on the scene."

"How on earth do you know that?"

"I read the newspaper online." She removes the clips and my damp hair cascades over my shoulders. She picks up a hairdryer. "They've not said anything about the one from Liverpool, so I don't know about his family."

My fingers are so crossed my knuckles hurt.

"But not one of the other grieving relatives interviewed is a dad. No one's spoken up for poor Russell Hill, but Mrs Dougal up the road said something nice about his grandmother. Quotes about the other three are from mothers, wives, ex-wives and one stepdad, but no fathers."

My phone's still in my hand when it rings.

"Steph, there's been a development." Kevin's voice sounds urgent. "Siobhan Evans is briefing us in twenty minutes. Drop whatever enquiries you're on and get back here." He rings off.

# CHAPTER FORTY-FOUR

We chat, shrug and give the odd laugh. Waiting for Kevin to start the briefing is like waiting to go into an A level exam. Another unwelcome link to Amy Ashby; we sat English and History together.

Harriet talks quietly to Tony about the last few revisits she's done to people who attended the roundabout planning meeting. "No leads that I could see, I'm afraid."

She turns round and tells me that the Head of Boarding at Orchard Prep gave her Amy's matron shifts for the last two weeks. They're partial alibis only. Harriet is still waiting for a call back from the school secretary about the night Amy did the flower displays in the school's foyer.

Tony sits forward in his seat, elbows digging into his bulky knees. His face says he's spoiling for a fight, but we know it's the look he gets when we're on the verge of a breakthrough.

Kevin comes in and we sit up a notch straighter. "Siobhan's on her way, but first the bad news. The saliva found at the Alexandra Simpson murder scene is not John Barlow's."

"Get in," Tony mouths and clenches his fist. "Told you. It's a serial killer."

Kevin gives him a withering look. "Spanish Police have confirmed they picked up Barlow trying to use a stolen credit card in a bar in Torremolinos at eighteen hundred hours local time on Tuesday. Their enquiries linked him to frauds here and in London. He was held in custody overnight. In other words, a cast-iron alibi for Alexandra's murder."

"Where is he now?" Tony asks. "I'm happy to go out there and interview him about Stroud Meadows."

Despite the tense atmosphere, Tony's selfless devotion to Spanish sunshine raises a titter from most of us.

"He's already back," Kevin explains. "More bad news. The London fraud totalled three million, the one here just under two. London get first dibs. He's at Paddington Green as we speak."

"Bugger!" Tony says.

"Hold your expletives for the worst news," Kevin says. "Denny Simpson called in a favour with Alexandra's insurance company and found out John Barlow is the sole beneficiary of her life insurance policy to the tune of seven million. Even if he has to compensate everyone he defrauded, pay costs and serve a custodial sentence, Mr John Barlow is about to become a rich man."

Harriet tosses her notebook on the empty chair in front. "Double bugger!"

The despondent silence that follows is filled by the clack of Dr Siobhan Evans's kitten heels entering the room. Kevin, looking heartily relieved to see her, shakes her hand and pulls out a chair for her to sit by the computer at the front. She thanks him and logs in. A moment later, her dashboard appears on the big screen on the wall. Although she clicks swiftly through several files, the wait knots my belly. Like

Tony, I feel a breakthrough coming, and the sooner it gets here the better.

When she reaches a slide of what look like blobby barcodes, she stands up. Profiles of DNA. Six of them. After opening her briefcase, she pulls out a telescopic pointer, reminiscent of the probe she uses on cadavers. I swallow hard.

She taps the first profile. "This is from Sean Farrell's DNA. He isn't on the National DNA database. No previous interaction with the police."

My blood turns to ice. By becoming a murder victim, Sean will be added to the database. Jake's DNA must never ever be taken, otherwise a geek in a path lab could make a match that will rip our family apart. I give silent thanks that Jake is past the tearaway stage and pray to all the gods out there that his future is equally law-abiding.

Siobhan moves her pointer to the next profile. "This is the DNA from the saliva on the swimming pool floor. Not on the national database either. We've taken swabs from Mr and Mrs Simpson as well as from Alexandra, but no match."

"It's our killer," Tony says, and sets off a flurry of chatter.

Kevin brings us down to earth. "The family threw a pool party the weekend before they left for Spain. A pool maintenance company came in on Monday, scrubbed the poolside with cleaning agent and hosed it down. It depends how thorough they were. This spittle could be from one of the weekend guests."

Siobhan draws her pointer over four remaining images. "Christopher Talbot, Steven Baker, Russell Hill, Alexandra Simpson. None of them are on the national database, but what do you notice about their DNA profiles?" Her eyes scan the room expectantly.

Crap, it *is* an A level exam. "Just tell us," I blurt out. "Please."

"Yes, please," Harriet echoes.

"Can you." Kevin says. It's not a request, and Siobhan's role as quiz master is cut short.

The pointer goes to some of the markers in the profiles. It dawns on me what she's getting at.

Harriet gets it too. "They're related."

"That's right. This is familial DNA," Siobhan explains. "Not parent/child – hardly a surprise given they were the same age – but the percentage of shared DNA doesn't indicate full siblings either."

We all talk at once, expressing disbelief and excitement in equal measure, and hurl questions that Siobhan has no chance of hearing. Kevin gives us a minute in our pointless speculations, then raises his hand for silence.

"What's the next stage for forensics, Siobhan?" he asks.

"We've applied for approval to carry out a familial search on the National DNA Database. If we find a common relative with a criminal record it might help to explain the family tree."

Kevin's face gives nothing away, but he must be wondering what the chances are of getting permission. Normally it's only granted in cases where we have the DNA of a violent killer who's not on the database, and we hope to get them through a relative who is. The UK's had some high profile successes, like when a woman, brought in for a domestic, had her DNA swabbed. It led to the conviction of her father for a twenty-year-old murder. But a familial search based on victim DNA is rare.

After Siobhan logs off and puts the retracted pointer in her briefcase, Kevin walks her to the door. As they say their good-byes, Stella Partridge, the police liaison officer assigned to Christopher Talbot's mother, appears and whispers something to Kevin. The boss responds with a thumbs up. When he comes back to the front of the room, Tony asks him to load photos of the victims onto the screen.

Kevin smiles, and it's obvious he's already thought of it. After he's logged on, he opens a file he's prepared before the briefing and clicks slowly through a series of photographs. The first is Christopher Talbot's corporate portrait from his days with Highland and Bosch. Smart suit, pale blue tie, neat black hair. Steven Baker's image is a cut-price version of the same thing. From the council website, suit not quite so smart, grey tie, sandy hair and beard in need of a trim. The Russell Hill photo is the only one any of us have seen of him alive. The shy youth, in a shirt that's too big, next to his grandmother.

"Same hair colour." Harriet points out the only discernible similarity between this poor quality image of Russell and Steven's council photo.

"Alexandra's mother has provided two pictures." Kevin changes the image on the screen. "This one was taken when she and Barlow went to a charity ball. Don't worry, Tony, we've chopped him off."

A man's shoulder is visible on the far left of the picture. Alexandra is in a leopard-print dress that hugs her ample hips. The hair is in a peroxide up do and her mouth has the telltale lip line that ageing Hollywood actresses get with overreliance on fillers.

"This next one was taken long ago at Alexandra's twenty-first."

As one, we gasp at the contrast. In essence it's a much prettier woman. Goofy smile, thick rimmed spectacles and softly curled, sandy hair.

Tony stands up for a closer look. "Could be half-sister to Russell and Steven. Red hair is a mutant gene that prevents dark pigment. Christopher Talbot has inherited a dominant gene for black hair." He turns round and raises his palms

217

defensively. "My Nikki's doing an Open University degree. She tells me stuff." He shrugs.

Harriet raises her hand. "Where does Sean Farrell fit into all this?"

Kevin's about to reply, but Tony, who's still standing, takes the floor. "Different killer. He was forty-four – never part of the pattern. Our victims are forty-one."

"He's our victim too." It slips out before I can stop it. Without Sean there'd be no Jake. He deserves our attention, whoever killed him. Whatever he did to me.

Kevin gives me a quizzical stare for long enough to make me look away. Then he reports that two officers from Liverpool CID are already carrying out door to door near Sean's home address in search of known enemies. "But we could be looking at the same killer for that one as well," he tells us. "Although he's not a relative, his murder occurred in the same time frame as the others. Keep an open mind, folks. We don't know enough yet."

"Could the killer be another relative?" Harriet asks. "Like a mafia thing."

Tony laughs. "I'm not seeing Russell Hill's granny as matriarch of the Cosa Nostra. Besides, Siobhan Evans said the saliva poolside doesn't match with Alexandra or her parents, so it won't match with the others. Our killer isn't a family member, but is linked to the victims in another way."

With the spectre of Amy Ashby in my head again, it's my turn to speak. "We don't know for sure the saliva came from the killer. The pool was likely teeming with party guests only three days before Alexandra was attacked. The pool maintenance people could well have missed it. We shouldn't get hung up on a serial killer." We – I – shouldn't get hung up on Amy Ashby.

"Steph's right. We make no assumptions." Kevin stands up,

ready to pace while he doles out the jobs. "The rest of today is about background checks. Everything about the victims' families and friends. Copies of these photos are here." He lifts a wad of pictures from the desk. "Explore whether family members recognise any of the other victims. Did they meet once at a family wedding? Any rifts? Black sheep? Dig, dig, dig."

Chairs scrape back. Tony throws his jacket over his shoulder. We collect our batches of victim photos and file towards the door.

Kevin calls Harriet and me back. "Christopher Talbot's mother has been brought in and is waiting with Stella P in the canteen. Softly, softly, but I want chapter and verse on family history."

# CHAPTER FORTY-FIVE

Stella Partridge, the liaison officer, sees us enter the canteen and comes over. "All yours," she says, pointing to a woman at the table she's just left. "Give me a buzz when you're finished and I'll take Katrina home."

"Anything I need to know?"

Stella lowers her voice. "Christa is a touchy subject, but she'll happily talk about Christopher. And about her own early life in the Philippines. She's a family person."

We thank Stella and she leaves us to it. Katrina Talbot is sixty-five years old with a head of long, black hair. A few silver threads, not many. In front of her is a cup of tea, apparently cold and untouched.

"Mrs Talbot?" I hold out my hand. "Thank you for coming in. I'm Steph, an inspector here, and this is DC Harriet Harris. We'd like to ask you a few background questions, if that's okay."

Her handshake is surprisingly strong and she looks me in the eye. "I'll help however I can."

We sit opposite her. The Formica table top is unusually

clean. Five murders mean few police officers have time to stop for refreshments.

Harriet retrieves the council website photo of Steven Baker from her bag. "Do you know this man?"

Katrina pulls the photo towards her. "I've seen this somewhere. In a newspaper, maybe. I haven't read the newspaper much since Christopher... Lies and half-truths. I'll remember my son as I knew him."

I've never been one to hate the media. Our press office has their tussles with them, but publicity helps solve crimes. However, I can imagine the lurid Christa stories that this grieving mother has had to endure. If the radio rumour about me hadn't been nipped in the bud, I'd be siding with Katrina right now.

Harriet lays the recent photo of Alexandra Simpson beside the one of Baker.

Katrina taps it. "This is the woman who died in a swimming pool. Why are you showing me this? Did the same person kill Christopher?" Her brown eyes flash at us both.

"It's routine in a case like this. We have to consider everything, no matter how unlikely," Harriet assures her.

When she touches her bag again to get out the Russell Hill photo, I nudge her and shake my head, sensing that Katrina will become distressed if we pursue this. Stella said Katrina's happy to talk about family, so let's go there instead. Harriet collects the photos off the table and zips them in her bag.

"We'd like to ask about your family, if we may," I say. "We want to build up a full picture of Christopher."

"My family is almost gone." Her softly accentuated voice is sorrowful. "I have an aunt in Cebu. She's ninety-six. I lost my mother twenty years ago and my father died when I was a baby."

"Do you have brothers and sisters?" I ask. I doubt it's relevant, but Kev wants chapter and verse.

"My big sister was killed in the earthquake in 2013, along with my niece."

"I'm sorry you've endured so much loss," Harriet tells her.

Katrina touches the dainty silver cross on her necklace. "They are in God's house now."

I give a tiny smile. Harriet does the same. I'm glad this woman has the comfort of her religion. How would I manage if my family was wiped out in a disaster? What god could I cling to?

"Was she your only niece?" I can't help wondering if cousins' DNA would produce similar profiles to the ones Siobhan Evans showed us.

"Yes. Only my aunt survives. Christopher said he'd take me to visit this year but..." She lets out a sigh.

"When did you move to England?" Harriet asks.

"When I was twenty-one. I got a job in Hong Kong with a lovely Irish family. When the father's company relocated to England, they arranged for me to come too. I had three years in a big house in the Cotswolds, caring for two cheeky little boys." Her face breaks into a smile that fades almost immediately. "I left when I found out I was pregnant. Didn't tell them about the baby. They were Catholic like me."

"How did you manage?" I rack my brains to work out her immigration status. Without employment, why didn't she return to the Philippines?

"Christopher's father paid the hospital bills for Christopher's birth and then monthly maintenance. When Christopher was two, I found a job as a day nanny in Gloucester. I could bring him to work with me."

"And you and Christopher's father eventually married. Is that right, Mrs Talbot?" Harriet asks.

Katrina picks the teaspoon out of her saucer and stirs the tea. "I didn't marry Jason." Her hair is low over her face but I see the colour rise in her cheeks. I know what it means: she was with someone else's man. My face colours up to match.

Harriet rests her forearms on the table. "May I ask, for our records and in confidence, who Christopher's father is?"

"His name is Jason King. He worked for a big solicitors' firm in the city centre. He's probably retired by now."

The name rings a bell and I make a note to check the files. "You're not still in touch?"

"Jason stepped out of our lives when I married Charles Talbot. Christopher was eight. It was my idea to sever contact. Charles was a good man and wanted to adopt Christopher. It wouldn't have been fair to him or Jason to continue the way we were."

"How did Jason react to you saying he couldn't see his son any more?"

"I think he was relieved. Providing for us must have been a strain when he had his own family to support."

My ears prick up. Jason King's other family would be half siblings to Christopher. "Did he have more children?"

Katrina looks up; she must have heard the excitement in my voice. "I meant his wife when I said family."

"He talked to you about her?" Harriet sounds surprised. Has she never had a man tell her: *My wife doesn't understand me*? She's young. She will, she will.

The tea gets another stir. "Jason tried to make her happy. Even had a... procedure, but things were never right."

I bite my bottom lip. My head says he sounds like a slime ball. My heart recalls me in a bar when Sean approached. If he'd had the procedure I think Katrina means, there'd be no Jake.

"Did you ever meet his wife?" Harriet asks.

"I thank God I did not. Jason told me she suspected he was having an affair, but she thought he was seeing someone at work."

"You don't still have his address?"

She shrugs. "Never had it – we met... elsewhere. He might not even live in Gloucester now."

I'm not worried. Jason King is a distinctive name – one I'm sure I've heard – and there can't be many law firms in Glouces-ter. I make it a priority to track him down after the interview. A man who had one affair might have had others. A half sibling for Christopher looks like a distinct possibility. Then I remember about the vasectomy.

"Yet you had a child?"

She presses the necklace against her chest. "The mystery and miracle of God."

Harriet and I exchange a glance. And the treachery of a man who lies to get out of wearing a condom. I remember Katrina is a Catholic and might not have been fond of contra-ception herself. I see another source of half siblings. "Did you and Mr Talbot have other children?"

For the first time her eyes fill with tears. "We had a miscar-riage. After that my mother-in-law became ill and my husband had to drive to Scotland most weekends to see her. We couldn't think about trying for another baby. We carried on like that for two years until he was killed on the M6. It's been me and Christopher since then. I found work at the call centre where I still work. Charles left us well provided. Christopher was able to go to The Guild School and later he trained as a lawyer. Like his natural father; it must have been in the genes." Her voice descends into a gasp. Maybe she's wondering whose genes led Christopher to quit his career and become Christa. Life must have been unbearable for Christa trapped inside Christopher, but it can't have been easy for Christopher's mother either.

I stand up and offer my hand again. "You've been very helpful. Stella will take you home. Can I get you another drink while you're waiting?"

She stands up too. It's not often I tower over someone, but she can't be more than five feet. She takes my hand. "I'm not thirsty, thank you. I'll just wait." I sense resilience in her grip.

# CHAPTER FORTY-SIX

The afternoon is office-bound, making calls. Dig, dig, digging for Kevin. None of Gloucester's law firms have a lawyer called Jason King. One youthful-sounding receptionist says she'll get someone else to phone me back when I ask if they've ever had a Jason on the payroll.

We've made no headway with the other victims' families either. It seems my mother's right about there being no fathers on the scene, but Alexandra Simpson's stepfather has plenty to say. When I phone him, he recounts Alexandra's entire sorry childhood.

"A one-bedroom council flat. Lesley had to sleep on the couch when Alex got too old for them to share. Alex never had friends round to play. It broke Lesley's heart to hear the excuses Alexandra made to the kids in her class."

I murmur to show I'm listening but open another file on my screen. Time's ticking and this poor man's trip down memory lane won't solve his stepdaughter's murder.

"You could say Alex didn't start her childhood until she was twenty-five, when I met her mother," he says. "I married

Lesley and loved Alex as a daughter. They both happily took my surname. No other man had shown either of them the respect they deserved. No man has since." His tone hardens. "I warned Alex about John Barlow. From the beginning, I knew he was after her money, but she wouldn't listen. But I didn't know he was a killer."

"John Barlow has an alibi," I remind him.

"What's that worth?" he shouts, and I move the headset from my ear. "He buggered off to Spain with millions in scam money. He could easily have paid some low-life to do it. Don't you think it's suspicious he gets himself arrested hundreds of miles away at the exact time my daughter is being murdered? We've got to nail him for this. My wife is completely broken. She's lost her only child. *Our* only child."

"Well..." I find a lump in my throat. I hate talking to relatives. "It's one line of enquiry." I hesitate before asking my next question; I kind of know what response I'll get. "Is Mrs Simpson still in touch with Alexandra's father?"

I'm kind of right.

"*I'm* her father, not the low-life who got her mother pregnant. He wasn't even around for the birth. Is he the one grieving? Is he the one sitting up all night with her devastated mother? Is he the one offering a ten thousand pound reward?"

"Well, thank you..." News to me. I wonder if Kevin knows that Mr Simpson's put up a reward. Will he be pleased or pissed off at the added number of nutters' statements we'll have to wade through?

"Look, I know you're all doing your best," Denny Simpson says, calming down. "But with those other murders, there aren't enough detectives to work on Barlow. How about I finance a team of private investigators to bolster your efforts?"

"That's not the way—"

"Under the control of the Chief Constable, of course. The

police would still take the lead. You must have the names of some good civilians we can recruit."

Denny Simpson is clearly a man used to making things happen. I give him Kevin's direct line. This conversation is above my pay grade. I end the call and notice Harriet is on another line at her desk.

When she sees I'm no longer on the phone, she says to her caller, "Bear with me a moment, I'll just ask my inspector." She puts her hand over the mouthpiece and explains. "I've got the landlady of the Loch Lomond Guesthouse in Cathedral Street. She wants someone to collect Sean Farrell's belongings now we've finished going through his room and released it. What should I say?"

"Tell her you'll pass on her details to Liverpool police so they can put his relatives in contact with her." I speak quickly, wanting to shake off her question. Wanting to shake off Sean.

Harriet conveys the proposal, "...I don't know how long ... I can appreciate that. Perhaps box everything up and you can use the room for new guests ... Nowhere to store a box?" She looks at me helplessly.

I mime putting down the phone.

"I'm sorry, Mrs Chiles," she says. "I don't know what else to suggest."

A loud bell rings in my head. I grab my notebook, flick to the front and wheel my chair over to Harriet. "Ask if her first name's Tracey," I whisper.

"My inspector wants to know your first name ... Tracey, I see." Harriet turns to me, bewildered.

"Tell her we'll be right round to collect the stuff." I reach for my jacket.

———

*Tracey M. Chiles licensed to sell all intoxicating liquor for consumption ON the premises.* The plaque above the door.

A tub of white heathers are wilting on the porch, next to an umbrella stand in the shape of Nessie. Harriet rings the bell and it serenades us with the bonnie, bonnie banks before the urgent yapping of a dog drowns it out.

A woman I recognise opens the door. She bends down, one hand on the dog's collar. I recognise the dog, too. I patted it outside the Georgian Gardens' shop.

"Don't mind Hamish. He gets funny round strange women," she says by way of greeting. "I'll put him in the breakfast room." Slipping her hand round the dog's wagging behind, she slides it across the hall as its claws fail to make purchase on the tiled floor. A couple of protest barks as she shuts it behind a door, then silence.

"Right, there they are." She taps a cardboard box with her foot. The top is folded closed, but I can tell by the way it tips that it's not heavy. It's stacked on another. The sum total of Sean's presence in Gloucester. *Not quite.* I try not to think of Jake.

Her foot taps the box again. She clearly wants us to scoop up the boxes and scarper, her involvement with her deceased guest terminated.

"How long did Mr Farrell stay here?" I ask.

"Three weeks on and off. I think he was away home in between times." Her Scottish vowels mix with local ones. I'd say it's a while since she lived up north.

"Why was he here, do you know?"

"I didn't ask." Tracey Chiles shakes her head apologetically. "I assumed a wee cash-in-hand job. He was out a lot." She passes a box to Harriet, sending us on our way.

I don't budge. "Can we see his room?"

She frowns. "Your colleagues were in there yesterday. I've got it ready for another guest now."

"Won't take a moment." I head for the stairs. "Up here, is it?"

"Aye. Number three." She follows me, and we creak our way past prints of Scottish lochs and castles. Not bad, but the frames are heavy and twee. As I turn at the top, I'm face to antlers with a stag's head. Hope Tracey has this landing well-lit at night.

I'm not sure what I was expecting in Sean's room, but I get nothing except a whiff of Airwick. There's a Tartan bedspread over a single bed. A tray of kettle, cup and drink sachets on a dark, over-sized dressing table. A cramped ensuite where you could wee and wash hands at the same time.

Harriet has stayed downstairs and hands me the first box when I return. I clutch it to my chest. Will there be something inside that Jake should have? I shake off the thought. Sean's next of kin is strictly Liverpool, whoever that may be.

Tracey holds open the front door. Out of courtesy or to hurry our departure? I rest my box on a bookcase. Ian Rankin and Val McDermid are well represented. "I'm sorry your walk was ruined last week," I say.

Her skin turns the florid shade I saw when Izzy Hutton was interviewing her in the conservatory at the Georgian Gardens. "I'd never seen a dead body before," she says and swallows.

Harriet's expression is puzzled and I explain that Tracey was the one who discovered Christa Talbot while walking her dog.

"That's a long way from here," Harriet says. "I bet you wish you'd stuck to the town park." I must remember to thank her later; she's led us to my reason for coming here.

"Do you usually walk Hamish in the Georgian Gardens?" I ask.

Still blushing, Tracey pauses before answering. "Sometimes. I know dogs aren't allowed, but I keep the lead on and I always pay. I didn't have change for the honesty box that day. Sorry."

"So you go early before there's someone at the kiosk to take the money?"

"Well, I suppose so."

"Aren't you busy in the mornings, making the full Scottish breakfast?"

"I-I don't always have guests." The red in her face has turned neon, but I can't tell whether she's mortified about having too many vacancies, or hiding something else. I move on.

"Sean – Mr Farrell was here last week, wasn't he?"

"He was room only. I didn't have to cook." She sounds like she's back on more solid ground.

"How did Mr Farrell seem to you last Monday?"

"Well, Inspector..."

"Steph."

Her eyes widen briefly as if she recognises my name. "Well, Steph, I hardly saw him, but I'd say he was in a strange mood." She parts her feet. "It was like he was elated and angry at the same time."

Her gaze lingers on me and her lips curl into a smile. I have to look away, feeling suddenly hot. Did Sean say something? Does this woman know about Jake? I can't move, can't speak.

"Do you know why he was like that?" Harriet asks.

Tracey pulls her attention away from me and shrugs. "He was just a paying guest. Like I said to the officers yesterday, he didn't speak to me except to book an alarm call or request more toilet paper."

Breathing easily again, I shift the box in my arms. Tracey Chiles knows nothing about Jake, or the murders. She's just a woman coincidently connected to two victims. Like me. Like Amy. None of us serial killers. Probably. I head out of the front door then stop as a thought hits me.

"What does M stand for in your name on this licence plaque? Something Scottish, perhaps?" My pulse pounds to the beat of Morag.

She pauses and looks me in the eye. Something passes between us that I can't catch. "Clever guess. It's Mairi. My middle name is Mairi."

———

I get home and find that Jake has honoured me with his presence. He's cleaned the kitchen again, bless him. Still feeling tired, I'd made a low-energy go at it after the fingerprint team had finished, but Jake's got it gleaming. Blinking away tears, I banish the thought that he's unwittingly wiped off the last traces of his father.

He cooks me pasta with grated cheese – which I manage to eat by adding ketchup – and tells me about his Chemistry paper. He and I both know I don't have a clue what he's saying, but it stops us musing on the break-in.

When he goes up to his room to revise, I decide on an early night. But work has other ideas. As I'm cleaning my teeth, my mobile on the bedside table makes itself heard. I finish in the bathroom, check who called and sit on my bed to ring back. It's Kevin.

I suppress a yawn as I ask him what he wants. He tells me.

I'm suddenly wide awake.

# CHAPTER FORTY-SEVEN

Leaning back in his swivel chair with his hands interlaced behind his spiky, blond hair, Nathan Jackson protests, "Don't know why you lot got involved. And it was years ago. It was a domestic. We were both as bad as each other."

Normally when a cocky little git of a man says that, I mentally barbecue his testicles and I set my sights on finding something – anything – to arrest him for. But Kevin briefed me on the phone, and this particular cocky little git might just be telling the truth. Six years ago, his girlfriend found out he'd been playing away at the nightclub where he gigged. When he came home at four a.m., she was waiting for him with the first punch. The neighbours called us. According to the arresting officer, there were more bruises on him than her. Main thing is his DNA has stayed on the system ever since.

As the chair swivels, I'm itching to push it faster and keep hold of his head while the rest of him spins. He's the prat who hinted on air that a detective was involved in the murders. He told Harriet he'd got carried away by a crank call, but after what Siobhan Evans told Kevin, we think he's in it up to his strutting neck. When approval for a familial DNA search on the victims was granted, one more relative hit the bingo board. Nathan Jackson is quite possibly another half sibling and, as the last man standing, our new prime suspect. That's unless there are other siblings out there not on the police database. We're hoping luck is on our side with Nathan J.

"We want you to look closely at these four photographs," Kevin tells him. He lays them on the end of Nathan's desk, away from the sound decks and computer that Nathan is hiding behind. "Wheel your chair this way, please, sir."

Nathan hesitates, knows when he's beaten and scurries along.

"Thank you, sir." Kevin at his most neutral and most deadly. "Do you recognise any of these people?" It's the two photos we showed Katrina Talbot of Steven Baker and Alexandra Simpson plus the corporate shot of Christopher Talbot and the one of shy Russell Hill with his grandmother.

Nathan scoops up the pictures and tries to hand them back to Kevin. "Anyone in Gloucestershire would recognise them."

"Lay them down if you don't mind, sir." Kevin waits until Nathan has obliged before he asks, "Did you ever meet them before their deaths put them in the newspaper? I understand you meet a lot of people in your line of work. Did any of them come here to the radio station or speak to you at a club?" It's funny hearing "club" on Kevin's lips. Can't see him requesting "Bodak Yellow" or buying Jäger bombs from the shot girl.

Before Nathan can shake his head, I lift Alexandra's picture. "She was single for a while. Ever bumped into her on the club scene?"

He takes the photo from me. His fingers are squat and chubby. Much like his physique behind his jacket, waistcoat and cowboy boots, I suspect.

"Before I got this job, I played every club in Gloucester.

Had to turn work down in Cheltenham and Stroud. These days I'm paid to do P.A.s." He looks at Kevin. "There are always lots of girls, know what I'm saying? I can't be sure."

"You may have known her when she looked like this." Kevin lays down another photo.

Still holding the first photo of Alexandra, he lifts the new one to compare the two. From his expression, it's clear he prefers the plasticated version rather than the fresh-faced twenty-one-year-old. He snaps them down on the desk like a pair of playing cards. "Can't help you."

Kevin places one last photo on top of them as if he's playing trumps. "What about this woman?"

Nathan chuckles. "He's a looker, I'll give him that." He leans back, cupping the back of his head again. "I'm a man of the world, always volunteer to play Pride Night and I've gigged in plenty of gay bars. If I'd seen him/her in a bar, I'd have had a second look. But I don't remember." He hands the post mortem head shot of Christa Talbot to Kevin, apparently not noticing how lifeless her eyes are.

"What about away from work?" Kevin asks. "Could you have met any of them at, say, a family event? A cousin's wedding, maybe, or grandparents' golden anniversary knees up?"

For the first time the mask slips. "Don't have any cousins. Just a mum. Don't have grandparents either. Their loss. They could be doting on a famous grandson by now if they'd stayed in touch." Cocky Nathan makes a return. Does he really think a graveyard shift on local radio makes him Dermot O'Leary? But I catch a glimpse of something else. Regret? For all his bravado, is this a little boy who wants a nanna like all the other kids?

"Are you in touch with your father?" Kevin asks.

"What you've never had, you never miss." There's a catch

in the cockiness.

"We'd like to talk to your mother."

Nathan stands up. "What is this? Leave my mother alone. She's elderly. You can't go harassing a pensioner. I'm not having it."

"Sit down, Mr Jackson."

Kevin's headmaster voice does it again. Nathan gives a sigh of defeat, sits down and gets out his phone. "This is her number, but she's on a cruise of the Balearics right now. I don't know how good reception is."

I note it down. Can't wait 'til I'm a pensioner.

Kevin moves on. "We'd like to ask you about your whereabouts last Wednesday, the sixth, between six and eight a.m."

"I'm a DJ; I don't get up before noon. Alas no one can verify that."

So no alibi for Christa Talbot's murder. I keep scribbling.

"What about the next day, early evening? Where were you then?"

"How should I know? Wait, yes, Thursday, I was at Red Rose youth club. I help on Mondays and Thursdays. I teach the kids how to play the decks." He tugs his waistcoat.

"What time?"

"Six."

I know the manager at Red Rose. Jake did a football skills course there one summer before his sudden switch to rugby. Easy enough to check, but it's only a partial alibi at best. Steven Baker could have died as early as four thirty p.m.

"What about last Saturday night, after midnight, early hours of Sunday?" Where was he when Russell Hill died?

Nathan's grin tells us he's got this one. "I was on air until one. My producer can confirm that." He glances at the clock on the wall. "She'll be here soon." He looks at Kevin with the rest of his answer. "After work I went to ATIK, stayed 'til three, had a kebab at the Spice Shack and got to bed about four. Loads of people must have seen me." Of course, everyone in Gloucester knows Nathan J.

"Thank you, sir." Kevin waits until I've finished writing. He doesn't ask for an alibi for Alexandra's murder. Or Sean's. It was a Monday evening, when Nathan claims he's always at Red Rose youth club. Not rock solid, though. Like Steven Baker, Sean could have been dead as early as five. An alibi from six p.m. might not stand up in court. But I can't see a way to challenge his alibi for Alexandra. Nathan J was on air when she died on Tuesday night. Unless there was something in that business about him playing non-stop music for the first hour.

Nathan wheels his chair back to the computer. "Can I get back to my work now? I've got tracks to cue."

"Go ahead. We'll wait out there for your producer." Kevin stands up, tilting his head at Nathan. "Is that your natural hair colour, sir?"

Nathan brushes his hand over the gelled spikes. "It's not against the law for a ginger to hide his roots."

Unease tickles my shoulders. "How old are you, Nathan?"

"Thirty-five."

I smile. "How old are you, Nathan?"

He sighs.

Before he can reply, there's movement behind the glass and a mic switches on.

"Ten minutes to air." The bossy female voice strikes me as a cheek when the talent – I use the term loosely – has been here a good hour and she's flounced in at the last minute.

"Thank you, Mr Jackson. We'll be in touch," Kevin says, and we go out to speak to the producer.

Louisa Brady is one of those middle-class twenty-some-things with a grating drawl that ends every sentence on a question. The silverware in her ears and nose looks quality. Rebel

Without an Overdraft. For a minute, it looks like it crosses her mind to deny that Nathan was on air last Saturday when Russell Hill was killed. Reluctantly she confirms they were both here until one a.m.

"But we went our separate ways at the end of the shift. My friends and I went to Cheltenham. Nathan probably stayed in Gloucester with the older set."

Looks like one of us will be trawling the clubs tomorrow to alibi Nathan for the rest of the night of Russell Hill's death. Who shall I give the job to? Harriet, probably. Tony won't want it. I still can't believe he's in a committed relationship.

Kevin's phone rings. "Hi, Jordan. What have you got?" It's one of the detectives working the late shift. As he listens, Kevin's face grows grave. He walks away with the phone to his ear.

I make small talk with Louisa. I ask how she got into radio. Media Studies with Drama degree, she tells me. As the clock ticks closer to Nathan's show, she loses interest and adjusts the switches on her desk. I catch snatches of Kevin's side of the phone call.

"Why are you telling me this now? ... What other evidence? ... From the cat. I see." He glances at me, then turns away. "No, don't wait. I'll come back and apply for the warrant." He comes off the line.

Even when we get out to the car park, he doesn't volunteer anything.

"Well?" I ask.

"Another line of enquiry. I'll brief everyone tomorrow. Go home and get some sleep."

Back at home, I'm so tired even superglued matchsticks couldn't prop my eyes open and I fall asleep as soon as I hit the pillow, despite the pinch in my belly that says Kevin is withholding something.

# CHAPTER FORTY-EIGHT

It's gone eight o'clock when I wake fug-headed. Jake's bag is gone from the hall. He must be at the revision club one of the teachers runs on Thursday mornings. I make toast, partly because the painkillers are really supposed to be taken with food, but mainly because my appetite is finally back.

I'm on the mend but my head doesn't clear as I drive to work. The pain hasn't been there for a couple of days and I slept through the night, but something in me doesn't feel right. My unease grows as I go through the gates at police HQ.

To get to the office, I walk past the canteen. Through the internal windows, I see Tony in the thick of it with a crowd of uniforms, but his expression is serious, arms folded. Has there been a riot I don't know about or a drugs raid? Otherwise, at a time like this, the only way this many officers would be at base is if the killer had been caught.

Unusually, Kevin's door is closed and there's no one in the CID office. I hang my bag and jacket on my chair and log on, hoping for something on the system to explain what's going on.

Harriet appears at the door. "We brought her in at seven.

She's refused a solicitor and is doing a 'no comment'. The boss is getting nowhere; he wants you in there." Her voice is excited but her eyes look cautious, like she's approaching a firework that might go off. "I'll brief you on the way down," she says.

My blood thundering, I follow Harriet.

———

A uniformed constable stands inside the interview room. Kevin sits at the table, and opposite him is Amy Ashby.

She probably wasn't awake when police went to pick her up, but she's slipped on a floaty cream top and navy linen trousers. Without mascara, her eyes are tired, but her lips defy her predicament with their statement lipstick.

Kevin speaks into the recorder. "Entering the room are..."

I clear my throat. "DI Stephanie Lewis."

Harriet says her name after me.

"Leaving the room is DCI Kevin Richards."

He can't leave! I want to jump on his arm and haul him back with my full weight, but the door clangs shut behind him. Thirty-eight years after Amy and I met, I'm scared of her for the first time. Thanks to my last visit, she knows my deepest secret. Her gaze into mine is unwavering. Harriet turns her chair my way, waiting. All eyes on me then.

"Has someone offered you a cup of tea?" My voice is in a pitch I don't recognise.

"You love this, don't you?" she hisses.

With our history, I have to let that pass. But five people are dead and that's the reason Kevin has put me here. That's all that matters.

Five people killed and a traumatised cat. I glance at the briefing papers Harriet has given me, needing to get my facts straight even though I get the gist. It was my idea to test the cat in the first place, but I didn't know it would lead here.

When I look at Amy, my thoughts are a trembling mush. I decide to read from the page; somewhere safer to look. "At seven this morning, police officers with a warrant searched 17 Anscott Close where you currently reside. They took away a pair of brown moccasin-style shoes with a view to matching traces of fur on them to a cat found at the location where a forty-one-year-old woman, Alexandra Simpson, was murdered. Do you have anything to say?"

"My, what big sentences you have."

She had to go there. GCSE English. Mr Grant used to say it to our class. Mostly to me. Said I was scared of full stops.

I'm scared of them now but I wait. Suspects often fill a silence with rickety lies or early confessions. But Amy clearly hasn't read the police manual. She stares at me, glances at Harriet, admires her nails.

It's Harriet who plugs the void. "When DCI Richards asked you earlier if you wanted a solicitor, you declined. You can request one at any time. We will stop the interview immediately and wait for one to arrive."

*Say you want one now*, I silently beg. That way, by the time the interview resumes, I'll make sure I've relapsed into another migraine and got as far away from this room as possible.

Amy folds her arms. "I'd like to hear what Steph has to say first." Sounding catty after all these years.

Cat. I put myself back on track. "If you have anything to say regarding the moccasins, it's best to say it now. Co-operation could work in your favour."

Her expression shifts to something almost gleeful and I'm right back in Mrs Hardcastle's office, taking the bollocking I'm due, and in my sightline is the vindicated smirk of my so-called prey. The memory makes me snap. "You can't play the..." I stop myself saying victim. "You can't play with us. This is serious."

The smirk is still there. "The shoes are comfortable. Thanks for asking. I put them on for driving and when I'm in the boarding house at school. I do not wear them to attack felines."

"You're denying you came into contact with a cat in an indoor swimming pool at the home of Alexandra Simpson? So you're saying that our technicians will be unable to match your footwear to the crime scene?"

Leaning towards me, she whispers, "Remember my viola?"

I colour up and I feel Harriet's curiosity to my left. Afterwards, I'll make something up so I don't have to tell her how it was Amy's word against mine, and I was found wanting. Is Amy trying to say I planted evidence on the moccasins?

Ignoring the taunt seems like my only course of action. "Can you confirm that you wish to say nothing about the footwear at this time?" God, I sound like Mrs Hardcastle.

Resting her palm on her chin, she says, "I reiterate my earlier answer: although immensely comfortable, their suitability with cats has not been tested."

I feel myself being tied in knots and have to sit on my hands to stop them balling into fists. Something in the briefing notes catches my eye about her alibi for Steven Baker's murder. "Going back to last week – Thursday between five and seven – where were you?"

Amy looks at Harriet. "Don't you people speak to each other? You've already checked my whereabouts. I was arranging flowers at Orchard School as I do most Thursdays."

"We went back to the school and asked again," Harriet explains. "The secretary confirmed that the flower displays had been changed when she arrived at work on Friday morning.

But, as she left work at five the previous evening, she can't verify what time you carried out your work."

"It was five thirty, it always is." Finally Amy's familiar petulance is here. "It took me two hours. I put in extra gerbera. Orange complementing yellow." Her sleeve rides up as she rubs her arm, the skin delicately pale.

Detail, like last time I asked her. Devil in the detail, and also in the lie? "Did anyone else see you?" I ask.

"One of the gap year students probably. It's their job to lock up. The school was open when I arrived and I punched the code pad when I left. I created eight pedestals and a table top for reception."

Detail again, but I latch onto the first thing she said. "A gap year student *probably* saw you. Please give us his name and we'll ring the school and ask."

Amy crosses her legs. "I don't know their names. They come and go. But I was there." She hesitates. "Believe me, I'm telling the truth."

Her pause is eloquent. Another echo of school clangs in my ears. *Believe me, I'm telling the truth.* My stock phrase, and Terri's. It meant squat all.

The notes rescue me again and I revert to reading aloud. "You had a grudge against Steven Baker's roundabout plans and your car was in the vicinity of the Georgian Gardens where Christa Talbot was killed."

Amy tries to push back her chair and finds it's fixed to the floor. Her feet slap harshly against the tiles. "Is this payback, Steph? Shouldn't it be the other way round? Thirteen school years of unrelenting bullying. Then when I think I'm rid of you, back you come and steal—" She stops suddenly, apparently remembering Harriet's presence. Spittle from her outburst glistens on her upper lip.

It reminds me what else I've got to ask. "DCI Richards

requested a DNA swab from you, which you have so far declined to give. If you're unsure, you can discuss this with a solicitor. It's not too late to halt the interview to appoint one."

Amy looks me straight in the eye. "You know me better than anyone else in the entire West Gloucestershire Police Force. You know I'm not a killer and we both know why you want this interview terminated."

"What about the sample?" I talk through my quavering voice. "It's a simple process. Doesn't hurt."

I brace myself for Amy's comeback. Instead she asks, "If I give you the sample, will you let me go? My mother is on her own."

I scan the notes. It will be Kev's decision, but the evidence is flimsy despite the apparent excitement in the canteen. Attending a council meeting, driving past the Georgian Gardens, wearing moccasins that might have cat fur on. Only a match on the saliva could nudge her into the frame. Would she be prepared to give DNA if she's guilty? Plenty of suspects think they've left no trace.

"Please bear with us. The DCI will be with you shortly. Shall I tell him you'll give a sample?"

She folds her arms. "If I must."

I turn. "For the benefit of the tape, DI Stephanie Lewis is leaving the room."

Leaning against the wall in the corridor, I let out a breath. I've got what Kevin brought me into this interview for: Amy's insistence on her flower arranging alibi, denial of murder and agreement to give a swab. But I can't help feeling I'd have come out more like the winner if she'd continued to say "no comment".

# CHAPTER FORTY-NINE

Expecting wee and cabbage, I'm surprised when the nursing home smells of furniture polish. I wait in the foyer while the care assistant checks that Mr Baker senior is happy to see me. A vase of carnations on a hall stand makes me think of Amy's flowers. Did she kill Steven Baker? And four others? Until forensics come through on the moccasins and saliva, there's nothing to link her to Alexandra Simpson. In the meantime, Kevin is going after her because of her flimsy alibi for Steven Baker. My gut doesn't buy it. Feelings were running high at the St Giles roundabout meeting, and even my mum said Baker was an idiot, but why would Amy kill him? Council traffic policy won't change because the chief planner has died. Whoever battered Steven to death had a personal motive. I've sent Harriet and Tony to interview his widow again and I'm trying my luck with his eighty-six-year-old grandfather.

The care assistant returns and says Mr Baker will see me upstairs. "I tried to persuade him to come down, but he hasn't left his room since he arrived."

I follow her unflattering utility trousers up a thickly

carpeted staircase into a sunny corridor with bedroom doors open on both sides. I catch glimpses of floral bedspreads, zimmer frames and the odd head of grey hair. David Baker's room is at the far end, and unlike the other doors, his is closed. The care assistant knocks and walks in.

A man sits in a high-backed chair by the window, a tripod stick by his left arm and an empty trolley tray to his right. Dapper is the best word to describe him. Navy cords, purple sweater, cream checked shirt. A man for whom, I suspect, looking good has been effortless all his adult life. It would be more of a struggle to let his standards drop. Against the opposite wall is a single bed, at hospital height, with half a dozen pillows. Does he sleep sitting up?

Refreshingly, the care assistant addresses him without raising her voice. "Your visitor is here. I'll make you both some tea." Before she heads out, she pulls a plastic chair away from the wall so it is about a metre from the man.

"Thank you, Judy." His strong voice, together with his luxuriant white hair, make me wonder why he's in a nursing home, but when he creaks to his feet and holds out a frail hand, I see his vulnerability.

"Please don't get up," I say.

"Young lady, you're trying to catch my grandson's killer; you deserve my manners at the very least." He returns to his chair and lets out a sigh at the effort. "What can I do to help?" He points at the plastic chair and I sit down.

"We're building up a picture of Steven's life and family. I'd like to ask you about Steven's parents."

He nods sadly, as if he expected the question but answering it will be no less painful for knowing. "His mum was my only daughter. Died of cancer when she was fifty-seven. My wife, June, stayed in Nottingham to care for her in her final weeks. The strain affected her health. Within two years I'd lost her too. And now Steven." His eyes drift to three framed photos on a dark-wood dressing table. A black and white portrait of a woman with curled hair, presumably his late wife. Another, a fading colour photograph, shows a young woman in a graduation gown, holding the hand of a small boy. The third, a more recent graduation photo, is of a sandy-haired youth recognisable as Steven Baker.

David sees me looking. "It's all I have left of them."

I want to squeeze his hand but can't risk damaging the paper-thin skin. "I'm sorry you've suffered so much."

"Don't mind me." He brushes an imaginary crumb from his lap. "Sentiment doesn't solve murders. What else do you need to know?"

"How long have you lived in Gloucester?"

"June and I lived here all our lives. Our daughter, Michele, went away when she was eighteen. She had a place to study teacher training at college here but at the last minute she announced she was going to Trent Poly instead. This was in the days before they all got called universities. We didn't see her again that year, always a different excuse why she couldn't visit and why we couldn't go to her. She started coming home after that but never for more than a few hours. It wasn't until she got her degree and a teaching job in Newark that she admitted why she'd stayed away."

He gives me a wistful smile and waits for me to say something.

"Because of Steven?" I say.

David Baker nods. "He was four years old before we found out he existed." He looks at me. "Am I such an ogre of a father that my daughter was too scared to tell me? We would have been disappointed for sure, but we'd have supported her. She didn't have to do what she did."

Even I can't put myself in Michele Baker's shoes. Was it

because I was already twenty-five when I found myself pregnant and single? My only anxiety in telling my parents was having to admit that all the efforts they'd put into preparing my new business would go to waste. I would never get the beauty salon we dreamed of.

"My wife and I were deeply hurt by what Michele had done, but we were proud too. As a very young single mother, with no support apart from a few student friends who minded Steven when she visited us, she'd got a degree, a job and a place to live. And Steven was an absolute credit to her. June and I fell in love with him as soon as we saw him." David Baker's eyes shine. "When he was older, he came to stay every summer. We'd build go-karts in my shed. He was more like a son than a grandson. When I had my stroke last year, he relocated with his family to be near me."

"How did his wife take the move?" I'm clutching at straws. We know the wife was working at a school parents' evening when Steven died. Even if resentment was a motive, she didn't have opportunity.

David shakes his head. "I thought she was fine about it. She was friendly, happy for me to spend time with Steven. But she's put me in here, so I must have read her wrong."

Gripping my pen, I scribble on my notepad. I don't ask him what legal right she has to do that. It's none of my business and not a police matter, although it damn well ought to be.

Judy comes back with a tray that she puts on the trolley and wheels it between my seat and David's. A brown teapot in a pink tea cosy, white cups and matching milk jug, sachets of sugar on another saucer, and a plate of digestives.

David thanks her, and after she's gone I pour our tea. The pot dribbles onto the sugar. I push the saucer aside and ask if he wants milk.

"Just a dash. I'm watching my waistline." His mouth turns

up in a tiny smile. I feel that it's a joke this slim man is used to cracking. But he's only going through the motions, no mirth left in him.

I push his drink to where he can reach it. "The staff seem nice."

"Lovely, but I wish they'd stop asking me to go downstairs."

"Not keen on company at the moment. I understand." And I do. A week ago he was in his own home, receiving frequent visits from his adoring grandson. The raising of a piece of Cotswold stone against Steven's skull has changed David's world to one of mourning and incarceration.

"I'm sure Judy means well," I say.

"Not worth making friends." He stares at the photographs. "I won't be here long."

His face gives nothing away, but my gut tells me he's not talking about moving back home. I make a mental note to ask Judy to keep a close eye, and I change the subject.

"Did Michele ever marry?" I ask.

"It was always just her and Steven."

A warm feeling reaches me. Like me and Jake. It grows cold when I formulate my next question. "What do you know about Steven's father?"

"Michele never told us anything and we never asked. We found her documents after she died. No father is named on Steven's birth certificate."

A dead end. And given that she kept Steven's existence from him for four years, it sounds like her father is the last person Michele would confide in. Poor old boy. He deserved more faith. I change the subject again. "Did Steven talk to you about his job at the council?"

"I don't think he liked it much. He told me once he wished he'd pursued his dream to be a fireman."

# CHAPTER FIFTY

How many lines of enquiry have I let slide on this case? Three days ago, I told the fire station that I'd ring back in the morning to speak to the officer who paid the safety visit to Russell Hill. It took David Baker's mention of his grandson's childhood ambition to jog my memory. I make the belated phone call and arrange to meet Matt Ward at Caffè Nero.

We've met before – when my nasal cavities were filled with smoke – but neither of us refers to our encounter outside Russell Hill's burnt-out house.

"What can I get you?" he says when we take our seats at a table outside.

"I'll get these," I say, keeping the interview formal, reminding myself I'm not on a date, however appealing that might seem. Amy's done well. If the fire service do a calendar, Matt Ward would be May through September. "Is coffee all right?"

While I wait in the queue, I admire him as he checks his phone. Why am I here? Acting on a hunch? Or filling time away from the police station, so there's no risk of being forced to interview Amy again before she's either charged or released?

When I return with the drinks, Matt says he's only got half an hour. "Text from the ex. I have to collect our son from school as she's stuck in a meeting."

"No problem. This won't take long." My voice is dispassionate, but my heart ticks to the encouraging beat of ex and family man as if I'm appraising him as a possible partner. "What can you tell me about your fire prevention visit to Russell Hill?"

His face is grave as he looks straight ahead, no doubt focussing his mind on what he saw. "Piles of newspaper, floor to ceiling. Access to each room was a sixty centimetre gap at the top of the doorway. You see some sights in my job, but that one scared the hell out of me. With good reason as it turned out." He lowers his eyes. I know that look. Coppers get it when an abuse victim drops charges and goes back to the abuser for more damage. A guaranteed disaster we fail to avert. Matt looks ashamed. Inexplicable and fully understandable at the same time.

"What was Russell Hill like?"

"Intelligent, articulate, well-informed and stubborn as seagull shit on a windscreen. He ran that house on his own lines of logic. Nothing I said got close to getting through to him. If I'd been able to foretell the future and give him concrete proof the place was about to be razed to the ground with him in it, he'd have still had a convincing answer why I was wrong."

"Did he say anything about his neighbours or friends?"

"According to him, the neighbours were small-minded and feeble thinkers. I doubt he had any friends. The only visitors he'd had apart from me were two social workers and they'd been about as welcome as I was."

I know about Clare Burgess, the social worker who

requested the fire visit. Kevin spoke to her early in our enquiries.

Matt gives a sad smile. "Russell called them interfering busy bodies who didn't know arse from elbow. His expression, not mine. The second social worker didn't know the first one had been. That must have made him mad. He didn't strike me as the type to suffer fools."

"Did he give you any indication that he was worried about anything? Did he feel threatened in any way?"

"Not the worrying kind, I'd say."

"I'll give Clare Burgess a call, see if he said anything to her or the other social worker."

He checks the time on his phone and drinks up. "That was good coffee. I've never been in here before. I usually go across the road."

"With Amy?" It slips out. Have I crossed a line, letting my personal curiosity creep into the interview? But it's a legitimate line of enquiry. My interest is professional.

He narrows his eyes, scrutinising me. "You've done your homework, inspector."

My job title sounds like an insult in that tone.

"There are good reasons for asking," I say. Truth and lie merge.

He shrugs. "I met a woman called Amy a couple of times. We didn't click."

Am I relieved or plain smug? Whatever, I'm caught off guard and my mouth runs on. "Just as well. If forensics come through, she might be charged with murder."

Matt's firm jaw slackens and his pupils grow as dark as the coffee still in my cup. I shouldn't have said that, but he's almost a colleague, isn't he? The fire service have collaborated with police on this case.

"You think she set the fire that killed Russell Hill?" The

colour drains from his face. "I told her about him. I said I'd visited a hoarder." He puts his head in his hands.

I, too, want to bury my head. I'm not here in search of another nail for Amy's coffin, but it looks like Matt's hammered in an unexpected one. He's just confirmed her connection to Russell Hill, another victim.

But then he looks up. "What forensics? I've read the fire report and I was at the scene. We found nothing."

"Not from the arson site. We have forensics at another murder scene, Alexandra Simpson, on Tuesday night. Forensics there are being checked against Amy."

He's so pale I think he might pass out. "Are you telling me I dated a killer?"

"She's a suspect, that's all. You're not in danger." Is that true? If it is Amy, how would I know what her warped victim selection criteria are?

Matt's forehead knits into a frown and his eyes go distant again, as if he's picturing something else. "Tuesday night? What time did Alexandra Simpson die?"

"Around ten p.m. Why?"

He sits back, folding his arms. "It can't be Amy then. I saw her in Tesco. My shift finished at nine forty-five and I went to the supermarket. A lot of shift workers shop late. I know it's juvenile but I ducked into another aisle before she saw me."

"Which Tesco was this?"

"Brockworth."

My head gets out its calculator. A drive from the fire station to Brockworth at that time of night would be about fifteen minutes. He'd have got to Tesco just after ten p.m. Amy would not have had time to electrocute Alexandra in Wrenswood and calmly stock up on fennel at that time. Is he telling the truth? Why would he lie to give her an alibi when he's just implicated her in Russell Hill's murder? Perhaps he's mistaken about spotting Amy. I see a trawl of supermarket CCTV coming Harriet Harris's way.

"Can you come into the police station tomorrow to give a statement?" I'd like it done today but I remember he's got to pick up his boy. And if forensics on the saliva and cat fur at Alexandra Simpson's come through, tomorrow will be another day.

# CHAPTER FIFTY-ONE

"Do you need a lift?" Steph asks, no doubt trying to sound neutral, but Amy detects the gloat.

Amy doesn't turn round and, as she continues to take back her belongings from the desk sergeant, her knuckles whiten on the strap of her handbag. The bitch and her police cronies have had her locked up in here all day with no thought for her mother alone at home.

"How will you get home? Let me help."

Steph's second question sends her back to school.

———

"Do you need a hand with something?" Terri asks, eyes stretched to innocent. Amy clings to her satchel, sports bag, sewing kit and viola. The way lessons fall on Mondays, she's always weighed down like a pack horse.

"Come on, Ames, we're walking the same way." They've reached the edge of Manor Park. The short cut to Tuffton is across the grass and down the steep hill. "Easy to slip with a banjo on your back," Terri adds.

Is it a threat? Surely Terri would draw the line at breaking the expensive instrument, but there's nothing to stop her 'accidentally' tripping Amy as she picks her way down the slope. Amy weighs her options. Limited.

"Thank you. You can carry this." She offers the plastic bag of needlework, thinking Terri will decline because it's not the viola, but too late Amy realises her mistake. Terri takes the bag, a wicked grin forming. She moves a few feet away and peers in.

"What the hell is this?" She holds out the embroidered canvas in front of her like an opened newspaper. All Amy can see is the hideous criss-cross of knots and threads across the back. Terri finds fault with the front. "Is that supposed to be a horse? It's got three legs."

"It isn't finished." Amy advances, arm outstretched awkwardly, the weight of her other bags unbalancing her.

"Nah. It's not your best work." Terri waves it above her head. "You ought to start this one again."

Amy makes a run at her, but unencumbered, Terri is quicker. She trots first, taunting her with the canvas between finger and thumb, but then she speeds up. Amy drops the satchel and sports bag. She takes the viola case off her shoulder, lays it gently on the grass and sprints after Terri.

Amy soon gains on her tormentor, her eyes on the flapping embroidery. Suddenly Terri stops and bends over as if she's playing leapfrog. Amy crashes into her and sails over the top. Coarse grass grazes her wrists as she puts out her hands to break her fall. She sits up, trying not to cry at the burning sting in her skin. Terri stands over her. Before either of them speak, there's a shout from behind.

"I've got it." Steph stands with the viola over her head, a malevolent grin on her fat mouth.

———

"Not this time, Steph," Amy says now as she pockets the money and bank cards the sergeant has returned to her. "I'm not playing your game."

Steph and the sergeant exchange a glance, and the gesture ignites a fury in Amy. How dare Steph make out that she – Amy – is the unreasonable one? Everything she's ever done has had an absolute logic towards a long-term goal. What has Steph ever done except fritter her time on childish amusement?

"Is that it for now?" Amy asks. "Can I expect you back in another eighteen years?"

Another glance is exchanged. Then Steph says, "You're released pending further enquiries."

"Further. You always did carry a joke too far." Amy snaps on her watch and strides away. "This time the joke will be on you," she whispers as she quits the building.

# CHAPTER FIFTY-TWO

Nathan lifts the lid on the truffle box and feels that it's loose. "Why has this been opened?"

"You begrudge me one, do you?" Lulu's sarcasm comes loud through his headphones.

"Spat on them, have you?"

"Nah, just dosed them in arsenic." She looks at him through the glass. "Eat up."

He closes the box and shrugs. "Not hungry."

"Too suggestible. That's your trouble."

He wondered how long it would take her to go there. Ever since the police visit, she's been threatening to tell the radio station controller he was duped by a crank call. So far the high-ups haven't found out about his visit from the police or what he said on air.

Enough of her sniping. Time to fix her. The record finishes and he takes the mic. "*There goes Florence in her machine. Now, as you heard on the news, a volcano on Hawaii has erupted, spewing ash miles into the air, with rocks the size of cars raining down. Well, listeners, we've had our own eruption right here in the studio. Lulu, my producer, has gone off on one. You should see her now."* He keeps his head down, not looking through the glass. *"Her face is as purple as the lace bustier she's wearing. And – get this – she's threatened to poison me. You'd never think something that cute and cuddly could be so deadly. Here's Little Mix with 'Black Magic'. Lulu would know all about that."* He starts the song.

Lulu stands up, face screaming *wanker*. "I've transferred the phone. Any calls on *hashtag Wedding Rehearsal* will come straight to you."

"Where are you going?"

"Toilet. I may be some time."

The hairs on Nathan's freckled arms stand on end. What's she up to? Last time she left him was during the Tuesday Smooch. Then she threatened to tell the police she couldn't vouch for him being in the studio. What if she was the one up to something? Where the hell is she going this time?

To quell his nerves, he scrolls Twitter, but there's nothing coming through. People don't like the theme. Lulu's idea. Boring. Boring. She can't keep him on a tight lead forever because of one lapse of judgment. He picks out a truffle, throws it in the air and catches it in his mouth.

Does it taste funny? He dismisses the idea that she's done something. The coating's softened in the heat of the studio, that's all. Still munching the truffle, he plays James Bay without speaking a link.

When Lulu isn't back by the end of the song, he puts on Chris de Burgh, eats another truffle and opens the bottle of dandelion and burdock. He takes a swig from the bottle. Some of it goes down his throat before his taste buds activate. He spits out the rest, leaving spatters on his waistcoat and a mini puddle on his deck desk. The drink is even more bitter than usual. Lulu wouldn't have peed in it, would she? Not her style, surely?

She still isn't back by the time he's played Wham! and The Commodores, and he can hear his nerves in his voice as he speaks the links between tracks. His heart speeds up in fury. He'll kill her for this.

The phone rings. Instinctively, he looks for Lulu through the glass, but she still isn't there. He'll ignore it. No one will know. But the Twitter feed stays empty and there's nothing new on email. Without listener interaction, his material is thin. The call might be Chaz@up4a3some ringing with a risqué anecdote to pep up the show.

While the song is still playing, he picks up the receiver. "Hi, you're through to Nathan J. What would you like to talk about?"

"Did you get your gifts?"

Morag. The woman has sent truffles and soft drinks last night and tonight, but there've been no phone calls since Tuesday when he aired her tip-off. He and Lulu figured she'd taken the joke as far as she wanted.

Nathan clears his throat. "Good evening."

"I've been... occupied since we last spoke," the voice says. "Have you missed me?"

"Always wonderful to hear from our loyal listeners." Nathan sets his patter to gushing, hoping she'll detect insincerity and ring off.

"The police inspector is still at work. It's your chance to be remembered for speaking out against police corruption. You'll be famous."

"I don't think..." He looks to the glass; Lulu's still not there. The penny drops. This isn't Morag at all. Nice try, Lulu.

"But what can I say on air?" he asks theatrically. "Tell me, Morag. What should I say?"

There's a pause on the line. Does she know he's onto her?

"Just say: a female police inspector was romantically involved with one of the victims."

She's a trier. Does she think he's dumb enough to bad mouth the police a second time after that fit, blonde police woman warned him off?

Nathan suppresses a laugh. Where does Lulu get her inspiration? "And you want me to broadcast this live?" Maybe he will do as she says. If the police come calling he'll tell them who put him up to it.

"Do it now," Morag says, "when the record finishes. Before you open the gifts." She rings off.

Heart racing, Nathan takes the mic. *"Before we continue with the show, I've something important to share."* He cups the mic, looks at the empty producer's chair and breathes out a long breath. *"I'm sure like me you've listened in horror to the unfolding drama of five murders in our city. I'm a great supporter of the police and believe they do a good job in difficult situations. But I've been told something tonight that has made me see them in a different light. I'll tell you more after the next track."*

Letting out another breath, he sits back in his swivel chair. No one can ever say he doesn't play fair. Lulu has got three minutes and twenty seconds to come back and come clean. And in the meantime he'll have some fun, he can think of a few choice words of voiceover to get her going. The broadcast can be heard everywhere in the building so she'll be getting the Nathan J treatment in the loo, if that's where she really is.

But before he can get to the mic to interrupt the song with a new piece of mischief, the light dims. His head throbs as if bees are buzzing to get in. Zizz, Zizz. He tries to shake them off but he's dizzy. The headphones land on his desk – two coiled, shiny black snakes. The track deck and the brown drink stain merge, loom closer to his face then fall away. Heart galloping, his lungs struggle to keep up. The world wobbles and he's on an inflatable carpet above the computer screen. He reaches for the keyboard but all he sees is his red, shaking hand. The view in his desk mirror is worse. Jowls bulging and puce.

Thirsty. Mouth dry. He can't swallow. Heart faster, like the blade of an electric fan but without the cooling effect. Hot, feeling too hot. The room speeds, his breathing slows, his heart rockets. Terror overwhelms him.

A face.

Morag?

Marble white. Metal ring through the nose.

Lulu?

Hands lean over the track deck.

A voice. "I've cued 'Stairway to Heaven' and 'MacArthur Park'."

The same hands catch and roll him. On his side now, he's still floating, boiling, racing.

"We've got at least fifteen minutes until dead air."

# CHAPTER FIFTY-THREE

Tony picks me up at two a.m. and we drive to the hospital in silence. Is he beating himself up too? I detest my own incompetence. We found out Nathan Jackson was related to four out of five murder victims; we knew he'd broadcast comments about the cases; and police interviewed him twice. Why the hell did we only see him as a suspect and not a victim?

We queue at Accident and Emergency behind an abusive drunk with a cut forehead. Tempting though it is to flash a warrant card, an arrest would delay us. Eventually the drunk staggers to the waiting area and lands in a seat beside a woman who grips her handbag tighter.

Tony explains to the receptionist why we're here. She tells us to take a seat until the doctor arrives. Among the swearing, crying and groaning, it's like being at the police station after pub closing time but without the benefit of toughened safety glass.

"Which part of the apocalypse do you want to sit in?" Tony asks through gritted teeth.

"Maybe we won't have to." I nudge him when a grey-haired

man in a white coat, stethoscope slung round his neck, walks towards us.

The man holds out his hand, but before I can shake it, he steps between us. With his back to me, he shakes Tony's hand. "You must be Inspector Lewis. I'm Dr Andreou, the A&E consultant."

"This is the inspector." Tony steers the good doctor my way and manages not to grin.

My unshaken hand has already dropped to my side and I can't be bothered to raise it again. "What can you tell us?" I ask.

"My office is this way." No apology for his presumption.

We follow the white coat down several dimly lit corridors. Away from the mayhem of A&E, the hospital seems deserted. I'm glad Tony's with me. For all we know, this doctor could be bogus, luring us from the relative security of vagrants and junkies.

We pass a door marked *Neurology*. Is that where they carry out brain scans? And operations. My skin prickles. I rub my forehead.

When we get there, the doctor's office is tidy and functional. The only splash of colour radiates from a poster for the diagnosis and treatment of mushroom poisoning on the wall above the desk. It's a small room but, as there's no consulting couch, there's space for four easy chairs. When we've occupied three of them, Dr Andreou explains Nathan Jackson's condition.

"He's ingested a poison that's had a serious effect on his heart rate and breathing, and he's in a coma. He's presenting as an atropine overdose. We're ventilating him and giving him physostigmine to counteract the effects."

"Will he pull through?" Tony asks.

"The next few hours are critical."

"Can we see him?" I ask.

He turns to Tony. "He's unconscious; you can't interview him."

I curl my fists. Does he think the little woman doesn't know what a coma means? The reason I want to see Nathan Jackson is because too much has gone pear-shaped on my watch in the last two weeks. A man has nearly died because I didn't assess the risk. From now on, I check and double-check.

I stand up. "Where is Intensive Care?"

My tone says don't argue. The doctor sighs, taps his pen against his teeth. "I'll take you to him."

We retrace our steps down the corridor and are nearly back where we started when he veers off through a set of double doors. Two women and a man at the nurses' station straighten in their seats, looking a little nervous. Dr Andreou nods and sweeps past. Tony and I mouth a hello. An alcove next to their desk leads to another set of double doors with instructions to wash hands before entering.

The doctor rubs his palms with disinfectant suspended from the wall. We copy and follow him inside. It's a short walk to Nathan's room. Kevin's ordered a guard on Nathan in case the killer finds out he's clinging to life. Our colleague, PC Smyth, stands up when he sees us.

"Thanks, Ned," Tony says. "You can stretch your legs in the corridor for a minute."

Only the spiky blond hair makes Nathan recognisable and even that's clammy and stuck in clumps to his head. Small squares of banana-coloured paraffin gauze obscure his eyes and a translucent tube is in his mouth. An optic line of liquids suspended on metal frames drip through tubes. They enter his body at points in his forearms and bare chest. His face is red, with an ugly rash covering his cheeks and neck down to his collar bone. A drain of yellowy gunge oozes down another pipe, presumably collecting on the far side of the bed but not visible from where we are.

The doctor scrutinises the monitor above the bed and seems satisfied with the wavy lines, flashing icons, beeps and squeaks.

There's movement in the corner of the room. Louisa Brady, the radio producer, sits on a plastic chair against the wall. She wakes and gives a gasp at seeing us. I beckon her out to the corridor where we can talk. We all take one last look at Nathan before assembling outside the room. Ned Smyth goes back in.

"The patient is stable." Dr Andreou starts by addressing Tony but corrects his gaze to me. "I'll review his condition in a few hours. I'll leave you now to your investigation."

After he's gone, I ask Louisa if she's been here all night.

"After I phoned for an ambulance, I had to finish the show. We can't have dead air," she says apologetically. "By the time I got here, Nathan was in intensive care. They let me stay because I said I was his daughter."

I suppress a smile. Nathan wouldn't like that. I hope he gets to ask her why she didn't say sister or girlfriend. I suggest we go and look for a coffee machine. It's bound to taste like creosote but at least we might find somewhere to sit.

Louisa shakes her head. "I can't leave him; I feel responsible. It was me that brought in the chocolates for him. He'd had them before so I didn't think..." She glances at me and seems to sense the need to start from the beginning. The middle-class snottiness that irked me last time we met has deserted her and all I see is an anxious kid.

In a hesitant voice, she explains what happened. "A fan started sending truffles and sometimes soft drinks – dandelion something. Nathan ate the truffles – we both did. We should have chucked them away as soon as she started the phone calls. It was the woman who said a police officer was mixed up in the serial killings. She didn't phone again after he broadcast it but she carried on with the gifts."

"Did you meet her when she brought the gifts?"

"Our security guard got calls to say they'd been left at the back door. He brought them in and gave them to me. I passed them to Nathan."

"Were they unopened when you got them?" My mind pictures a CCTV scenario showing no one but the security guard at the back of the radio station. We must PNC him.

Louisa nods. "I usually ate a couple before I gave them to Nathan. Just to annoy him; I didn't even like them much." She gives a half-hearted chuckle. "I ate one last night."

Tony makes a note. The lab is checking the truffles and drink. Until we know, we can't rule out either, but if Louisa ate one, the truffles seem unlikely. Unless we have an indiscriminate killer who likes Russian roulette with individual chocolates, not caring who gets poisoned on the way to Nathan.

"He told me off for eating it," she continues. "To get his own back he said something horrible about me on air. I stormed off to the loo, which wound him up as he hates being left without a producer." Her face crumbles. "When I came back he was on the floor. Bright red. His pulse was raging. *He* was raging."

"Was he conscious? Did he say anything?"

"It sounded like he said 'You're Morag.' Like I said, he was raging."

My skin prickles. "Why would he say that?"

"The woman who rang up and sent the truffles said her name was Morag."

Rubbing my eyes, I discover how much my hand is shaking. How could I be so dense? I even heard Nathan on air on Tuesday appealing to Morag to get in touch. I didn't make the connection. I daren't look at Tony but feel him primed beside me. I steady my breath.

"It's a made-up name, isn't it?" Louisa says. "We weren't sure the caller was even a woman until she said that. Is it important?"

# CHAPTER FIFTY-FOUR

After Tony dropped me home, it wasn't worth going back to bed, so I reread all our references to Morag. There weren't many. Morag was the mystery number – the only stored number – on Christa Talbot's pay-as-you-go mobile. Extensive enquiries with Christa/Christopher's family, friends, pupils, ex-colleagues and the LGBTQ community had drawn a blank. Until Louisa Brady said Nathan's crank caller was Morag, I'd written it off as a dead end. Now I'm wondering if the caller from bogus company Radley Development, who lured Steven Baker to his death at the old hospital, was a Morag too. Either that or a Jason King.

I finally remembered why the name of Katrina Talbot's lover rang a bell. An internet search confirmed that Jason King was the flamboyant character in a TV show of the same name from the early seventies. Back then, there would have been very few women he could have duped with that alias, as the character was a household name. But a young Filipino girl who didn't watch much English TV would have been none the wiser.

I was alert while I was thinking all this at five a.m. but I'm paying for it now. Kevin's briefing in the incident room is technical and monotone. I have to stop myself nodding off.

"...still in a coma but stable. Poison has been confirmed as atropine in this." A bottle of dandelion and burdock appears on his computer screen. "It hinders the normal actions of the parasympathetic nervous system. He ingested a hundred milligrams. The bottle contained several times that dose. Spitting most of it out saved him. It would have tasted unpalatably bitter."

Our poisoner probably chose dandelion and burdock, hoping its strong flavour would mask the taste. My nan used to give me the same drink. I had to pinch my nose to get it down.

Kevin scours the room and allocates a detective to visit the manufacturer. I notice Harriet isn't here. It's not like Harriet to be late to a briefing.

"More than likely it was tampered with locally rather than at the factory," Kevin says. "Find out from the company who stocks these bottles. It's not as popular as it used to be so I'm hoping there won't be many outlets to visit and sales will be low. There's an outside chance we can locate the killer on CCTV making the purchase."

"Where would they get hold of the poison?" Tony asks.

He picks up his notes. "The hospital has given me a chemistry lesson. Atropine is found in deadly nightshade. Belladonna – beautiful woman – is another name for the plant. Italian women used to put it in their eyes to dilate their pupils to make themselves more attractive. Ophthalmologists still use a solution containing atropine to dilate pupils when they need to see into the eye. Some medications to prevent inflammation of the iris contain it.

"There are other medicinal uses: irritable bowel, cough mixture. Surgeons use it in operations to stop airways getting blocked with secretions. The military issue atropine in self-injecting combipens as a counter to chemical weapons poisoning. And belladonna grows wild all over Britain. So take your pick: our killer could be optician, doctor, soldier, or a randomer plucking the stuff out of hedgerows. Until we get more results from the lab, we can't speculate on the source."

The door opens and Harriet enters. Instead of creeping to a seat at the back, she hovers by Kevin.

He keeps talking. "With this one, it might be easier to find the source of the drink than the toxin." He turns to Harriet. "Find anything?"

"Two things." Harriet addresses us all. "The boss asked me to look back through city centre CCTV footage for the last week. I got lucky. Twice."

Tony coughs but mostly keeps the innuendo to himself.

"Last Sunday morning, ten twenty," Harriet says. "Eastgate Shopping Centre. We got a clear view from the first floor balcony camera of a man fitting Sean Farrell's description meeting a woman. Her back is to the camera but she's small and wearing a turquoise top. She appears to hand over her phone. Farrell taps something into it and hands it back. They part and she heads towards the Southgate exit, but CCTV wasn't working so we don't have a view of her face. We've got to check other CCTV in the area to see if we can pick up a better view of her, but most of the other footage is black and white so she won't be easy to spot."

"Amy Ashby, d'you reckon?" Tony says.

I rub my forehead. If it is Amy, she lied when she said she hadn't seen Sean for eighteen years. What else has she lied about?

"We found something else." Harriet continues the briefing. "The builders at Greyfriars have installed CCTV because of thefts of the Cotswold stone. A woman in an orange tunic on

Thursday the tenth at ten fifteen pauses by the building materials. She could be picking up a brick, I can't tell. Then she turns round. I'm pretty sure it's Amy Ashby."

"Get her in," Kevin says. "Put it to her that we've caught her red-handed selecting the murder weapon that killed Steven Baker. See what she has to say."

I look at Kevin. "We can't be sure the stone came from that site, and we've only just let Amy go. A lawyer would drive a coach and horses through fuzzy CCTV footage of a woman walking by Greyfriars. Unless the lab turns up her DNA in the saliva at Alexandra Simpson's house, I don't think we've got anything."

"Lab results still not back?" Tony asks.

"They're re-testing," Kevin explains. "The first result might have been compromised. A risk of cross-contamination apparently."

I roll my eyes. If the lab has cocked up, I'm not going to be the one to ask Amy for a second sample.

Kevin stands up. "Right. Tony, you're with Harriet. More city centre footage to trawl. Steph, back to Intensive Care. Be there when Nathan Jackson wakes up."

——————

PC Izzy Hutton has taken over from PC Ned Smyth, and it's another doctor on duty when I return to the hospital. This one seems happy to overlook my obvious shortcoming of being female and explains that Nathan, despite still being in a coma, is doing well as his system works itself clear of the poison. His daughter – as the doctor calls Louisa Brady – has gone home for a shower and change of clothes, promising to be back soon. I thank him and say I'd like to sit with Nathan for a while.

Time to think; comatose witnesses have their uses. Except

that all thoughts lead to Amy. The net is tightening. After all these years, am I going to be the one to fix the knot at her neck?

My phone goes and I instinctively look at Nathan as I snatch the noise out of my bag. But his body stays still and the lines on the monitor don't change. The caller is Clare Burgess, one of the social workers who visited Russell Hill.

"I had a message to call you," she says.

"Thanks for getting back to me. I wanted to ask what you and Russell talked about."

"He did all the talking. He was polite and I didn't feel threatened – other than by his precarious newspaper towers – but he made it clear he was angry. He didn't want me there, but then no one wants me there. I'm a social worker."

"I get you; I'm a police officer."

We share a hollow laugh.

"What was he like?" I ask.

"Well-spoken, bright. Could argue white was black."

Just as Matt Ward described him. "Did he say anything that struck you as odd? Any run-ins with neighbours or other visitors?"

"He hated his neighbours and didn't speak to them if he could help it. But he was convinced another social worker had called a few days earlier. I told him that wasn't possible but he wouldn't have it."

"Why wasn't it possible? Another member of your team, perhaps?"

Clare laughs. "What team? There are only three of us and one is on long-term sick. My other colleague is male. Russell Hill said a woman visited."

"Did he catch her name?"

"A Scottish name, was all he said, although she didn't sound it."

Morag? My heart speeds. If I was hooked up to Nathan's

machine, the lines on the screen would be in a bouncing frenzy. "Did Russell say what this other social worker did during her visit?"

"Same as me, I think. Chatted at the front door and inspected the rest of the house from outside. I wasn't about to go newsprint mountaineering so didn't go inside. Don't suppose she was either, whoever she was."

"Did the other woman go to the back of the house?" The broken dining room window was where the fire started. An arsonist might well have chosen the site in advance.

"I don't know. Mr Hill didn't say."

"Did he describe her?"

"Said she was bossy and tactless. I knew as soon as he said that she wasn't one of ours; that's not how we operate. He referred to her as a baggage. I took that to mean she was older than me. I'm thirty-one." She pauses on the line as if thinking something through. "I can put out a cross-county email in case a social worker from a different district visited him, but it's not likely. No social worker is going looking for work out of area."

I thank her and put the phone away.

Who the hell is Morag? Tracey Chiles, perhaps, Sean's Gloucester guesthouse landlady and the dog walker who found Christa Talbot in the Georgian Gardens. Morag as her middle name, not the Mairi she said it was. Is that why she rifled through the victim's bag in search of a phone? To create a reasonable excuse for her DNA to be on the body if forensics turned it up? Did anyone check that she didn't have her own mobile with her as she claimed? Too full of headache at the time, I never thought of it. Did it occur to Izzy Hutton when she interviewed her? Or Jess Bolton, who has popped up at three murder scenes in the last week? Not sure I saw that much action when I was a PCSO.

Could Morag be Louisa Brady, Nathan's producer? Too

young, surely. But didn't Louisa say she'd studied drama? Russell Hill didn't get many visitors, so she might have been able to convince him she was a middle-aged social worker. Could theatrics also have explained her show of distress at Nathan's bedside? Maybe I should have trusted my gut and gone with the dislike I felt the first time I met her.

A flurry of concern sends me out to speak to Izzy in the corridor. "If Nathan gets any visitors, make sure you go in the room with them. No one must be alone with him."

"No one? What about staff?"

"Not even the chief consultant." If Louisa Brady could play social worker, she could pull off doctor or nurse.

I start to walk away and then turn. "Are you sure Tracey Chiles didn't have a phone with her at the Georgian Gardens?"

A frown furrows Izzy's forehead. "She said not. Is there a problem with her statement?"

"Course not," I shrug. Just my imagination running on super-strength painkillers. "Any problems, contact me at the station."

Izzy smiles. "Don't worry, I won't leave anyone alone with the patient. And I won't let Amy Ashby within a million miles."

I walk away stiffly. Even an experienced officer like Izzy has convicted the prime suspect. She might be right. Russell Hill told Clare Burgess that his other visitor was 'bossy and tactless'. Amy to a tee.

# CHAPTER FIFTY-FIVE

A parallel universe has materialised in my kitchen. It's not yet eight a.m. on a Saturday, but Jake is up, dressed and wearing a tie.

"Rugby Club do, isn't it?" He kisses my forehead on his way to the toaster. "The service starts at twelve but it's on the telly from nine. We want to get settled."

He sees my blank face, not yet awake after a restless night, and explains that the Rugby Club is having an all-day party to celebrate Prince Harry's wedding. So wrapped up in work, I forgot about the royal nuptials despite falling over Meghan and Harry bunting in every tat shop in town. I wonder if I'll be home in time to watch the highlights. They're bound to have the *Match of the Day* slot.

"By the way, I took a call for you yesterday," Jake says as he reaches into the fridge for the marge. "Access Centre or something."

The doctors' surgery. "Probably a wrong number. What did they want?" I ask, squeezing every ounce of nonchalance into my voice that my racing heart will allow.

"No idea. They said it will be in a letter on Monday."

"Monday," I echo, my mouth suddenly dry. So soon.

"You all right, Mum?" He's looking at me quizzically.

My phone goes, making us both jump. Jake picks it off the kitchen top where I've left it and hands it over.

"Morning, Tony." I sip my coffee, for once happy to hear his voice. A reason to stop thinking of brain scans. "What's up?"

"I have some damning news about Amy Ashby."

I put down my cup as a tremor passes through my hand. No way. Despite the mounting evidence, I never thought... "You're saying she's a match for the saliva found at Alexandra Simpson's?"

"Not that. The lab still isn't happy with those test results. But what's turned up is a game changer."

My gasp makes Jake look up. I've known Amy since she was five years old. What could my colleagues have on her that I don't? And even if it has changed, just what game is she playing?"

"Are you still there?" Tony asks. "The boss wants her at the station. Kevin thinks you'll have a better chance than anyone else of bringing her in quietly. I'll pick you up at yours and brief you on the way."

We agree to meet outside the Bell Tower. Kevin's a poor judge if he thinks anything between Amy Ashby and me is done quietly.

"Shall I cancel this toast?" Jake asks as I put down the phone. "I'm guessing that was work."

"Thanks, love. I've still got time for breakfast." Anything to delay what's going to happen. Something's off. Until I know what Tony's going to say, I turn my thoughts to the DNA at the murder scene. How many times are they going to test the saliva sample before they accept it doesn't match Amy? All the talk of cross-contamination is cover for saying the test isn't giving Kevin the results he wants. I pick up the phone and find Siobhan Evans's number. She'll give me a straight answer.

———

Twenty-five minutes later, Tony and I turn into Anscott Close and park in front of the Ashby bungalow, my guts churning. Tony didn't brief me in the end; I heard the shocking news from Siobhan and I've been trying to process it ever since. Tony was right about it changing the game. Siobhan also told me what the test of the saliva from the poolside showed and seems as baffled as everyone else. The lab was re-doing it on Kevin's instructions, but Siobhan expected the results to be the same. She assured me there would have been no mix-up, but convincing a jury would be harder.

As Tony turns off the engine, lightning strikes. A blinding flash of how I could have been so stupid hits me. DNA never lies, they say. I never believe a never, but I have faith in Siobhan Evans. I scroll the internet on my phone and find what I need.

Then I phone Harriet. "I don't care what you're doing..."

"CCTV."

"Stop that. I'm sending you a link to a photo. Show it to Katrina Talbot and Alexandra's mother. Make sure the stepfather, Denny Simpson, is out of the way when you speak to her." Let the monkey talk without the protective organ grinder.

"What shall I ask them?"

"Nothing. If I'm right, you won't need to. Their response to the photo will be enough." I put the phone away. Heart booming with excitement and dread, I get out of the car with Tony and we knock on Amy's door. As we wait, I tell Tony

278

we're no longer bringing Amy in for a quiet chat. This will be an arrest.

"But the boss said..."

I raise my hand to silence him as we hear movement.

A vision in apricot chiffon answers on the second knock. I laugh. I actually laugh. I'm here to arrest a serial killer but all I see is Amy from school at her pretentious worst. What's that on her head – a fecking fascinator?

"It's for the Prep School." Amy touches her hair. "We're having a Royal Wedding party in the boarding house. I'll be late if I don't leave now."

Tony turns my way, expecting me to make the arrest. It's the obvious place to do it; easy to get her out of the house and into the car. But Amy and I don't do easy.

"Can we come in for a minute?" I ask.

"I've just settled my mother. She's watching the Royal Wedding."

"This won't take long." I step past her. The hall is heady with whatever perfume Amy has applied for her school party, but the scent hasn't travelled to the lounge. That still smells of old woman and talcum powder.

Eileen Ashby doesn't look round when we come in. Her chair is three feet in front of the TV. The screen shows Phillip Schofield on a grey sofa that is superimposed on the crowd line at Windsor Castle.

"Would you mind wheeling the chair round?" I ask.

"She's watching."

The woman's head is slumped to the side. I can't see her face but I imagine the eyes are closed more often than they're open.

"Please, Amy," I say softly. "This is important." I ignore Tony's quizzical expression. We're trained to make arrests with minimum fuss and no audience. I'll explain my cruelty to him one day.

As soon as Amy's turned the chair, I launch into the spiel that we're arresting her on suspicion of the murder of Steven Baker. That's enough to be going on with. We'll hit her with the entire back catalogue once she's at the station.

"Why?" Amy's eyes flood with tears. "You let me go yesterday. I... Is this about school? Is that why you're doing this, Steph?"

Shaking like hell, I manage to stay monotone. "I'm here on the instructions of Detective Chief Inspector Kevin Richards. We would also like to question you in connection with a number of other incidents." I pause and glance at the wheelchair. "Expect to be with us quite some time."

"I can't leave my mother again. You kept me for too long yesterday"

"She can come with us."

Tony's head flicks towards me. I was expecting that reaction and ignore it. "We'll look after her while officers question you." I point at the coffee table. Tissues, orange juice, spectacles, medicine bottles, packets of pills. "We can make sure she gets her medication. Do you have a travel bag for it?"

Amy pulls out her fascinator and tosses it on the sofa. "It's in the bedroom." Her lacquered hair sticks up where the hair grips have been.

# CHAPTER FIFTY-SIX

Mother and daughter are mute as Tony drives us to the police station. Amy's one act of defiance is to watch us struggle to lift the wheelchair out of the boot. She doesn't offer to help.

After Amy's been processed, she's led to an interview room. She reluctantly has to leave her mother with us. I ask Tony to fetch Kevin.

"He wants you and me to do the interview," he replies.

"Not this time," I say with all the authority my rank can muster. "I have to look after Mrs Ashby. If anyone wants us, we'll be in Interview Room Two." I push the wheelchair away before the desk sergeant can challenge my breach of protocol.

I park Mrs A in the interview room, promising to find her a cup of tea. The woman doesn't react. Hasn't done anything but blink since we entered her bungalow. A moment of panic hits me. What if she needs the loo? I'd better get on with this quick.

Out in the corridor, I phone Harriet. "Where are you?"

"Station car park. Lesley Simpson and Katrina Talbot recognised the photo. You'll never guess who."

My fist curls in a jubilant punch. "Harriet, I need you to

281

come down to the interview rooms, and if Izzy Hutton's not on duty at the hospital, bring her with you."

My heart's pumping. Now we're getting somewhere. If I play this right, I'll be able to close this and head home for the wedding highlights.

"Steph." The shout echoes off the corridor walls and Kevin advances, eating up the space between us. "The Ashby interview, now."

I swallow hard. "No can do, Kev. We've a frightened elderly woman whose daughter's been arrested for murder. If we don't look after her, Amy's lawyer will have us for neglect."

Kev's eyes narrow. "What's she doing here anyway?"

"She may be old, decrepit, short of the odd marble, but she can make or break Amy's alibi. Get her to co-operate and we might come out of this with a full confession."

Kevin rubs his chin. "The way to a murderer's heart is through her mother." He hesitates and I can see the wheels turning. "Okay," he says, "You've got twenty minutes. I'll start Amy's interview with Tony, but then I'm sending someone else to babysit Mrs Ashby."

"Can I have an hour, fifty minutes even?"

"Push it, Steph, and you'll get ten," he shouts as he storms away, almost colliding with Harriet and Izzy.

I thank them for coming and ask Izzy if she'll make us some tea in a while, when I give her the nod. I also tell her how I like it. Both she and Harriet pull a face.

We have to sit side on to Mrs Ashby because the chairs in the interview room are fixed to the floor to avoid violent suspects having an officer's eye out with a chair leg. The wheelchair only just fits under the side of the table. Mrs Ashby's knees and Harriet's must be almost touching. Izzy remains standing by the closed door.

I start the tape and give the date and time. Each officer introduces themselves.

"I'm making this a formal interview because I believe you can help us," I say. "I'm going to explain the evidence against Amy so you understand how serious this is."

Eileen Ashby continues her steady blinking. Is she looking at me? It's hard to tell; her eyes are red and sore.

"For the benefit of the tape, Mrs Ashby remains silent.

"Our first victim was Christa Talbot, also known as Christopher. We didn't have anything to connect Amy at first. We do now but I'll come back to that. I have to say I missed another piece of evidence. Amy uses your car, a Toyota Corolla, doesn't she? When I called at your house on..." I fish out my notebook, fumbling, unprepared. Somehow I flick to the right page. "...on Monday the fourteenth, the tyres and undercarriage were chalky white. My car was the same. I got my son to clean it." A lump blocks my throat as I regret bringing Jake into this. "The drives and car park at the Georgian Gardens are chalky. The victim, Christa, had chalk on the soles of her shoes. I should have spotted that sooner. Tests could have placed the Corolla at the crime scene. Amy must have driven away from the Gardens before our witness arrived and found Christa."

Eileen blinks on. I reckon she'd slap me if she could.

"We've arrested Amy for Steven Baker's murder because the evidence is stronger. Amy attended a meeting chaired by him, wrote a letter of protest against his traffic plans, can't account for her whereabouts, and had access to the murder weapon." I cock my head at her. "You won't know that. We have CCTV footage of Amy with some Cotswold stone a few hours before Steven was killed.

"Then we have poor Russell Hill. No connection with Amy, you might think – apart from the piece of evidence I'm going to tell you about later. But she did know of him and how he lived. We've a witness who can confirm that." Matt Ward came in to make his statement, giving Amy a Tesco alibi for Alexandra's murder with one hand and taking it away with the other through details of their date conversation about Russell.

"Things get more concrete when we come to Sean Farrell's death. Between you and me, I expect DCI Richards to charge her with that one before the day's out. Our experts are checking the Corolla. Amy washed off the chalk and goodness knows what else after she ran over Sean, but there'll still be traces of his DNA."

For a moment, Mrs Ashby stops blinking. I press on before my eyes water. I can't dwell on Sean's death. He's not so completely nothing to me.

"Amy lied to us," I say. "She made out she'd had no contact with Sean for eighteen years. But she called his phone and we have footage of them meeting in the city centre last Sunday.

"The thing is..." I lean across the table and lower my voice. "...if she'd only killed Sean, the sentence might have been lenient. The French have special arrangements for crimes of passion. We don't have that here, but judges can still use discretion. Sadly that won't help Amy. Electrocuting Alexandra Simpson and poisoning Nathan Jackson were passionless, premeditated acts of evil." I stare at Eileen. "It gives me no pleasure to say that about your daughter."

I cock my head again, studying her for a moment. "I notice your eyes look sore. The travel case of medication Amy packed when we left your house could have interesting stories to tell. Can we have your permission to send it to our laboratory?"

Toad-like, she blinks again.

"You don't have to decide now, Mrs Ashby. We can come back to that. But I'd bet my police pension your eye drop solution contains only water."

I feel Harriet's head shoot towards me again. Behind me, Izzy shifts the weight on her feet. Pity I'm getting more reaction to this revelation from them than from Eileen Ashby.

I press on. "I'm no doctor, but I'd say your treatment isn't working. How long have your eyes been sore and scratchy like that? It must be months if Amy's been stockpiling enough atropine to kill a grown man." I flick my notebook. "It's written in here somewhere. We've got a very good pathologist in this headquarters. You can ask her anything medical and she knows the answer. She told me this morning that one bottle of typical eye drop solution contains only a few milligrams of toxin, but if someone had access to the prescription, they could, over time, collect enough bottles for murder."

The eyes look redder now. Tears? Or has the talk of eye drops made her condition feel worse? Time for a break.

"Tea or coffee, Mrs Ashby?"

Silent blink.

"I'll get my colleague to make a pot of tea." I turn to Izzy and thank her. "PC Isabel Hutton leaves the room. Interview suspended at eleven fifteen."

By Kevin's allowance, I've got only a few minutes left. I hope Izzy is quick with the drinks. Harriet busies herself, writing in her notebook. I stare at Mrs Ashby and she stares back. Her face seems paralysed. Another shadow of worry casts over me and I count the seconds until Izzy returns.

# CHAPTER FIFTY-SEVEN

Without taking one for herself, Izzy pours out three mugs from the large metal pot. Canteen staff don't usually let their teapots out of captivity so Izzy's done well to coax one away. No one speaks until she's removed the empty tray and returned with a jug of milk.

"Sorry, Mrs Ashby, did you want sugar?" she asks.

No response.

I put my mug to my lips and blow across its surface. "I'll leave yours here until it's cooled down," I say, placing a mug in the centre of the desk. I pass the third one to Harriet.

She sips it. "Ouch, hot," she mutters and puts it down.

Izzy resumes her position by the door. We switch on the tape and I begin again.

"In the police, we don't condone lying, but if you'd said Amy was at home with you at the time of Steven Baker's murder, we might have left it there."

The eyes stop blinking. Something going on in her head? Regret? Confusion?

"And if we'd left it there, we would never have asked Amy to provide a DNA sample."

For a split second, the eyes widen.

"Didn't Amy tell you we took some of her cheek cells? I expect she didn't want to worry you, but after all that family history research she did last year, she must have known what we'd find. You can get home DNA kits these days. Dangerous, I think, don't you, DC Harris?"

Harriet nods. "You never know what you might find."

Good girl; she's keeping up.

"We think that's what happened to Amy. What she found out with her family history research was so shocking, she destroyed all her research files. But sadly her rage didn't stop there and she destroyed all live, human evidence too."

Not a flicker of recognition. If anything, the face looks more paralysed.

"Bear with me a moment." Fingers rattling, I scroll through my phone until I find the image I sent Harriet to show the mothers of two victims. I place the phone on the table and push it towards Mrs Ashby. She doesn't look at it. I don't expect her to.

"For the benefit of the tape, DC Harris will explain the photograph I have shown Mrs Ashby."

Harriet speaks clearly. "It is a photograph retrieved from Amy Ashby's Facebook page. It depicts Amy with her mother and father. This morning I showed this picture to Katrina Talbot, mother of Christa, and to Lesley Simpson, mother of Alexandra. Although they knew him by different names, they both identified Amy's father as the father of their child."

I take over from Harriet to reveal the stunning news Tony was on his way to tell me but I heard from Siobhan first. "The DNA evidence from Amy's cheek sample showed that Christa and Alexandra, and three other victims are Amy's half-siblings."

Silence.

"When Amy found out her beloved father had sired five other children, she went on the rampage." I look at Eileen. "Did you know any of this? Is that why you kept silent?"

Harriet picks up her tea but almost drops it again. "Still hot."

"Is that why you haven't come to Amy's defence through all this?" I continue. "Because you know she's guilty?"

Nothing. Still no reaction. Enough now. Time for Plan B. Heart in my throat, I lean over the table towards the giant teapot. Before I can ask myself whether my hare-brained action is a good one, I tip over the pot. Harriet slides out of her seat and backs away as liquid cascades down her side of the table.

As a police officer, Harriet has fast reflexes, but she's nothing on Eileen Ashby. The woman has bolted from the wheelchair and stands beside Izzy at the door.

"It's okay, Mrs Ashby," I say. "The tea wasn't hot. It wouldn't have scalded you." Harriet's a cracking actress; the tea is stone-cold undrinkable, made the way I requested.

Eileen doesn't move except to put a stoop into her stance. After months of defrauding the disabled community, is she still at it? I think of the crap Terri puts up with for being deaf, but force down my fury.

"You know that clever pathologist I told you about? She thought her team must be losing their touch. We got DNA from spittle at Alexandra's murder scene, and when Forensics compared it with Amy's cheek cell sample, the result was a partial but not complete match. The lab re-tested but the result was the same. It was like one of those logic puzzles Amy and I got at the end of term when the maths teacher was fed up with spoon-feeding the curriculum and gave us something fun to do.

"If Amy's sample indicates she's closely related to the person who spat at the crime scene and also to Christa, Steven and Russell, how is it that the spitter isn't also related to Christa, Steven and Russell? Are you keeping up?"

The woman is still stooping.

"You, Eileen Ashby, are closely related to Amy but not to her half-siblings, who share a father but not a mother." I stare into the woman's watery eyes. "You are the killer caught in a furious spit of anger aimed at a cat."

Harriet's eyes widen in apparent bafflement. I'm not sure she's as keen on logic puzzles as I am. I move on.

"Do you see the flaw in playing the invalid, Mrs Ashby? If you hadn't lost the power of speech, you could have saved Amy from all this. If you'd given her an alibi for the times of the murders, you'd have given yourself one too. And you've only ever wanted to save Amy, haven't you? Even in her school days, Amy had you there to do whatever it took to protect her. Come and sit down and tell us why you had to protect her again, all these years later."

Eileen Ashby straightens her back, eschews the wheelchair and sits in the chair opposite me. In a strong, clear voice she says, "I want my solicitor."

"We'll sort that out for you. Then you can start by telling us about Morag."

289

# CHAPTER FIFTY-EIGHT

Dampness seeps through the chiffon at Amy's armpits and a track of moisture trickles between her breasts. How long has she been on her own since the detectives were called away? Except she's not alone; the silent female sentry stands by the door. When Amy was younger, she used to watch *Prisoner: Cell Block H*, but never thought she'd be living it. Her sweat ducts gush again. If they don't believe her, this will become her everyday life. It will be in the newspapers. She'll lose her job, her freedom. It will be the death of her mother.

The detective constable thought he was clever, trying to trap her with his inferences and asides. Amy didn't care for his tone. The older one, the senior officer, sounded so sure of his facts she came close to doubting herself. But whatever he accused her of, she vehemently denied.

Is this another of their interrogation techniques: leave the suspect to stew?

Her head shoots up when the door opens, and her legs ready themselves for flight though she can't go anywhere.

Wiping the drips from her temple, she waits for the duo to reappear.

But it's not them. Steph Lewis steps round the door. Amy keeps her hands in her lap, trying her hardest to look composed.

Her expression neutral, Steph slips into the seat opposite. She takes a breath and looks Amy in the eye. "We're releasing you without charge."

The relief cascades through Amy and comes out of her mouth in a gasp. But another emotion follows and she curls her lip. "You said that yesterday."

"You're no longer a suspect." Steph clears her throat. "Someone has confessed."

"What?" Amy lets out a breath. "You drag me – and my elderly mother – in here on Royal Wedding Day. I miss work. I miss lunch. And that's all you can say: no longer a suspect."

"I'll take you home."

Amy folds her arms. "Last time you made that offer, I declined. My preference hasn't changed."

"If not me, then let DC Harris – Harriet – take you. Is there someone she can call to be with you when you get there? A neighbour or a friend?"

Amy studies her. Steph's snide face is imprinted on her memory, but this isn't it. This is the expression that the young constable last year wore when he broke the news about her father's death.

"Has something happened to my mother?" she asks.

Steph lowers her head, takes another breath and then raises her gaze. "She's confessed to six murders and one attempted murder."

Amy slides out of the chair and backs to the wall, shaking with rage. "You're sick. What the hell happened to you? You wouldn't have sunk this low at school."

Steph's expression doesn't change. "DCI Richards is going through her written statement now. I'm not joking, Amy. Not this time." Her eyes are almost pleading.

Amy scoffs. "Even if she was physically capable – which she isn't – why would she kill a series of random people in the space of two weeks?"

"They weren't random. As DCI Richards must have explained, four of them were your half-siblings."

"And I'll tell you what I told him. That's utter nonsense." She paces along the wall, looking at the paintwork. Amy's always dreamed in colour, but this nightmare is a greying shade of magnolia.

"You'd better sit down." Steph stares at the table, her shoulders hunched. "The mothers of two of the victims have identified your father as the father of their—"

"Don't say that. Don't you dare." Amy stays standing.

"Your mother was worried you'd find out through your family history research. That's why she destroyed the files on your laptop."

Amy thinks of the day she couldn't find her files, recycle bin empty. She'd sought comfort from her mother, who was still able to speak back then. Quietly, repeatedly, her mother suggested she throw her energies into her flowers instead.

"All your half-siblings were forty-one years old, born within a year of you. Your mother found out about them when she was sorting through your father's papers after his death. She came across a draft of a will in which he left his estate equally between his six children. Obviously she destroyed it, but she couldn't be sure he hadn't lodged a signed and witnessed copy somewhere else, so she put a plan into place that would remove the five rival heirs and ensure you inherited everything."

A shiver takes the heat out of Amy and she has to sit down to stop the room spinning. If she goes along with Steph's cruel fantasy for a moment, it explains why her mother burnt old paperwork and wouldn't let Amy help. And why her father supposedly died intestate and why Amy's inheritance hasn't come through. Her mother couldn't apply for it until all contesters were out of the way.

"Why would my father have so many...?" A lump at the back of her throat makes it hard to speak. "Why all the same age?"

"After you were born, your mother didn't want to go through childbirth again and wouldn't let your father near her unless he had a vasectomy."

Amy squirms to hear intimate details about her parents. From Steph, the biggest liar in the school. She grips the table edge. "My mother told you all this, did she? An old woman, who struggles to breathe most days, said all this?"

Steph doesn't react to the change of tone. "He asked for a six-month stay of execution to come to terms with the idea. We're pretty sure his medical record will confirm he had the snip eventually, but in the meantime he set about impregnating other women. Your mother found his diary and photos of the babies. There's a name for it – some sort of god complex – I don't know what."

"Are police allowed to do this?" Amy addresses the young woman by the door. "You know she's lying, don't you? Did you see my mother when we arrived? She's in a wheelchair. Can't even dress herself."

The constable's blank expression doesn't change and she shakes her head. "I'm so sorry. I was in your mother's interview earlier. I've seen her walking."

"She duped us all, even you." Steph bites her lip. "But you must know how manipulative she can be. I remember at school..." Her voice trails off as if she's slipped into a memory.

And Amy catapults into one of her own. The viola.

RACHEL SARGEANT

———

By the time Amy gets home, her tears are thick and flowing. Her sewing bag and viola case land on the hall carpet, and she stomps upstairs with her satchel and sports bag. Slams her bedroom door, casts off the bags and launches onto the bed. She lowers the volume of her sobs long enough to make sure she can hear the flack-slap of her mother's moccasins on the stairs.

A moment later, Mother enters her room without knocking. "Whatever's the matter?"

"They got my viola."

The mattress gives as Mother sits beside her. "Say that again." She tugs the pillow from under Amy and places it upright against the headboard.

Amy shuffles up until her back is against it, but she continues to cry into her hands.

Mother taps her thin fingers along Amy's shin. "Who was it? The usual suspects?"

"Steph and Terri." Amy looks at her mother, nearly smiling in her eagerness to tell her tale. "They threw it in the air. Taunting me, calling me names."

"Did anyone see?"

Amy nods. "Loads of us were walking home."

Mother stands up, straightens her apron. "Your head teacher will have to expel them. No excuses for stealing."

"Even though they gave it back?" Amy's enthusiasm wanes, but she still hopes Mother will go to school and speak to Mrs Hardcastle about the name calling.

Mother narrows her eyes. "Did they break it?"

Amy shakes her head. "They'll get away with it again, won't they?"

Mother's gaze fixes on the wall above Amy's head. Her

294

make-up is immaculate, better than any of Amy's teachers even though she has no job to go to. Her face is unreadable. A frisson of nerves passes through Amy as the silence lengthens.

"Where is the viola now?" Mother says eventually.

"In the hall."

Without another word, Mother marches downstairs. Amy listens at her bedroom door. Hears the single chime of the house phone being picked up. Then her mother's voice.

"Is that Mrs Hardcastle? I thought I might still catch you in your office."

Amy can't resist smiling. Mother's going into battle again.

"Those awful girls have been up to their tricks, bullying Amy. ... Well, you might say that, but I call it systematic and persistent. And they've gone too far this time. ... Amy's viola is filthy and broken. Completely unplayable. The bow is beyond repair... They hit her with it. Amy is most distressed, as am I."

Amy strains to hear. Was that a sob?

"...Tomorrow morning at ten thirty? ... I'll be there with the viola so you can see for yourself what they've done."

There's another chime as the phone hits the cradle, and the next sound is the back door opening. Is that it then? How's Mother going to explain a self-healing viola to Mrs Hardcastle? The instrument isn't broken. Amy feels like crying all over again and wishes she'd never told her mother. They'll look like fools. More ammunition for Steph and Terri. Mother has made everything worse.

Maybe the girls did make a few scratches on the varnish or even snap a string. Amy knows they didn't touch the bow or hit her, but will that be enough to convince Mrs Hardcastle to punish them? Amy goes downstairs to examine the viola, but the case lies open and empty on the floor. The bow is still in the velvet pocket of the lid, but snapped. It must have happened when Steph dropped the case on the grass and ran away. Some of the curled hairs are sticky and red. It looks like blood. How could Amy not have noticed?

The backdoor closes. Mother's brisk steps move through the kitchen and she emerges in the hall. Her right arm is ramrod straight by her side. The viola hangs from her hand like a slaughtered pheasant. The strings are loose, ragged over a clump of muck and weeds. The wafer-thin bridge has slipped, and half of it is missing. A nick on the back of Mother's hand oozes blood that meanders across the surface of the instrument into the mud, grass and varnish.

Mother replaces the viola in the case and snaps shut the metal catches. "We'd best put a bandage on your arm before tomorrow. We'll tell Mrs Hardcastle it's your blood on the instrument." She gets to her feet and wipes her bloodied hand on her apron. "I'm protecting your interests. One day you'll understand."

———

"You're saying she faked her illness?" Amy asks Steph, even though she knows the answer. Her mother really is capable of anything. "To me? To the doctor? For all these months, her health becoming worse?"

"What's wrong with her eyes?" Steph asks. "Have you noticed her getting through her eye drop prescription faster than usual?"

"A chronic condition. She's had it for years but lately she's been a bit clumsy, mislaying bottles or knocking them over."

"It's likely those were filled with water. She would have already decanted the toxin."

"Toxin?" Amy can hardly breathe. What now?

"One of your half-siblings was poisoned."

Amy sees a hole in Steph's story. "I don't remember reading about a poisoning."

"We've kept it out of the press. He survived."

"Thank God." The words come out automatically but she means it. She doesn't know this half-sibling, but doesn't want him dead. A feeling of hope comes over her. She has a brother. The idea pleases her despite the horror of what she's being told. "Can I meet him?"

The question seems to floor Steph and she hesitates, apparently collecting her thoughts. "That will have to be his decision."

Amy stands up, suddenly wanting to be out. Away from Steph drip-feeding her with things about her family, her life. She needs the haven of home. Will she be allowed to sell the bungalow if her mother goes to prison?

Steph clears her throat again. "There's something else I have to tell you. Please sit down."

Amy slides back into the plastic chair, hating herself for following an order from Steph Lewis, but she senses she can't get out until she's heard it all.

"Your mother also told us about Sean. He came to the bungalow."

Amy covers her ears. She can't hear that name from Steph. But when Steph carries on speaking, she moves her hands to listen.

"After he was unfaithful..."

"With you, you mean." Amy flares, not letting the woman side-step that one.

Steph glances at her colleague by the door and colour creeps up her neck. She turns back to Amy. "After you got engaged, your mother threatened to kill Sean if he didn't get out of your life."

297

"That's ridiculous. How could a sparrow the size of my mother threaten a grown man?"

Steph shakes her head. "I don't know, but he left, didn't he? When he came back three weeks ago, he thought it was safe now she's in a wheelchair. But he made the mistake of going to confront her. He was angry you'd used her as an excuse for not meeting up with him."

Amy winces. The stupid phone call. If she hadn't phoned him, if she hadn't changed her mind mid-call, citing her mother's needs as a reason to hang up, would he still be alive?

"When he went to see her, she told him about..." Steph's skin darkens. "...things he didn't know."

"About his son?" Amy fires the question like a bullet and is pleased to see the torture in Steph's face.

"After he left the bungalow, your mother followed and mowed him down. She's admitted she still drives. We expect to find CCTV proof if we look hard enough. Think about it, Amy: all the murders took place when you were away from the bungalow and your mother was unattended. You really did take the bus home from work that Wednesday morning. It was your mother driving when the Corolla was clocked near the Georgian Gardens. And your mother wearing the shoes that picked up cat hair."

Amy stops listening as a swell of pride rolls through her. It's dawned that she's won. Sean chose her not Steph. He visited her mother to set out his intentions. It was Amy he wanted. "Did Mother tell you what he said to her? Did he say he still loved me?"

Steph opens her mouth. There's silence. The constable looks at the floor. Steph gazes at the ceiling. "I'm sure," she says finally.

Amy smiles graciously. Of course. She was prime steak; Steph was only ever burger. When her smile falls on the sombre-faced police constable, she remembers Sean's dead. Her one chance of happiness extinguished by her mother.

"I suppose it was all done to shield me. You can't blame a mother for protecting her young. Two weeks of madness in an otherwise blameless life."

"I'm afraid there was one more victim," Steph says, admiring the table again. "Christopher Talbot's mother told us that years ago, your mother suspected your father of an affair with a woman at his office.

"Your mother has now confessed to pushing that young colleague into the Severn. Her death was ruled accidental at the time. Morag was three months pregnant."

Bile fills Amy's throat. Her own mother. All her life she's lived with a murderer. A liar, an arch-manipulator who tricked her into giving months of intimate care. She straightens her back. "Did you say DC Harris would take me home?"

Steph stands up. "I'll go and find her for you."

When she reaches the door, she turns. "By the way, your mother was right. There was an authenticated will and an offshore account. You'll have to share it with your half-brother, and possibly Christopher Talbot's children, but you're going to be all right for money."

Tears stream down Amy's face as she waits for DC Harris. But even the worst days have flickers of sun. When she gets home, she'll catch the end of the Royal Wedding and tomorrow she'll search through the remains of her father's papers to see what other nest eggs there might be. On Monday, she'll go to the estate agents. She'll buy her little apartment in the Bell Tower and never have to see Steph again.

———

We hope you enjoyed *Her Deadly Friend*. The next book in the series, *Her Charming Man* is available from book retailers or the Hobeck Books website.


Happy reading!

Rachel Sargeant (and Rebecca and Adrian at Hobeck Books)

# AUTHOR'S NOTE

Gloucestershire provided inspiration for my setting. I used real landmarks, renamed some, moved a few around and invented many others. I hope readers, who – like me – know and love the county, have fun spotting familiar places and forgive me for playing with the geography. There is no Georgian Gardens, although you'll find Painswick Rococo Garden on the edge of Painswick village. Dogs are welcome on leads but there is no out-of-hours honesty box. It is not yet famed for its developing collection of bluebells, but the snowdrops in January and February are a beautiful sight to behold.

# ACKNOWLEDGMENTS

Thank you for reading *Her Deadly Friend*. I hope you enjoyed the story.

I would like to thank my publishers Rebecca Collins and Adrian Hobart for liking "Steph" enough to welcome her and me into the Hobeck Books fold. It is a pleasure to be working with them and with marvellous cover designer Jayne Mapp and eagle-eyed copy editor Sue Davison.

I would also like to thank fellow writers Fergus Smith, Peter Garrett and Jessie Payne for their advice on early drafts.

Once again, I'm grateful to the book bloggers, authors and readers who have variously blogged, reviewed, tweeted and hosted me on their websites. Thanks to everyone who has taken the trouble to comment and spread the word about my books. I would also like to acknowledge the contribution of the Hobeck Advance Readers Team (HART) who provided important feedback and support for this book.

And grateful thanks to Iain Robertson of Gloucestershire Fire and Rescue Service for advice on fire service procedure. All errors and omissions for creative licence are entirely my own. The fire service and police force featured in my story are of my own invention and not based on members of the real blue-light organisations that serve Gloucestershire, or elsewhere.

Thank you to my fellow Hobeck author Brian Price for his advice on chemicals and poisoning, and to my other fellow members of the Crime Writers' Association for their ingenious suggestions on how to poison a victim. They recommended two excellent books:

- *A is for Arsenic: the poisons of Agatha Christie* by Kathryn Harkup
- *Wicked Plants: the A-Z of plants that kill, maim, intoxicate and otherwise offend* by Amy Stewart

A big thank you to my family for, well, everything really.

Best wishes

RACHEL

## ABOUT THE AUTHOR

Rachel Sargeant is a full-time writer of thrillers and crime fiction. Her novels have been translated into other European languages and sold worldwide. Her short stories have appeared in women's magazines and anthologies, and she is a winner of *Writing Magazine*'s Crime Short Story competition. After many years in Germany, Rachel now lives in Gloucestershire with her family. She likes visiting stately homes, country parks and coffee shops, and she has a PhD from the University of Birmingham. She loves reading in a range of genres and chats about books on her monthly blog.

Visit her website at: www.rachelsargeant.co.uk

Twitter/X: @RachelSargeant3
Facebook: @rachelsargeantauthor
BookBub: @rachelsargeant3

## HOBECK BOOKS – THE HOME OF GREAT STORIES

We hope you've enjoyed reading this novel by Rachel Sargeant. To keep up to date on Rachel's fiction writing please do follow her on Facebook, Twitter/X or BookBub.

Hobeck Books offers a number of short stories and novellas, free for subscribers in the compilation *Crime Bites*.

- *Echo Rock* by Robert Daws
- *Old Dogs, Old Tricks* by AB Morgan
- *The Silence of the Rabbit* by Wendy Turbin
- *Never Mind the Baubles: An Anthology of Twisted Winter Tales* by the Hobeck Team (including many of the Hobeck authors and Hobeck's two publishers)
- *The Clarice Cliff Vase* by Linda Huber
- *Here She Lies* by Kerena Swan
- *The Macnab Principle* by R.D. Nixon
- *Fatal Beginnings* by Brian Price
- *A Defining Moment* by Lin Le Versha
- *Saviour* by Jennie Ensor

- *You Can't Trust Anyone These Days* by Maureen Myant

Also please visit the Hobeck Books website for details of our other superb authors and their books, and if you would like to get in touch, we would love to hear from you.

Hobeck Books also presents a weekly podcast, the Hobcast, where founders Adrian Hobart and Rebecca Collins discuss all things book related, key issues from each week, including the ups and downs of running a creative business. Each episode includes an interview with one of the people who make Hobeck possible: the editors, the authors, the cover designers. These are the people who help Hobeck bring great stories to life. Without them, Hobeck wouldn't exist. The Hobcast can be listened to from all the usual platforms but it can also be found on the Hobeck website: **www.hobeck.net/hobcast**.

# ALSO BY RACHEL SARGEANT

As well as writing the Gloucestershire Crime Series, Rachel also writes psychological thrillers.

## *The Roommates*
When a university student disappears during freshers' week, her new flatmates search for her, not realising the danger ahead. Four roommates, four secrets, one devastating crime.

## *The Good Teacher*
A popular school teacher lies dead in a ditch. On her first ever case, DC Pippa 'Agatha' Adams visits his school and meets families who've learned a shattering lesson. Maybe even the good have to die.

## *The Perfect Neighbours*
Helen joins a British expat community abroad and is welcomed by the charming family across the way. When tragedy strikes, she realises her perfect neighbours are capable of almost anything.